Larkin Cunningham

THE MURK BENEATH

WHITE GATE PRESS

Published 2016
by White Gate Press
Ballyvolane, Cork, Ireland
www.whitegatepress.com

ISBN: 978-0-9956964-0-2
eBook ISBN: 978-0-9956964-1-9

A catalogue record for this book is
available from the British Library

2 4 6 8 10 9 7 5 3 1

Printed by Ingram Lightning Spark
Typeface: Garamond 12/14

For Caroline and Conor

I STOOD OVER THE dead boy and remarked how angelic he looked. Detective Sergeant Cotter grunted, then said, "You'd think he was asleep."

There was a December chill. Frost shrouded grass, branches … fingers. The early morning sun cast long blade-like shadows over the crime scene.

"Why take the clothes?" Cotter asked, shining a torch on the boy's corpse. "Why leave him naked?"

I shrugged. "Dunno. Maybe he ejaculated all over them, took them for disposal, left the boy like a piece of rubbish."

Cotter grunted again, said, "Savage called. Says there's a witness saw this fat bastard yesterday fiddling in his pants near the playground."

I knew such a fat bastard, had been rattling his cage of late, maybe too much given recent events. Cian Chambers was his name, a child molester out on parole, living not ten minutes' walk away. His last offence had been public masturbation within ten metres of a primary school, so the MO fit. It had been my informal responsibility to ensure he kept his nose clean, that he knew the Guards were on the lookout for him. But it may only have served to ferment those sick urges of his, like agitating the beer in a pressure vessel.

I looked at the boy again. Robbie O'Meara. Taken from a playground the day before while his mother was busy rummaging for his Santa sweater in their nearby car. I looked in his eyes – innocent, bewildered eyes. I looked at the ice-dusted twigs protruding over his body from a bush, as if the hands of Death itself were eager to snatch the boy into eternity. I wished those twigs would blind me. I felt rage. I felt guilt.

"I've seen enough," I said. "I'll head back, talk to the Chief."

"But we haven't talked to the dog walker that found him yet."

"You're well able, Barry. Get Murphy to tag along. It'll be good experience for him. Let me know if the techs find anything interesting."

Barry just nodded, didn't seem impressed by what might have seemed like disrespectful disinterest given the seriousness of the case and the nature of the crime scene.

I signed myself out of the crime scene and took a detour to Chambers's flat. Not exactly standard procedure, I'll admit, but I felt responsible in some way for Chambers's actions, felt I owed the boy some debt.

As I walked, I remembered how people had looked blankly at us as we patrolled the streets looking for the boy. They must have sensed he was already gone. I think that's the first reaction nowadays – to assume the worst of humanity, to plan a funeral before a homecoming party.

What I should make clear up front is that I didn't intend to strangle Chambers, but it was those eyes of his, you see. Those dead eyes. I wanted to choke some life back into them.

When he answered the door, I only said I wanted to ask some questions. But when he tried to close the door in my face, I lost it.

It didn't take much to restrain him. I mounted his flabby bulk, pinned his arms down with my knees. I looked at his red face. I looked in his eyes. I saw nothing. No spark. No sense there could be remorse.

I wanted to strip him naked, sodomize him with whatever I

could lay my hands on. I wanted him to know what it had been like for the boy. Only he could never know, because he was a grown man and the boy had been only six.

I went to work on him. I beat him until the fat folded over on his face, the cheeks peeled from the bone. Still there was nothing in his eyes. I got up. I kicked him in the ribs.

"Can you feel nothing?" I shouted.

No response. I got back down. I wrapped my hands around his fat neck. I squeezed hard. I could see little sparkles of light flitting before my eyes as I further tightened my grip. His eyes bulged, didn't blink despite the blood pooling in the sockets. I kept squeezing.

And then eventually, perhaps more out of pity for myself than Chambers, I stopped. My hands were shaking, dots of blood peppered along my shirt sleeves, my knuckles lost in the messy pulp of my fists.

I read him his rights. His arms were limp by his side, one eye closed, the other staring through a split eyelid at the ceiling. As it turned out, I'd choked and beat him right into a coma – brain damaged, baby food through a tube, piss and shit into a bag.

I looked up at the hall table beside him. Next to a telephone was a small brown teddy bear, a red ribbon around its neck tied into a bow. A lure to tempt little boys away from their mammies. The blood drained from my brain and I almost passed out.

I got off light, relatively speaking, my many years of service taken into account, apparently. I was dumped out of the force without a pension, but there was no prison time. Front-page news for all of a day – PAEDO STRANGLER, DI MICHAEL BOSCO, CLEARED OF CRIMINAL CHARGES, EXPELLED FROM GARDAÍ. Thereafter, I was largely anonymous.

As fucked up as things had become, however, I was at least comforted by the certain knowledge that no one had yet managed to molest or murder a child from a coma.

1

Doc O'Reilly and a Machete

I FOUND OUT PRETTY soon that there were few careers open for a disgraced Guard. I got a few slaps on the back for doing in a child killer, but they didn't add up to a proper job, at first. I eventually picked up one as a security guard with a company called Solid Security. I worked the graveyard shift minding a warehouse in Churchfield. I'd have considered it beneath me had I not been so desperate. After all, I'd gone from putting it up to gang bosses to sending loitering hoodies on their merry way.

I barely made ends meet over the next two years. The rent on my one investment property fell short of the mortgage repayment, but I could just about make up the difference from my wages – much of it cash, under the counter.

One thing in my favour was a sense of timing. I sold the investment property, a rat-infested hovel near the top of Blarney Street, to some guy who might have been Armenian or Algerian or something. I'd been plagued by weekly calls about leaky pipes and smells from drains, so I was glad to be rid of it. I made a tidy profit of forty grand, but twelve months later had only twenty left. The arse had fallen out of the property market by then, so

I didn't feel so bad about frittering away twenty grand I might never have had. I blew it on drink. On the hounds too.

I became so accustomed to trouble that it was like a blood relative. It invited itself around like the randy uncle everyone dreads. The one who turns up at your wedding or your child's christening uninvited, reeking of alcohol. The same uncle whose funeral you go to anyway, because the sick bastard shared some part of you.

Trouble had been taking its toll, though. I figured mostly it was the security job, my internal clock being out of sync, not seeing the sun nine months of the year. Only that doesn't make you put on four stone in weight. Drink does. Curried chips at the dog track too.

I felt crappy enough that I'd been to the doctor a couple of weeks prior, had some bloods taken. Now I was back for what I assumed was bad news. I mean, when do you ever actually get good news from a doctor? Nothing wrong with you that we can detect is probably as good as you can hope for.

After waiting nearly forty minutes in the waiting room, and tolerating the smell of stale piss that was obviously emanating from the old guy sitting across from me, the 96 FM hourly news report was interrupted as the doctor called out my name over the speaker.

An Asian kid in short pants and with Bart Simpson on his T-shirt, maybe four or five years old, and with his tongue lolling because of whatever was eating away at his throat, watched as I rose from the seat. The kid's mother slapped the back of his hand and told him to put his tongue back in his mouth before she pulled it out.

I walked into Doc O'Reilly's office. I couldn't tell you his first name – he's always just been Doc. The old man – I would have guessed he was seventy or only slightly south of that – was sitting in a squeaky swivel chair. It was the same chair he'd sat in the first time my mother brought me to see him when I was just a young fellow – when she had been convinced I had TB when all I had was a dose of the sniffles.

He wore slacks that were the colour of stomach bile. He had

grey hair, grey skin, grey eyes, grey teeth. Like a black and white mugshot. His face was thin and his skin stretched out like Rizla paper so that I could see the sinew beneath.

He was studying something on the screen of his laptop, some kind of spreadsheet. I guessed it was my blood results. My very essence reduced to tabular format. He looked up and waved me to a chair next to his desk.

"Feck sake, Michael," he said without so much as a prior pleasantry. "Have you cut down on the black pudding like we talked about last time? Not judging by your cholesterol level. Or your ALT count. You have fatty deposits in your liver."

I regretted telling him about my penchant for Clonakilty black pudding at the previous visit. It would probably be the stick he would beat me with every time the blood counts came down on the wrong side of improvement. I like the Clonakilty, the way the oatmeal falls apart in your mouth, the way that blood mash melts and releases the intense flavour.

Doc keyed awkwardly on his laptop, muttered something in frustration, found what he was looking for, and frowned. He was holding a promotional pen for some drug in his hand.

"156 over ninety-four last time. Right, get your sleeve up."

Doc put a rubber tube around my arm and fastened it with Velcro. He pumped it until it felt like my nails would pop off, muttered again, waited for the pulse to stabilize. I think he derived more enjoyment from dishing out pain than curing it.

"Shite," he said.

"What?" I said and straightened my back.

"Gone up. 162 over ninety-seven."

Doc coughed a rasping smoker's cough that sounded like rusty ball bearings in a brown paper bag. Sixty a day, no inkling of quitting. A self-confessed hypocrite.

"You've cut down on the fags too, I hope," he said.

"Uhuh." I was lying.

"Remember what I keep saying about that?"

"Do as you say, not as you do?"

"Exactly. I'm an addict. I give myself ten years if I'm lucky.

Can't quit. But you can, right?"

I had my doubts. It wasn't like I hadn't tried before. Doc was motioning the drug pen towards me like he was shaking the ash off a cigarette.

"Uhuh," I said after a pause.

"Keep it up. And cut down on those builder's breakfasts too. Or you won't see sixty. Does that spell it out for you?"

Right then sixty seemed like bonus territory.

"Got it."

Our conversations were always this candid. I'd hate to get a cancer diagnosis from him. *I give you three months, at most, of rapidly deteriorating quality of life, then a painful death where you will spend your final hours crying out for morphine*, I could imagine him telling me. He might even have pissed on my grave for good measure.

"No dicking around, Mickey. Come back to me in three months. No significant improvement and you'll need to be medicated. For blood pressure *and* cholesterol. That's a lifetime deal. You take that shite, you stay on it. That clear enough for you?"

"Yeah, crystal."

He hadn't mentioned meds before. I hate taking pills – the fucking things seem to treble in size as I swallow them – so it freaked me out a little.

"Go on, clear off," he said.

Charming as always.

Later that morning I was at home in Blackpool Village. I prefer to call it the Village because to do otherwise would be to admit it was just a suburb. And I'm not the suburban type.

The house isn't fancy – a two up, two down with a small bathroom in an extension to the rear with a toilet that backs up every other week; an iron bed that wouldn't look out of place in a Victorian insane asylum; a fourteen-inch black-and-white TV; nothing so modern as a dishwasher. A CD player with a tape deck and radio, though – I'm quite proud of that.

I took a bottle of Jameson from a kitchen cupboard, put it on the table. I sat down, stared at it for a bit. I consider it a noble drink. It's what real men drink, especially when alone.

I still had the doc resonating in my ears. *Fatty deposits in your liver.* I put a double measure of whiskey into a tumbler. I sniffed it, felt it burn my sinuses. *Gotta quit*, I thought. It wasn't that I was running headlong into a coffin – I was staggering there, wheezing like a deflating balloon.

I sipped from the glass. It burned my lips. Then it burned the inside of my mouth. I swirled it, allowed it to singe my tongue. I guess I was punishing myself, torturing myself. I dared myself to swallow. I chugged it, almost coughed it back up, and threw the crystal tumbler at the sink. It shattered everywhere.

I buried my head into my palms, combed my fingers into my hair, scratched my nails on my scalp. It felt like zero Kelvin in my head, the synapses inert, nothing firing. I felt a cold gloom descending over my brain like a fire blanket, deadening everything.

Fuck it. I'll get back on that horse. Stick my two fingers up at … at … everything. Fuck it!

I picked up the bottle and walked to the sink, avoiding the tumbler shards. I emptied the remaining whiskey into the sink, some going down the plug hole, some of it mixing with the putrid dishwater trapped in dirty bowls and mugs. *It's a start.*

I went to the drawer below the cutlery one, opened it, and took out a pack of Benson and Hedges. *One step at a time, one step.* I slid out a cigarette and lit it. The hot smoke seemed to permeate my brain, get it all firing again. I sat back down.

I'll do something tomorrow. Make a difference. It was early – my late, of course, given the night work – only eleven-thirty. I felt tired, more so than normal. I dragged myself upstairs and lay on the bed.

I fell asleep with my clothes on.

I woke at six drenched with sweat, my legs cocooned in the bed sheet. I'd had a recurring dream again – one with my father calling to me from the boot of a rusted car. It was almost dark. My joints ached and my heart was labouring to squeeze whatever rancid juice I had that passed for blood around my withering body.

I got up and scratched and stretched myself. Working nights was definitely taking its toll. 6 p.m. was breakfast time in my world.

Have you cut down on the black pudding?

I'd made a start with the whiskey; I could allow myself the black pudding. I cut two slices of Clonakilty instead of the usual three. A little thicker than normal, though; maybe a fifteen-percent reduction overall. *One step at a time.* Two slices of lightly-buttered toast, mug of Barry's Classic Blend tea. Two slices of fried … no *grilled* Clonakilty black pudding.

I had a twelve-hour shift starting at 8 p.m. I worked five nights a week – forty taxable hours above board, twenty hours under the table in cash. The job just about paid a living wage. I wore a Solid Security uniform – blue shirt under a dark navy sports coat that had a portcullis crest on it, navy heavy-duty pants, boots that laced up above the ankles. Nothing but a torch for protection.

The warehouse was a distribution centre – Druid Distribution. Lorries came and went, wheeled long trailers to loading bays where conveyor belts brought goods for the manual workers to shift onto the trailers. But from about 10 p.m. till 4 a.m., the place was usually deserted.

I decided to dispense with my hip flask. *Or you won't see sixty.* But it was late October and the wrong wind could put a chill through you, so I brought a scarf. The Bensons would help too, but I couldn't afford the speed at which I knew I would want to smoke, so I just brought the one pack. I would have to pace myself, allow myself just the one fix every thirty-five minutes. An addict like myself calculates down to the second.

Walking kept me warmer than sitting on my arse, so I moved about a lot, circling the compound over and over. It made me wonder why I kept putting on weight. I had a walkie-talkie and checked in with the base every hour. I had a mobile phone too, just in case. I had the number of the head office and the nearest twenty-four-hour Garda station.

The wind was northeasterly, probably Siberian, and took little nips at exposed areas of my skin. I pulled the scarf up around my cheeks.

The work suited me. I was on my own, the boss of myself, in effect. But there was a lot of time for thinking too. I'd see things out in the dark. Flashes. Something in the corner of the lot. A little boy's grey corpse. I couldn't shake those images.

A couple of hours passed. I took a piss in the southernmost corner, watering dog leaves that had found a home in some cracks in the concrete. I looked out over the city through the chain-link fencing. The lights winked in a light mist that was rolling over the city from the direction of the harbour. A bat flew by near enough for me to hear the swoosh of its wings.

There came another noise somewhere out in the dark. I quickly zipped up my pants as if the lack of decorum might offend whatever cretin might be out there. The sound came from my side of the fence. I'd seen things, yes, but never heard anything that wasn't there. I arced the pale yellow glow of my torch, but couldn't make anything out. Another noise, this time from another direction – a shoe sole rolling on gravel, I was quite certain. I turned the beam of light to see what it was.

My heart bottomed out when I saw the man in the balaclava with the machete in his hand. The machete caught the light of my torch and reflected in my eyes, ruining my night vision. My feet seemed to grow roots and I felt a tingling sensation in my groin. Some drug addict with a two-by-four I could handle, but this guy had come prepared and it was clear he meant business.

Balaclava man just stood there as if waiting for me to advance, the machete held at an angle across his chest. When I felt like I could move my legs again, I began to retreat slowly as if he was somehow an animal that would startle easily. I backed into something … *someone.* Less than a second later I was lying crumpled in a heap after something had been rapped against the back of my head. The pain was like a spike had been pushed down through my skull.

Things became disjointed then, all at once happening at speed and in slow-motion. My ankles and wrists were bound with plastic ties. Three men, maybe, all in balaclavas, were busily moving in and out of the warehouse taking boxes to a van that had been driven into the compound. Another stood by me, initially emptying my pockets – car keys, mobile phone, walkie-talkie – then just standing over me as if I were carrion and the masked man with the Doc Martins was a bird of prey. Those boots would prod me occasionally with steel toe-caps, just to see if I was still conscious. I was, barely. That I could see the comings and goings appeared to be of no concern.

Not a word was spoken. There was no doubt among the raiders about the location of their loot. The operation was precise – there would be no messing around to see what else caught their fancy.

They made five trips in all, making off with fifteen boxes. Then two of them got in the back of the van and the other into the driver seat. The man with the Doc Martins gave me one last prod, more forcefully this time. I looked up at him, dazed, but somehow with enough of my wits intact to look at the man's eyes. I couldn't make out the colour, but I could see their shape. I'm good with eyes, me. I hoped they would register in my mind despite the bang to my head.

"That's quite a fetching outfit," I said, for some reason noting how sleek he looked. "Black is slimming on you." I got a kick in the ribs for being a smart aleck.

The van driver gesticulated for the guy to get out quickly. Doc Martins looked at the driver, then down at me again before moving away, finally, mercifully, to take his place in the passenger seat of the van.

"Yeah, that's what I thought!" I screamed after them. "Fucking … black ops wannabes."

And then, at last, they went. I could feel the warm trickle of blood tickling its way down the back of my head and inside my collar. What in the name of Christ could I do then? I struggled to free my hands, working the wrists, tightening my thumbs inward to make my hands as narrow as possible. This only succeeded in drawing more blood. I wormed my body along the gravel until I reached a forklift and used the fork to rub the hand tie against. I eventually got free when the tie gave. With my hands free, wearing down the tie around my ankles was quicker.

What then? Run? Hide? A phone. The office. I ran to the site manager's office, forced the door open and raised the alarm with HQ and they called the Guards. I sat in an office chair and waited. Then came the unmerciful pain in my skull. I put my arms across the desk and slumped my head into them.

It took less than five minutes for the Guards to arrive. A patrol car at first with a couple of low-ranked uniforms, both young women, then a couple of minutes later an unmarked Mondeo from which stepped a uniformed sergeant that I recognized. I'd never liked the guy. He never seemed to have his shirt buttoned up properly. For me, sloppiness is the first rung on the ladder to corruption.

"As I live and breathe. If it isn't my old pal Mickey Bosco," Sergeant Dave Savage said.

The way he said *breathe* was elongated, slithery.

"Give us a look," he continued.

He twisted my head around like he was handling a coffee mug so he could see the wound. It hurt like a motherfucker. He sucked air in between his pursed lips.

"Oh that's nasty. I think we should call an ambulance."

I could smell mouthwash on his breath.

"Forget it," I said. "I'm fine."

If there was one pig I wouldn't be showing weakness to, it was Savage.

"Standard procedure, I'm afraid. Sorry to make a fuss, you know."

He gestured to a junior Garda officer.

"Call an ambulance for my old pal here, will you, Dom?"

Dom looked like he wasn't long out of Pampers. His uniform was pristine, his gait erect and stiff. He had a high forehead and very little hair for a man of his age. He looked like a Guard should, but I could imagine him naively hoovering up Savage's nastiness as if it were somehow part of an unwritten Garda code. It was Savage's ilk that gave the Gardaí a mixed reputation. I could only hope that maturity and a sense of inner decency would prevent Dom ending up like him.

Savage asked me for an account of the robbery while we waited. I gave as much as I could remember: black balaclavas, black jackets, dark camouflage cargo pants, black boots – like uniforms. *Dressed more neatly than you, you sad excuse for a Guard.*

Savage asked me for any more specific details. I gave him the number plate of the van – which would no doubt turn up a couple of miles away burnt out. There was the blow to my crown and the prodding Doc Martins. The robbers never spoke, knew exactly what they were coming for, and where the boxes were stacked. Very professional. Inside knowledge for definite. But that wasn't for me, the ex-Guard, to theorize about.

The first two Guards that arrived returned to tell Savage that they had checked the centre and the scene was secure. They had a country look about them. They looked at me like I had just fallen off the end of their shoes, one of them smirking with an uneven grin. Savage said something to them out of earshot and I could see the four of them sniggering while glancing in my direction.

Savage walked back to me and thanked me for the information just as the ambulance arrived. His words rang hollow. He looked at me, up close to my face and said, "The old Bosco I knew would never have been taken from behind like that." That was rich coming from a back-stabber like Savage. "What happened to that guy, eh? Have you gotten soft in your old age?"

An EMT interrupted Savage's rambling when she came over to me with some kind of toolbox. Like I was an old motorbike. She opened the box and put something white and spongy on my head, then asked me to apply pressure, which I barely had the strength to do. As the EMT led me to the ambulance, Savage called out, "I'll be in touch, Bosco. You can count on it."

They took me to A&E where I was stitched up, observed until the morning, and sent home.

Later that day as I fiddled with the dressing on my head wound, I decided I'd put myself in harm's way one time too often. I called HQ, asked for the boss, and quit on the spot. The guy said something about a notice period, but when I pointed out, in a slurred voice that was not entirely put on, that brain damage was grounds for a law suit, he promptly granted my wish.

Just before 1 p.m. a couple of sharp raps on the front door ricocheted inside my aching skull like bullets in a bank vault. Bleary eyed, I made my way to the door and could see from the side window that Sergeant Dave Savage and a plain clothes detective – I can tell them a mile off – were waiting impatiently for me. Another knock on the door just as I reached for the latch made me pause. I shook my head to clear the resultant ringing in my ears and finally opened the door.

"Have you no pity for the walking dead?" I said.

Savage, looking as dishevelled as ever, just chuckled. The other guy, a grim-looking man in a grizzled suit, wore rectangular glasses that seemed to offset his eyes too much. He was all arms and legs and I imagined his suits had to be specially tailored. His sinewy face made it difficult to put an age on him, but his demeanour suggested at least early fifties.

"I'm DI Halloran," he said, not so much as offering a hand to me. "I'd like to ask you some questions concerning the robbery last night. Do you mind if we come in?"

I stood aside to let them pass. Neither man moved.

"After you, Mr Bosco," Halloran said, beckoning me towards the kitchen. A brief smile creased Savage's mouth.

In the kitchen, I offered both a glass of water. Both refused. A decade earlier I would have been in a position to offer something stiffer, though the newer breed of Garda were apt to refuse such an offer.

"Please sit, Mr Bosco," Halloran said as he took a notebook from the inside pocket of his furry suit jacket. "This won't take long. Sergeant Savage has filled me in on the details of the case, but I just have a few follow-up questions. I'm sure you understand, what with you ..."

The pause was an embarrassing reminder of my past indiscretion. "Yes. I'm pretty familiar with the procedures. Go ahead."

Halloran began by asking about the events of the previous night and I gave as good as verbatim to him what I had said to Savage. While Halloran wrote something into his notebook, I decided to fish for something on his background.

"I don't think we've met, Detective Halloran," I said. "What division are you assigned to?"

"NBCI," he replied with some authority, and without looking up from his notebook, as if to suggest he was above assignment to one of the districts.

"A bureau man, then. What interests the bigwigs in Dublin about this particular case?"

Halloran looked up from his notebook. "You're out of the loop, Bosco. It's no concern of yours. Just answer my questions."

I'd be lying if I said his reply didn't hurt. Out of the loop. An *other*.

"Did anything suspicious happen in the days leading up to last night? Someone out of place, maybe taking a bit of interest in the facility?"

I shook my head. But I had to question my attitude as a security guard. As a Garda officer, I could be sure I'd notice if some goon was casing the place. I was in service, responsible to the citizens that walked the length and breadth of Cork. It was my *duty* to notice such things. Solid Security, on the other hand, was a *job*, a cheque at the end of the week. I did the minimum, could barely see past the end of my nose, to be plain about it.

"It must have been tough, Bosco," Halloran said. "You put your life on the line and there's no second chances. You do the country a favour—"

Savage, unusually silent all this time, finally piped up, interrupting Halloran. "I always knew you were a ticking time bomb, Bosco. If it wasn't Chambers, it was going to be someone else. I'll bet you loved it, years of frustration coiled around his neck, squeezing the—"

Halloran put up his hand suddenly to hobble Savage in full

gallop. I noticed my right fist was clenched so hard that the nails were embedded in my palm.

"That's quite enough for now," Halloran said. "If there are any follow-up questions, I'll be in touch."

I saw them to the door and watched as they got into a marked patrol car. Savage drove them away.

Something struck me as a little odd about the house call, though. Halloran was a long way from Dublin's Harcourt Street HQ. The way I saw it, relatively minor robberies like Churchfield were handled by the local plods. There had to be more to it than the apparent routineness that Halloran conveyed.

My phone rang a day later while I stood weighing up whether to go for a cereal or a fry up. The caller identified himself as a *representative* of Jim Jordan, chairman of the holding company that owned the distribution centre in Churchfield. It didn't twig with me at first exactly who this Jim Jordan was. It should have.

"The boss wants to know why the sudden walk out, Mickey. He doesn't like how it looks."

"Were you expecting a protracted walk out?"

"Enough with the quips, Mickey. Why'd you quit?"

"I got beat over the head. Why do you think I quit? Anyway, I don't work for you. I worked for Solid Security. How'd you even get my number?"

I leaned back against the fridge. The fridge groaned. My head still hurt and it seemed the radiation from the phone made it worse.

"That's a dumb fucking question, Mickey."

His voice had a thick Cork accent. From somewhere in the city, maybe south of the River Lee. Somewhere on the Southside that belonged on the Northside. Togher?

The guy was going all lackey on me. And that's when it did finally twig with me. The Gentleman. Of all the places to end up minding, it had to belong to Jim *The Gentleman* Jordan, a supposedly gone-legit former crime lord, someone who'd slipped from the public consciousness. I took a second to compose myself.

"All the same," I said, "what business is it of yours or anyone else's?"

"The shades have come up with fuck all. The boss was wondering if you were feeding a load of shite to them. He's beginning to worry about you. Do you know what I'm saying? I mean, a secure facility and a gang of crooks just drive in the front gate?"

"That's a pile of horse manure. You should see the gash on my head. Hurts like a motherfucker."

I instinctively ran my hand over my head and felt the bump that no amount of ice, it seemed, could reduce in size.

"Fifteen grand's worth of TVs, though? I'd consider taking a slap on the noggin for a piece of that," the representative said.

"The cunts could have left me brain damaged. Or worse. Even fifteen K wouldn't cut it for that kind of risk. Now, fifty K, maybe."

Truth was, I had been in kind of a desperate situation, so who knows what I might have done.

"Look, you gotta work with me here. The boss just wants to make sure. You gotta see how it looks from the outside, right?"

"Yeah, right. What did you say your name was?"

I knew he hadn't, but I had to try something to shift the focus of the conversation.

"Never you fucking mind. All you need to know is who I'm speaking for. Capische?"

Jesus Christ, who did the guy think he was – Don Corleone? The guy was acting tough, with an emphasis on the word *acting*.

"I got that part loud and clear, Marlon," I said. "Now I hope I've made myself clear. I didn't do nothing your boss need worry about. I'm clean. OK?"

"If you say so, homes. Look, you take care of yourself, OK?"

I cringed when he said *homes*. He'd gone from Italian mob to Latino street gang in two sentences flat.

"Yeah. No one else will."

I gently placed the receiver onto its cradle to end the call. Then I picked it up again and banged the table hard three times with it before replacing it. A tightening of my chest muscles and a labouring of my breath reminded me that there were only so many of these hard miles I could travel.

Churchfield had just been an assignment from the security company. Why was a lackey of The Gentleman calling me? Besides, I knew shag all about the robbery. But guys like The Gentleman went with their gut and if they smelled something they wouldn't hesitate to act. He only had to be paranoid all the time for him to be right some of the time.

I sat back at the kitchen table again. I thought about buying another bottle of Jameson. Instead, I stuck a Benson in my mouth and fired it up. It was one or the other, I decided; no way was I going cold turkey.

I listened to the radio for a while in the hope that my wheeziness would subside as I relaxed. Daniel O'Donnell – Ireland's favourite mammy-loving crooner – was interviewed at one point and I felt like taking a hammer to it. I just didn't know what to do with myself. *Pull yourself together.* My arse was killing me from sitting on the knotted wooden chair. I didn't understand why anyone would make a chair without a cushion.

First Savage and Halloran, and now this heavy of Jordan's. It was enough to make me feel sorry for myself. Rather than wallow in self pity, I decided that I had to do something that would move my life forward. And where better for a fresh start than the pub.

2

A Crucifix of Suffering

AN CAPALL BÁN – THE White Horse. A bar with more characters than a typewriter. My local haunt is frequented by the dregs of Blarney Street and Gurranabraher and has all the charm and comfort of a tinker's caravan. It lives up to the tradition of Cork as the rebel county by defying the smoking ban – the health inspectors dare not visit unannounced.

Behind the bar, a single barman washing glasses. At the bar, a row of half-passed-out men, some with pints, most with harder stuff, some with newspapers open on the horse racing pages, hands black with ink, others absently watching a replay of a soccer match between nobodies on the TV An assortment of collectors' items on shelves around the bar – old lanterns, old road signs, old bottles, old pictures of old sports teams. The floor sticky, the air stale with spilt drink, wafting cigarette smoke and the body odour of men who seemed to live there but never shower.

As a Guard I had become friends, in the loosest sense of the word, with a retired bagman by the name of Moggy Mac. Mogs had collected loan repayments around Cork's Northside, the interest rates often dwarfing the amounts owed. I would slip him a ten or a twenty for tidbits of information – who'd been seen around that shouldn't have been around, who was beating whose wife, and so on. Enough to keep the Bosco almanac up-to-date.

When I was a Guard I drank only with my own mob – the blue mob. I found friends hard to come by once I had been kicked out. If for no other reason than familiarity or continuity, I remained on good terms with Mogs.

I noticed that Mogs was sitting there pint-less. He looked about the same as he always did: hair slicked back to cover his bald patch, skin drooping from his cheekbones like melting wax, rotting teeth amongst white ones that looked like tombstones on a full-moon night. He wore a cheap checked sports coat that made him look like a news reporter from the seventies.

I wore unassuming clothes. I wanted to blend in. A simple pair of blue jeans, striped grey shirt and black shoes. I think I lacked the confidence to wear anything remotely snazzy.

"I'll get them in so, will I?" I said.

I wondered how long Mogs had been sitting there waiting for the Bosco tab to walk in. It was all very well him taking other people's money, but he was very slow to part with his own.

I jostled my way to the bar, knocking elbows with a dome-headed guy who had a thirty-two-county tattoo on his crown. This tilted the man's pint of Murphy's sending the frothy head slopping onto the floor. The bald guy looked at me with his fist at the ready, but then he must have recognized me as the ex-cop who'd put Chambers in a coma. He relaxed, giving up his position at the bar.

I ordered a Bud and a Howling Gale Ale. I like stuff that has been brewed or distilled locally. I'm not a lover of stout – Beamish and Murphy's are out – so I opt for a Howling Gale when it's on tap and I'm in company. Whiskey is something I drink alone. Whiskey is for thinking – and remembering things. Like Dad.

I sat opposite Mogs at a table that would barely have qualified as a stool in most respectable pubs. I shook his hand. It was like rattling the bones of a skeleton.

"Who's Humpty Dumpty?" I said.

Mogs looked blankly at me.

"The guy with the tat on his head," I clarified.

"Oh him? That's Geoff Cooney. Scoobs we call him. He's harmless. Male nurse in Holy Cross hospital."

"Well, he's hardly a female nurse now is he? He'd put the frighteners on you if he came in to give you a sponge bath. Anyway, how are ya?"

"Ah you know, scratching my balls along the road as usual. You?"

"Same old, same old."

"That bad, eh?"

I played around with a sopping wet beer mat, tore at the edges of it. I smiled blithely.

"Yeah. That bad."

Mogs opened his mouth like a pelican and took an enormous gulp of beer. He wiped the back of his hand across his beak and dried it on his jumper.

"Well, maybe this'll perk you up, boy," he said. "You remember Johnny Fitzmaurice – Johnny Moolah?"

"Vaguely. Wasn't he like a wacker or something?"

"He was in your day. Anyway, he graduated from cornerboy to fully-fledged dealer. Rumour has it he took a shipment of heavy stuff off a yacht near Nohoval Cove."

"That's all very interesting, Mogs, but I'm not in the cop game anymore."

That might have been true, and they may have sent me packing, but they couldn't take the cop out of me. That's something that splices with your DNA, changes you forever, turns your blood blue.

"Listen, Mickey, the guy got wacked a couple of days ago. You must have read it in the papers, like."

"I stopped reading papers a long time ago."

I had not picked up a newspaper since I'd seen myself writ large in The Examiner that time I put Chambers in the hospital.

To say I had fallen out of touch with recent goings on would have been an understatement. I only had my own world, kept to myself.

"Ah right. Anyway, guess who put the green light on Moolah?"

"Get to the fecking point, Mogs."

I supped my pint.

"Jordan."

That caught my attention. I swallowed some beer and a gas bubble caught painfully in my chest.

"The Gentleman," I croaked.

Pain radiated around my upper chest and across my shoulders. It joined up with the ache on my head. It was a crucifix of suffering.

"None fucking other, boy."

I buried my hands into my hair and felt the scar. I picked at it, pulled at the stitching, opening it up just a bit. I felt something seep from the wound. I suddenly lost my appetite for drink. I needed to take stock for a moment, weigh up what this could mean.

"I'll be back in a minute, Mogs. Gotta drain the old weasel."

Mogs smirked. "As long as that's all you do with it, boy."

The lavatory stank to high heaven. The only stall was free and I went in and closed the door. There was a seat on the toilet, which was somewhat of a surprise given the condition of the rest of the lavatory, but no lid to sit on. I took a leak, then stood and thought for a moment.

The word on the street, something Mogs was very close to, was that The Gentleman had ordered a hit. What I also knew was that I was on Jordan's radar now. For a while I'd been flying low, below that radar, minding my own business. Now my altitude had risen and I'd hit unexpected turbulence. I was already recovering from one plane crash – I didn't need another.

I flushed the toilet. I desperately hoped I wasn't flushing my life away with my piss. Maybe it was already too late to worry about that. There was no soap in the dispenser and I knew from experience that the hand dryer was busted, so I gave my hands a quick rinse and wiped them on the back of my jeans.

Back at the table, I noticed that Mogs had already reached the end of his glass. Without asking, I ordered another pint for him. I still had most of the Howling Gale left and it was as much as I could stomach.

"They really should do something with that jacks," I said. "Just because no one else bothers to wash their hands doesn't mean I shouldn't be able to."

"Fuck sake, boy, who ever died from not washing their hands? I'm still here."

Barely. He was gaunt with all the appearance of an Egyptian mummy. His skin was like old saddle leather and I remembered that he used to rub a lethal mixture of olive oil and vinegar into his skin to promote tanning. That was before they cut three cancerous moles from his skin and told him to apply a liberal daub of factor fifty any time the sun shone.

"C'mere to me, Mogs. Who's been talking about Jordan and the Moolah in the same breath?"

Mogs grinned. "Just rumours, boy. Tittle-tattle."

I really wasn't in the mood for much idle chat after hearing what Mogs told me. We changed the subject to Premier League football for a bit, then watched the Six-One news on the nearest telly – another minister had resigned citing "health reasons". I got restless after that and looked at my watch.

"I'm sorry, Mogs. I've got to go."

"Ah hang on. I was going to get a round in."

"You were in your fuck."

I left nearly half a pint of the Howling Gale behind.

I decided to walk the mile or so to my house in Blackpool. The cloud cover was threateningly dark and it was getting cold, so I zipped up my anorak. Saint Anne's Steeple loomed in the blue-grey murk as I walked down the hill. The limestone and sandstone building made a big statement among the small dwellings that surrounded it, but dubbed *The Four-face Liar* because of the inability of each of its four clocks to keep in sync, it also reminded me that I could trust no one, that there was never one reliable version of the truth.

Live music blared from an open apartment window. A jam session with tin whistle, piano, and guitar. I did a little jig and banged my left heel against my right ankle making me wince with pain. Someone shouted, "Up ya boy ya!"

I called an old acquaintance from the force, Barry Cotter. The last time we'd worked together was the Robbie O'Meara disappearance. Barry had been a partner of mine when we were in uniform some years before that. I had been five years his senior, had shown him the ropes. We mostly just walked the beat around Bishopstown, then later Togher. I trusted Barry more than anyone I worked with since.

"Jesus, Bosco. I heard about Churchfield. How are you doing? I've … I've been meaning to call."

Sure you were. I knew I was *persona non grata* in police circles.

"I'm grand. Just a couple of bumps and bruises. You?"

"The usual shite. Drugs, guns, murders."

"Oh yeah. I remember." I actually missed them. "Listen, Barry, I was talking to an old friend of mine from the street. Said something about some guy called Moolah coming to an untimely end. You hear anything about that?"

"From the *street*?" I could hear Barry chuckling. "It's my business to hear. I'm assigned to the Fitzmaurice case. Why, what you hear?"

"Oh, you know … just that Jordan might have been up to his old tricks."

Having risen to the position of Cork's organized crime kingpin by the mid-eighties, Jordan was suspected in a number of hits on up-and-coming dealers. As well as being called The Gentleman, a moniker that was a hangover from his boxing days, he was sometimes called The Nipper, because he would eradicate potential competitors before they could lay down a serious foothold – nip them in the bud, so to speak.

"You know I can't talk about it, Mickey. Not even for an old friend like yourself. Anyway, who told you this?"

"Sorry, Barry. Can't say. You know, not even for an old friend."

There was that familiar chuckle again. We'd shared plenty of jokes, many of them x-rated, on our foot patrols. The laughter kept us just that little bit warmer on cold nights. Can't beat a blue joke when you're going blue from the cold in a blue uniform, is what we used to say.

"Ah fuck it. Look, what if I said that we weren't looking for anyone for the hit?"

"I'd say you weren't looking because you'd already found who you were looking for."

Barry just grunted something into the phone that sounded like it might have been an affirmative.

"There's something I have been meaning to ask you, though," Barry said as I passed by the North Cathedral where my first holy communion and confirmation ceremonies had taken place. "Jordan owns that place up in Churchfield where those guys hopped you. How'd you get the job?"

"I dunno. I just got assigned by the security company."

"How many guys work for them?"

"The security company? About twenty-five I'd say."

"Bit of a coincidence, don't you think? That of all of them, you get assigned to Churchfield."

I pretended like it hadn't already crossed my mind. This just made it front and centre, though. Something I'd need to confront. I couldn't discount the conspiracy theories on how I ended up minding stuff in Jordan's warehouse.

"Hmm. Maybe. When you put it like that."

"Well, just watch your back, Mickey."

I decided to fish for something on Halloran.

"You hear of a DI called Halloran? He was round yesterday asking questions. Questioning my involvement, to be more precise."

"Dick Halloran. It's funny you should bring him up. He's been seconded to the Bridewell for the foreseeable. Says he's working the Churchfield case, seems to think it may link to something bigger."

"It wouldn't be the first time some langer from the Bureau had a hidden agenda."

"Anyway, I don't see why he would be too interested in you. Just stick to your guns and he'll not be on your back for too long."

"I hope you're right, Barry. I can do without his shite."

Rain began to pelt down suddenly, landing in the puddles like mortar fire. I pulled up the hood of my anorak. I said my good-byes to Barry and searched my pockets for my pack of Bensons. I found it. Smoke filled my hood as I lit up. All of two minutes later and I was home. I flicked the fag butt into a puddle and there was a brief sizzle.

"That's it," I said out loud. "The last one."

I don't know why I quit right then. Maybe I had grown tired of seeing everything through a cloud, either psychological or the one I was blowing out in front of me. I took the pack from my pocket and emptied the remaining three cigarettes into the puddle. I didn't trust myself to just bin them. I'd probably scavenge them out from amongst the rotting vegetables and spent tea bags and smoke them whatever condition they were in – God knows, I had in the past. At least you couldn't light a wet fag – and I'd tried that too.

I went inside to spend a smoke-free night with a good book and some relaxing music. But I knew I'd be climbing the walls before too long, craving just one last drag, one final hit of nicotine.

The next morning I was tired and my body clock was still adjusting to normal waking hours. I scanned the ever-shrinking jobs page of The Examiner. I wasn't exactly sure what I was looking for. I felt maybe I'd know the job when I saw it, but nothing stood out. For the time being I was drawing down my savings to pay the bills and such. I don't believe in the dole – not unless I'm totally on my uppers. I don't like people poking into my affairs. *How much savings do you have? How much is your house worth? Any dependants?* I'd know soon enough if I needed to get off my arse and settle for another security job.

I was on the porridge now. I decided I would only partake of the Clonakilty and such at my mother's, just to appease her. She thought I was too thin, needed bulking up. That's mothers for you.

My mother, Adele, is devoutly Catholic. I was baptized, even served as an altar boy, but by the age of ten I found priests creepy. There was one particular priest who would put cold, wandering hands up your shirt and rub your bare chest. Thankfully, for my sake, I wasn't one of the priest's favourites. That would have been Declan. Mrs Bosco didn't want to hear about that, though. She wouldn't hear a bad word said against Father Bartholomew. He'd married my parents and baptized me *Michael Jeremiah Bosco*. I hadn't been to church in years, but would lie to my mother about going – about receiving communion, about confessing my sins. I had plenty of those to confess, but I was damned if it was a priest I would confess to.

There was one other memory of Father Bartholomew, however. He presided over my father's funeral mass. It was funny the things I was beginning to remember as my father's anniversary approached. And there was something different about this anniversary, something unresolved. It was inside my head now, scratching away, picking at fragments deeply buried, like the way I would occasionally pick at my head wound.

It wasn't that the memories were particularly different than before – they were the same every year. But I'd flooded those with drink. I'd smothered them before they could manifest into anything approaching true feelings. They had been pictures on someone else's wall, like holiday snaps. Not like now. Now they played in my head in full HD. Like I was feeling them for the first time again. The smells, the sounds. The tears tickling my cheeks.

The old anger I felt was coming back strong too. I didn't just feel angry at life, or at God, or anything non-specific. I felt angry with Dad. He'd somehow let me down, died meaninglessly, not been there at key moments in my life, like the Chambers incident. I could have handled him dying of ill health or by accident – eventually, anyway. But he'd put himself in harm's way for his job. For his job, for fuck sake! What about his family? I would immediately feel guilty for damning a dead man.

My father, seen by some as the archetypal sleazy newspaperman and by others as a crusading investigator, had shifted along the razor's edge of official society and the murk beneath and been cut down. He had quite a name back in the early eighties, a time of immense political instability and corruption. He became synonymous with the exposure of some of the biggest local scandals of the era.

Biggest of all was the time some Gardaí held onto the ransom money they were supposed to have paid to IRA kidnappers and instead went on a disastrous armed assault that yielded one dead hostage, one dead kidnapper, and three seriously-injured plain clothes detectives.

My father painstakingly documented the subsequent surge in lifestyles of those Special Branch detectives and interviewed a high-ranking member of the IRA's Southern Command who disputed the ransom payment. Unsurprisingly, I suppose, not one detective got suspended, let alone lost their job. Who was going to believe the words of an anonymous terrorist, after all?

I remember how those same Special Branch detectives came in their suits at seven in the morning, banging so hard on the door that they broke the letter box. We were supposedly suspected of harbouring one of the kidnappers who had fled during the botched hostage recovery operation. Convenient that they had someone to pin the loss of money on. That was the kind of carry on that went on back then when money was flowing into the Guards in the name of anti-terrorism. Two birds, one stone: harass a thorn in the side and get paid at the overtime rate for doing it.

They found his body in the boot of a rusting hulk of an Opel Kadett in a scrap yard on Dublin Hill in October, 1986. Of all the images of your father you want to be left with, a crime scene photo of his rotting corpse in that boot isn't one of them. But the report of his final moments in the case file paints an even more pathetic image: the frantic struggle for life, the defence wounds on his forearms, the scrapes on his hands and knees as he tried desperately to evade those final blows, then, finally, how he bled out.

I don't know much about the circumstances that led to my father's death. According to the case file, the senior editor of the Cork Evening Standard had described how my father was working on a cigarette-smuggling story. He went on to say that my father had been keeping things to himself, that he may have gone in over his head on the story. The long and short of it, however, was that the editor knew shag all of any consequence – or at least that was what he claimed.

The Garda investigation could hardly have been described as comprehensive: a few door-to-door enquiries, an interview with the owner of the scrap yard where my father's body had been discovered, an appeal for witnesses to come forward. Far from leaving no stone unturned, it looked as if they had lifted up a token pebble and placed it neatly back in its place. Nothing from informants about the word on the street, nothing about surveillance of suspected smugglers or dealers. They'd ticked the minimum number of boxes and buried the file in records. Besides, there were more pressing matters at that time, like IRA *sympathizers*.

That fixation on the IRA and INLA would allow others to quietly build their crooked little empires while the Gardaí had paramilitaries on their mind. The scourge of heroin that poisoned much of Ireland's urban areas – and still does – went largely unchecked. It led to The Gentleman, for instance.

I phoned a flower shop to order a wreath. Nothing special, just a standard round one with white flowers. Nothing too gaudy. The wreath was more for my mother than myself. I wasn't sure how much she cared anymore, though.

I spent the rest of the day moping around the house trying to distract myself, somehow trying to project myself beyond my insane urge to suck on a cancer stick – that's what I began to call cigarettes from then on – trying to fill the house with constant noise so that there wouldn't be any silence to fill with thought.

But nothing worked and the sweat poured down my forehead and stank my armpits.

I went to the kitchen, soaked a facecloth, and returned to the sitting room. I put the facecloth across my forehead, sank back in my armchair, and closed my eyes.

I went to see my mother the next day at her home in Gurranabraher. I went early enough that there were still some sausages, rashers, and of course black pudding, in the frying pan – that heavy, filthy old cast iron thing that had fed me since I was small. It was Denny black pudding, though – OK, but not my favourite. Obviously that would be the Clonakilty, but I would admit to an overly-discerning palate when it comes to the full Irish.

Most people think that any old fried shite will do, but I know that it takes the finest local ingredients, cooked in the right order, served at the right temperature, and presented appropriately, to count as a proper full Irish.

My mother's not your average blue rinser. Her hair's white, but not from bleaching, straight and cut shoulder length. She wears a house coat, but does so with panache. She's seventy-six, five-feet tall and obese, but mobile enough to drive to the farmers' market twice a week and mass every morning at eight.

"Look at you, Michael – all skin and bone," my mother said.

She lowered the drawbridge of a shelf on the dresser that seemed to have been in the kitchen for as long as I could remember. Nothing in the kitchen, not even the toaster, was younger than twenty years old.

"The doc wouldn't agree with you there, Mam."

"Hmm. Well, I never did like that O'Reilly fellow. It would be more in his line to practice what he preaches. He's a chimney. Always out the front of The Long Valley puffing away. Drink, fags, and curried chips on the way home. And then he tells you to watch what *you* eat."

"I know. He's a good doctor, but a lousy human being."

I cut a piece of black pudding into three segments and put one in my mouth. I savoured the texture and flavour; I didn't intend eating the stuff for much longer.

"You know what today is, don't you?" I said, chewing.

I didn't doubt she did. She nodded.

"I've ordered a nice wreath," I said. "I'll take us out to St Finbarr's."

"You're a good man, Michael. Whatever others say. I know you're decent inside. You're a good Christian … even if you don't believe that."

I didn't know what kind of man I was. I knew I was capable of killing a man with my bare hands. I didn't care much for my measurement on the Christian scale, though. I couldn't have cared less how the Miracle Man Himself rated me.

"I go now and again. You know – to give the Guy in the Sky a piece of my mind."

A blatant lie. I only went for funerals, just to pay my respects, to be seen by the bereaved. I didn't even bother with weddings – not that very many invites were forthcoming.

"You shouldn't talk like that, Michael."

"Why, because he's everywhere? Well, where was he when Dad died?"

A provocative line I'd used many times before. I wouldn't pretend to be the greatest son. Silence. It's the one line to kill a religious argument. Why does God allow the innocent to die? Only Dad wasn't so innocent. Even his death had the stain of suspicion about it. But I was close to him, knew he was decent inside, like my mother was fond of saying. If there was a foul whiff about his death, it was because someone had set him up, had made it look like a deal or a meet gone bad.

"Well," my mother said, finally breaking the impasse, "I baked some nice bread last night. I'll put a couple of slices in the toaster for you. And there's some fresh free range eggs in the fridge. I got them off the farmer this morning if you fancy a fried egg."

"No thanks, Mam. I think it's time I started heeding what the doc says."

I washed down the last of a greasy sausage with a sup of Barry's Gold Blend. There was time enough to heed the doc.

The drizzle was heaping down on us as we stood at the grave-side. The wet grass tangled around our shoes as we sank into the ground. The section of the graveyard where Dad's grave was looked unkempt, the grass badly in need of a cut. I craved a cancer stick. I didn't even care then that I'd started calling them that.

"It's like a cliché, isn't it?" I said.

Mam looked at me with one eye cocked.

"Rain at the graveyard. It's like some kind of film noir."

"Sometimes I have no idea what you're talking about, Michael. But if you were expecting rain, why didn't you bring an umbrella?"

I shrugged. "Twenty-five years, huh?"

I looked at the wreath I had collected from the flower shop. It was plain, with funeral-grade flowers. It would look tired by the morning.

"Maybe I should have gotten a better wreath," I said. "Something to commemorate the anniversary."

"He'd have moaned about the cost, your father. We didn't have two shillings to rub together back then."

"Twenty-five years, though. If you think about it, I've been alive for thirty-nine years and he's been gone for two-thirds of it. And before long it'll be—"

"Ah Christ, Michael. Let's just have a moment of silence."

We stared at the headstone – Cork limestone. Already the lettering was smudged as the etching was eroding. We stared as if waiting for a reply from the cold, wet stone.

"A touch of black paint would be good," I said. "It would bring out the letters nicely."

Mam stayed silent for a moment. She seemed to get more tired of the ritual each year. Then, perhaps having contemplated my words for a while, she replied.

"The way you're going, Michael, we'll have an engraver out here to mark your own burial. We can kill two birds with one stone then, save a few bob."

I laughed. It was a fatalistic laugh. In a brief moment I thought going for a nap next to my father wasn't such a bad thing. Not the way things were going. I tried to change the subject.

"Do you believe what the Guards said about his death?"

It sounded strange to my own ear saying "the Guards". It used to be *us* or *we*.

"Pah!" she said. "Your father wasn't exactly Mr Transparent. I could never tell what was going on in his head."

I could never tell what was going on in my own head, so I could excuse my father of that. But I had asked the question before and gotten the same answer. Maybe even exactly twelve months before … and twelve months before that. But my perspective had been shifting. Something about what happened in Churchfield, and what I had heard about Johnny Moolah, was powering it. And God knows I had plenty of time now for thinking. Too much time.

"But," I said, "do you believe what they said? That he was up to his elbows in the black market. A smuggler. A dealer. I mean, it's complete shite isn't it?"

"I don't know what to believe, Michael. I just don't know what to believe. There was a time I would have spat at anyone who suggested it. But I'm tired. I'm just so tired now."

"There's never been a follow-up investigation. You know, to rake over the leaves again to see if there might be any new leads or some DNA evidence. I asked about it … you know, when I was a Guard. I thought about doing my own investigation on the side."

The crime scene photo flashed into my mind. Dad was under the ground pretty much as he had been found. Understandably, it had been a closed casket affair.

Mam sighed. "You'd have gotten into a right heap of trouble. I'm sure that's not what your father would have wanted for you."

I laughed. "I might as well have. Better to be thrown out for that than what happened with … with Chambers."

Again she sighed. "Best to leave some things in the past, Michael. Some things are best not talked about. I'm sure God has his plan for all of us, a reason why we have to suffer."

"You mean you hope he has."

She said nothing.

At the entrance to the cemetery, a hearse arrived with a small procession of mourners. They walked slowly through the gloom like ants and forked onto a path to the far end of the cemetery. An expensive-looking wreath with flowers spelling SON dominated the display on the roof of the hearse. A smaller one had the Manchester United insignia. Some poor kid, I assumed, dead before his time. Like Robbie.

As the drizzle became rain, it seemed then that Death wasn't much of a one for sunny days.

"Come on, Mam," I said finally, when it seemed the damp had permeated every layer of clothing. "Let me take you home."

3

A Deal with the Devil

LATER THAT AFTERNOON I picked up The Examiner and looked at the jobs pages again. I focused in on positions with titles like facilities manager and premises officer. When you cut to the chase, though, they were just fancy words for caretaker. A mop and bucket, a card for the cash and carry to buy toilet rolls and Cillit Bang, and unsociable hours. I didn't think I'd get a sniff at an interview for those, though. I mean, how can you blag your way through a CV when you were front-page news not so long ago? But maybe I was just being impatient. Maybe I'd get a call out of the blue, maybe have two or three all at once. And there was always another security job – something where my reputation had been a positive – but I didn't know how that would pan out now that I was the guy who let Druid Distribution get robbed.

So, unemployed as I was, I had an entire afternoon to fill. I was still adjusting to daytime hours and would find myself napping during the day and rising in the middle of the night, restless and with the remnants of nonsensical dreams still fresh. Doc O'Reilly was in them a lot. Dad too.

I sat on the couch reading a book and listening to chillout music. Music with no words so that I could keep my train of thought as I read the words of *Billy Budd* by Herman Melville. I prefer to read old classics. At least those worlds are static, predictable, safe to retire into. Melville's *Moby Dick* had stuck with me from an early age and I had never read anything else by Melville, so I decided to try another of his.

The book was tattered and yellowed. I had inherited it from Dad. It was the one thing my father had been specific about in his will – Michael Junior was to be left his collection of books, some of them early editions, collectors' items even. I had read most of them in my teens, but they had stayed hidden away in a box in the attic ever since. Something had prompted me to climb into my mother's attic to retrieve them.

I got to the part of *Billy Budd* where Billy stabs the evil captain in the heart. *Good for you*, I thought. Then someone was knocking on the door using the flap of the letter box.

I opened the door to a stranger in a black suit. The morose, granite-like face of the man who stood there suggested, just for a moment, that this could have been one of the mourners from yesterday's trip to Saint Finbarr's. I would have put his age at about thirty.

"Mr Bosco." Not a question.

"Yes?"

"My boss would be grateful if you could accompany me to his premises where he would like to engage in conversation with you."

"What about?"

"It's not my place to presuppose the words of my boss."

He would have seemed like a very educated heavy had it not been for the fact that the words were spoken robotically, as if the man had been rehearsing in front of a mirror for an hour before driving to my house.

"Look, I'm in the middle of something. Please tell Mr Jordan that I'm busy and ask would he perhaps phone me in advance to make an appointment."

I smiled wanly.

The man, who I had no intention of finding out the name of, brought forward an enormous hairy hand and grabbed the shoulder area of my T-shirt into such a clump that it stopped the blood flowing to my arm.

"My boss doesn't need to make appointments," he said with a thicker accent, betraying his social background. These words were unrehearsed, but still, I felt, something the man had uttered many times before.

My smile disappeared quickly and I could feel my eyes widen dramatically. I could handle myself, but to a certain extent I had been living off my reputation. Beating and strangling Chambers into a coma had certainly made people think twice about messing with me. But this guy, all six-foot and some four or five inches of him, with an Eastern European-style buzz cut, had no respect for that reputation, if indeed he knew of it.

"Let me just get my coat," I said meekly.

I wasn't up for a fight and it wouldn't have been smart to pick one with one of Jordan's guys. Not when there were twenty more to take his place, every one as hard and uncompromising as the last.

The man led me to a black Mercedes that I thought of, what with the earlier visit to my father's grave, as a funeral director's car. The one that carries the family after the hearse. I sat in the back on cold, fresh-smelling leather. A loud clunk signalled to me that I was now locked in, a prisoner. I watched the man drive north from my home in Blackpool, then up Blarney Street, past Clogheen Grotto, and on into the north Cork countryside.

It took about forty minutes to arrive at the Jordan estate, some-where between the villages of Buttevant and Doneraile. We were buzzed through a heavy iron gate and drove up a tarmacadam drive that snaked between rows of mature trees – sycamore, oak mostly. I swore I saw a pheasant as something brown flashed by, but I couldn't be certain.

We came to the front of a big Georgian, red-brick house that seemed to be a perfect cube. Two pillars stood on either side of an enormous front door that had a large round black iron knocker on it.

Lying on the porch was a big white and grey ball that suddenly unfurled to reveal an Old English Sheepdog. It looked freshly blow dried, its fur sticking out like it was statically charged. It bounded over to the car and peered in the window where I sat – at least it only seemed to, because the windows were blacked out. I thought it looked benevolent, in a dopey kind of way. All the same, I would be keeping my guard up. Benevolent by nature perhaps, but in the hands of Jordan you could never know what to expect.

The driver shooed the dog away and then opened the door for me.

"Follow me," he said like I had no choice.

We walked to the porch where a woman who had all the appearance of an accountant greeted me. She was thin – a bit too thin – and baby-faced. She wore a grey trouser suit and had matchstick legs, so her trousers billowed about like sails. Her auburn hair was tied up in a bun. She ran her eyes up and down me like I was a balance sheet.

"You must be Michael. I'm Grace. My father has been so looking forward to seeing you."

She spoke softly with an indistinct, perhaps forced accent. She directed me into the hall where I could see pretty much what you expect to see in a country manor: stag heads, pictures of hunts, ancestors in formal dress – only these weren't *their* ancestors. No, they had bought their way into this realm. The only question was, how much blood had coated that money?

A wide granite stairs rose from the centre of the hall and split left and right like a snake tongue to the landings on the first floor. A floral carpet ran up the centre of the steps, held in place by twisting brass rods.

On the wall above the stairs was an enormous mural. It looked freshly painted and was entirely out of keeping with the other pictures. In it a man stood proudly in a riding outfit, his chin elevated, his riding helmet at his right side, a stallion to his left. At least it wasn't a ridiculous Napoleon on a horse type painting, but it still had something about it that was over the top by some way, like a horse clearing a fence in the Grand National by a far greater distance than it needs to, just to try and demoralize the other horses in the race. The subject of the painting was, of course, Jordan.

Grace led me along a corridor that had busts on plinths, a couple of suits of armour that shone from frequent polishing, and stained glass windows with scenes from the bible. At the end of the corridor a heavy oak door was slightly ajar and I could hear a man speaking.

When I finally saw Jordan, the thing that struck me immediately was how different he looked from his daughter. His daughter's face had sharp features – thin lips, pointed nose, narrow chin – and her father's, by contrast, had a boxer's nose, square jaw, and the look of a man who believed that heavy doses of vitamins would see him past a hundred. Without her deceased mother for comparison, it would have been impossible to imagine them as father and daughter. I had only ever seen Jordan in stock photographs that had graced the front pages of tabloid and broadsheet newspapers over the years. Not so much this millennium, though.

"Thanks, Terence," he said into his mobile phone. "I'll talk to you later."

He hung up and looked up at me from the armchair he was sitting in.

"Michael, Michael. It's good to finally meet."

He pointed to an armchair that was old and slightly tatty, but obviously priceless. I sat and sank down into the softly-sprung cushion, my elbows uncomfortably high on the arms. I felt like the seated statue of Abe Lincoln at his memorial building in Washington, DC.

"Drink, Michael?"

"I'm fine."

I could have murdered one.

"A little birdie tells me you like Jameson. I've got their eighteen-year-old limited reserve."

I wondered what little birdie that might have been. It seemed a lot of people were poking their noses into my affairs of late. And at a time when I had been going out of my way to keep to myself. To be anonymous. To fly below the radar.

"I'll bet you've got a flock of those birds," I said. "Maybe I'll have just a wee drop, then."

I smiled politely and hoped it didn't betray my contempt.

Jordan gestured to an ornate cabinet. I think it was pure teak or mahogany rather than just veneered. Hand-carved flowers grew from hand-carved urns and meandered the length and height of the cabinet.

"Be a petal, will you, Grace?"

Grace was an appropriate name for his daughter. She seemed to have it in spades.

Jordan's armchair was identical to mine. He nestled into it comfortably, his elbows at just the right height. He looked like the king of all he surveyed and I must have looked like his court jester.

"How have you been, Michael. I mean, since the robbery. I heard you took a nasty knock."

"The swelling's gone. Most of the pain too."

"That's good. The hospital treat you OK?"

"Yes. Fine."

Grace handed me a healthy measure of whiskey in a crystal tumbler and left us alone in the sitting room. As I looked into the glass, I thought that I had never seen a more beautiful colour.

"And the cost?"

"No cost. The state picks up the tab. One of the few times it does."

I forced another smile.

"Good, good. Forgive me for all the questions, Michael. You see, I'm just the chairman of Druid Distribution. I'm not au fait with the day-to-day goings on. You understand what a holding company is don't you?"

He said "au fait" in an exaggerated French accent that almost made me cringe. Did he think the French had a monopoly on class?

"You own a bunch of companies," I said, "but other people run them for you while you keep your distance?"

"More or less, more or less. In the case of Druid, that would be Martin. You know Martin, right?"

"Yeah. But mostly just to see. Mr O'Brien and I rarely crossed paths, what with me doing the night shift."

Mostly just to see. But I'd seen enough to know he was garbage. He was a fat, round man who wore shirts a size or two too small and whose tie looked like a noose around his neck. He treated his employees with disdain and walked by me like I was no more important than a cardboard box.

"Ah, of course, of course. Well, I'm glad to hear there haven't been any lasting effects. You never know with knocks on the head. Well, that's good, because I want to talk about what happened."

"The night of the robbery?"

"Yes. According to the Garda report, you say they took at least fifteen TVs?"

Garda report – what was Jordan doing with that?

"Eh … I would say *exactly* fifteen."

"Of course, of course. You were a copper, after all. Why wouldn't you be so precise? Facts, facts, facts. Just the facts, ma'am."

He laughed at his attempt at humour, baring a set of perfect teeth. With the tan from his obvious trips to sunny climes, he could have passed for a cheesy car salesman. He may have surrounded himself with the trappings of wealth, but he still came across as cheap.

Jordan looked down at his lap, seeming to ponder something deeply. He did this for about half a minute.

"You haven't worked since that night have you?" he said, finally.

"No."

"And you haven't signed on either. I know this because you haven't requested a P45."

And there was Jordan telling me he knew nothing of the daily goings on in his companies. Yet he had obviously asked Solid Security's HR person whether I had asked for my P45. What exactly was his relationship with Solid Security? And what was his interest in me?

"No. It's not my style."

Jordan smiled. "That's what I like to hear. You like to earn your keep. That's a good trait in a man." He leaned forward and the smile dissipated. "We've a lot in common, you and me. A lot in common."

I doubted it. "How so?"

"We've had – how can I put it delicately? – mishaps in the past. And we've tried to move beyond them. To rise above them, as I like to say. Isn't that what you've tried to do, Michael?"

I was beginning to lose patience. There was an ulterior motive to Jordan's ramblings and I wanted him to get to the point. Quickly.

"Look, I get it that you know all about me. It seems everyone knows me. Everyone wants a piece of me."

Jordan laughed a broad, throaty laugh. Then he smiled so widely that his eyes became slits and his face reddened.

"Let me cut to the chase then," Jordan said, much to my relief. "I have a proposition for you. Something suitable for a man of your background. A man of your talents."

I could sense where this was going. I didn't want to have anything to do with the guy.

"I'm not the lackey kind, Mr Jordan. I don't do the whole beck and call thing."

"I know, I know. You're very much your own man. I wouldn't have it any other way. Any other way. This proposition ... well, as you have guessed it is a job offer of sorts. But it's one of mutual interest I can assure you."

My interest was piqued just a tiny bit. "How so?"

"I've had my suspicions about Martin for a while. Little things here and there. Things he always has an excuse for. Too readily, though. I became – how can I put it? – a little untrusting. And now with the robbery ..."

"More than a little untrusting."

"Exactly," Jordan said, extending his arm suddenly like he was playing a game of snap. "And if he had something to do with you getting that whack ... well, I just figured you might want to be in on it."

"In on what?"

"Surveillance. I want him watched. I want to know who he meets, for how long, and what bad habits he has. I want a picture of his lifestyle. I want to know if he's living beyond his means."

I thought it was rich coming from The Gentleman. If ever there was someone who had lived beyond his means – his *declared* means, at any rate – it was Jordan. Certainly, he had filed his accounts for all his companies and had the appearance of legitimacy. But he had bought his way to legality with ill-gotten gains and I didn't like it. Not when he had been pontificating about *earning your keep*.

To buy myself some time to think, I took a laborious sip from the whiskey tumbler. I savoured it. It was good vintage. Beyond *my* means, though.

"I don't understand. Why not get one of your own lack- ... *employees* to do this for you?"

"I'm looking for a man of subtlety. That I do not have in abundance when it comes to my staff. But also a man of integrity. Ten years ago, I would have mistrusted such a man. But I have grown to understand the need for such men. It's why I'm sitting here in my comfortable home while others pace the corridors of Mountjoy or sit in their little terraced houses for fear of attracting attention to themselves."

Somehow Jordan had survived the best efforts of the Criminal Assets Bureau. In other cases the CAB had seized possession of cash, property, Land Rovers, horses, and all manner of assets that had been the fruits of organized crime. Many of his contemporaries had been prosecuted under strict new laws against criminal gangs, some of them, as Jordan suggested, pacing their twelve-foot by six-foot cells in Mountjoy prison. Others had been scared into driving battered old cars and living in dingy houses in order not to draw the attention of the authorities on themselves.

"I'm not going to pretend, Mr Jordan—"

"Jim. Please call me Jim."

"—that I would be thrilled to be in your employ. The fact is, I don't trust you. And I don't want you to take that personally, Jim. I just don't have the trust gene in my DNA. Not anymore."

Jordan seemed to sense my intentions. "But …"

"I'll do it. If there's some langer out there that had the temerity to fuck me up, then I want to know about it."

When it seemed that Jordan could have smiled no wider, he did.

"That's what I like to hear." He held up his own glass of the vintage Jameson to toast me. "I'll drink to that."

We discussed terms. They were most agreeable to me. Cash, though. This would be an under-the-mattress deal. No trace, no over-zealous spending to trigger suspicion.

We exchanged mobile numbers and agreed to twice-weekly updates. Then he handed me a manila envelope. He explained that it contained all the vital statistics about O'Brien, the stuff that I would just be wasting my *talents* collecting. It showed me that he had planned this well in advance, that whether I took the job or not, O'Brien was going to be watched.

When we had concluded our discussions, Jordan picked up a little brass bell with an old wooden handle and shook it. To the manor born, indeed. The tinkling sound brought Grace back into the room.

"Please see Mr Bosco to the car, would you, petal?"

She smiled like a little spaniel.

"Yes, Daddy."

In the hall, I spoke to her.

"You work for your Dad, then?"

She smiled sweetly, almost innocently.

"Yes. For my sins."

"You don't look like you've sinned a day in your life."

She let her guard down, fluttered her perfectly curled eyelashes. "Oh, I've sinned. Daddy doesn't know the half of it."

"He's quite the man, your Dad. Quite convincing."

She smiled again. "Give him a chance. He might just surprise you."

Not Jordan. Leopards and their spots, and all that.

She led me to the car where Mr Stone-Face had been waiting patiently for almost an hour.

"Take good care of Mr Bosco. And none of that KGB locking of the doors stuff either. Mr Bosco is a friend of ours now."

I guessed that was it, though: you were either their friend or their enemy, no middle ground. I'd tipped my hat, kowtowed to The Gentleman. I was his now.

Back home, I slumped into the couch and absently searched my pockets for the fags I had given up. The whiskey and the stress had made me tired and I almost nodded off. I put back on the chillout music and picked up *Billy Budd*. Reading calmed me every bit as much as the chillout CD. I would often fall asleep with a book across my chest and wake up as soon as it fell off and hit the floor.

A knock on the front door made me flinch violently out of a semi-sleep. I reluctantly pulled myself out of the couch where I had sunk down and begun to form a cocoon for myself.

It was only about ten minutes since I had been dropped home, so I assumed I must have left something in the Merc. I checked my pockets for wallet and phone as I made my way to the front door. But it was Barry.

This version of Barry was sporting a neatly-trimmed beard and had a discernible scar across his forehead – a far cry from the fresh-faced rookie that I had teamed up with more than a decade earlier.

"Jesus, Barry. Come on in."

I don't think I hid my surprise on seeing him. It was nearly three years since he had last called socially. It made me wonder if it was, in fact, a social call. I ushered him into the living room and offered him a drink.

"No thanks. I'm not staying."

He said this gruffly. He sounded different than he had the previous day on the phone when he had been jokey.

He left on his thick wool overcoat and sat on the arm of the couch closest to the door. I stood by the fireplace where a gas fire was just beginning to heat up.

"To what do I owe the pleas—"

"Where have you just been, Mick?"

His face was serious, his scar lost in the folds of his brow.

"What do you mean? I haven't *been* anywhere."

No way could I have told him where I was. It would raise too many questions, the answers to many of which would put me further out in the cold with one of my last remaining friends.

"Fuck it, Mick, don't dick me around. You were at Jordan's place."

I almost felt my bowels give way as Barry shot me a piercing look. One thing about Barry that you couldn't forget were the eyes. They were dark, unforgiving eyes. The kind that didn't reflect light. The kind that swallowed bullshit up whole.

"Have you been following me?" I asked.

"You're some thick cunt if you think you could go see Jordan without it being noticed. *You*, Mick. You didn't think it would raise a red flag you paying him a visit? He's under surveillance twenty-four seven. Didn't that click with you? Moolah, the hit, Jordan a suspect?"

He was right. The blue in me was fading. I was beginning to think like a fucking citizen.

"I didn't have a choice!"

"Jesus Christ, I knew this would be a waste of—"

"I'm dead serious, Barry! He had a fucking giant come fetch me. Finn McCool to the power of ten this guy was. Hands as big as frying pans."

I put a hand to my throat and simulated strangulation, just for emphasis. Barry sighed heavily and propped his chin on the heel of a hand. He gave me a deep, probing stare.

"Bad enough you strangled Chambers without strangling yourself now. The man is O'Keeffe," he said, the sound almost lost in his laboured exhalation. "William O'Keeffe."

Finally a name to put to the block of granite.

"You'd better start talking, Mick. From the beginning."

I'd only give him the bare essentials, try to account for my time. I didn't think it would fly, though.

"He just wanted to talk about Churchfield. He asked if I was OK, if I needed anything. He asked if I had any hospital bills or anything like that and I just said that the state had picked up the bill. We shared a whiskey and what's-his-face – this O'Keeffe guy – took me home. Then you turn up like the Spanish inquisition."

"And all that took fifty minutes?"

"He talks real slow."

I couldn't help my bravado. I'd been shipping blows from all angles the past few days, so I was beginning to lose my cool. Barry stood up and closed the distance between himself and me. We were almost touching noses.

"Well, maybe you think *I'm* real slow if you think I'm buying that crap."

I couldn't help myself at this point. I rolled my eyes exaggeratedly. Barry's arm twitched as if he were within a hair's breadth of grabbing me by the throat. I'd had quite enough of being manhandled for one day, so I was prepared to strike back.

"Stay away from Jordan," he said, little beads of spittle dotting around my face. "Or you'll land yourself in a small room with nothing but you, me, and a phone book."

I wasn't going to be intimated by that cliché. I held my ground. I felt roots under my feet again, like I had during the robbery, but good ones this time – ones that would hold me steady against an attack. Appearing to recognize this, Barry backed away from me a bit and began to breathe more easily. His face changed and he looked pleadingly at me.

"What did I say, Mick? Watch your back, I said."

I said nothing and just nodded. Barry shook his head and

walked to the sitting room door.

"Don't back me into a corner," Barry said, keeping his back to me. "I value our friendship, Mick. But let me be straight … I can't be seen within a country mile of you if you hang around with the likes of Jordan."

I wondered what the difference between a country mile and any other mile was, but decided the time for joking had passed. I considered telling him that Jordan had gone legit, that he was audited and everything. But I didn't believe it myself.

"Something goes wrong, Mick, and I can't be there to rescue you."

"I'm a big man, Barry. I can look after *numero uno*."

"Well … you better. I don't want to find you in some landfill somewhere, just another case on my desk."

And with that he turned and left without another word.

I tried to shout something after him, but it was like my mouth was gone. Like in my nightmares. Only now I was in my own living nightmare.

I sat back in the couch not quite knowing what to make of Jordan's offer, of why I so readily accepted it, or why I wanted to put myself into the centre of a maelstrom with Barry Cotter on my back. I decided that under the circumstances a stiff drink was in order. I had just enough for a double measure in an old bottle left over from the previous Christmas. I emptied it into a tumbler and sipped from it, then put it on the side table next to the couch. I started up the CD player again and the synthesized sounds of nature and electronica once again soothed me. I picked up *Billy Budd* and found the last page I had read before the interruptions. If there was another knock on the door, I was going to ignore it.

I read until I reached the end of part one. I remembered my father sitting in an old cloth-covered armchair he had been particularly fond of – *his* chair. His reading chair, worn through to the sponge on the arm where he used to balance the corner of a book as he peered intently at the page.

I turned the page to begin part two and … something fell on

the ground. A slip of paper. As crisp as a new bank note, like it had been written yesterday. On it was written the address of the scrap yard where his body had turned up in the boot of a car. Below the address was written: "20,000 Camels. Starman."

A shot of adrenaline hit me right between the eyes. Camels. Cigarettes. That story of his about the smuggling operation – it was true after all. 20,000 cigarettes. I did a quick calculation: 200 fags to a carton, so that meant 100 cartons. Not big enough for a main shipment, perhaps, but big enough for a local dealer. And what or who was Starman?

I remembered there was a film called *Starman* starring Jeff Bridges, but I didn't know if it had been released before 1986 when my father's body was found. And didn't Bowie sing about a "Starman"? That was much older than the film.

I had to slow myself down – too many thoughts were racing around in my tired brain. All these years later and there had been a clue lying there in my mother's attic, tantalizingly out of sight. One other thought hit me just then, one that made my hands tremble. Dad had put the note in the book, probably to mark the page, just before he went off to meet his killer. I tried to remember if I had seen my father reading that day or the night before, but nothing came to me.

I held the book in my hand and flicked through the rest of the pages. Nothing else dropped out. I held the book to my chest. It was a connection to Dad and for the first time since his death I could actually *feel* the connection to him. He'd read the same words, thumbed the same pages, very shortly before his death. It was the closest thing I had left to a touch of his hand.

It was too much to take in so suddenly. My hands continued to tremble and my breathing erupted into something approaching an asthma attack. A flood of tears came. Not long afterwards, I slept a deep, dreamless sleep.

$$4$$

The Sum Total of Nothings

I FIGURED THE BEST place to start the surveillance operation on O'Brien would be to stake out the distribution centre. I sat in my car, an old Fiat Uno with a nicotine-stained
dashboard, and which had seen nearly as many miles as Apollo
11. It was a wet week, even for October. Chilly too. The damp
made my ankles swell, so I'd not be leaving the car if I could help
it.

I was parked up near the post office in Churchfield with a
good view of Druid Distribution. I left the engine running so
that the battery wouldn't go dead as I listened to my Leftfield
CD. I also kept the heater blowing to demist a windscreen that
seemed to catch every cloudy gasp of my breath. I had O'Brien's
car – a puke-coloured seven-series – in sight.

I'd done some surveillance for the Guards. The advantage of
that, though, was that you worked in shifts and in pairs. Usually an eight hour shift, occasionally a double. But you got some
sleep, time to rest the eyes. And when you needed to go for a piss,
your partner covered for you.

It would be pot luck, I decided. I would cap my observations at twelve hours a day, less if I had something on, like my mother's birthday, which was coming up in a few days' time. I would take breaks whenever I wanted. I didn't fancy pissing into Coke bottles or squatting behind bushes with cows gawking at my arse. If I missed something, well that was all well and good. The pay was grand, that was for sure, but I didn't even know which side I was working for. Never mind your good and evil shite, maybe one was as crooked as the other – two rotten eggs, Jordan and O'Brien.

I didn't have a sense of what Martin O'Brien was about. Did he think like a criminal, or was he an amateur, even an innocent? Would he suspect he was being watched, or go about his business oblivious to the set of eyes that would be trained on his every move, assessing him, judging him, waiting for a slip? Did he have a heightened sense of awareness that would lead him to question every car that stayed in his rear-view mirror for longer than ten minutes?

I thought about one time, about a year after I'd been made detective, when I had worked on a task force whose purpose was to take down a small drug gang. For close to four months we had been all over the boss. We took photos of him shovelling chips into his gob, pissing in doorways after the pub, scratching his arse, but nothing to tie him to anything even remotely illegal. In the end, it was half a day's testimony in court by a snitch that brought him down.

The gist of the whole thing, as I saw it, was that if the mark was careful enough, even paranoid enough, you would get nothing but a whole heap of frustration and piles. That was the nub of it, though – you were glued to that fecking car seat, your finger on the camera button, itching, twitching for some action to snap.

I had been taught that it was the accumulation of it all – the routine, the meaningless things, the sum total of nothings which added up to something. I knew I might be in it for the long haul, so it was the routine I was going to begin with. That was the baseline. And it was only when you established the baseline that you began to see the deviations. These were the things to question, to follow up separately.

I wondered if O'Brien would leave to pick up the kids from school. He had two of them according to the background file Jordan gave me: Liam, aged five, and Monica, aged seven. Would he grab a six pack of beer on the way home? Maybe pick up a whore for some quick head? I would follow him when he left work, take note of everything he did between then and when he got home. If he drove straight home, then that was fine; I would wait for long enough and assume he was in for the night, or O'Brien would leave and the tail would begin again.

I waited, ready to roll when O'Brien did. Being in the car had its compensations compared to when I used to pace around the lot not a hundred yards away, the cold wind chapping my already weather-beaten skin. But sitting in the one spot made me stiff. I regularly flexed my toes to keep the circulation going. That deep vein thrombosis shite could kill, and with the blood pressure I had, even the tiniest clot would probably have stuck in my aorta or a lung, or wherever blood clots get stuck badly enough to kill you.

I was on edge; not from anything to do with the job – which, after all, was a piece of cake – but from a desire to suck on a ciggy. There was one thing I knew would quell that craving, dampen it so that it was no worse than a hunger pang. That was a swig of the caramel-coloured nectar. And I craved that like nobody's business.

It took three nights of bum-numbing drudgery before something of note happened. O'Brien left Druid Distribution in his BMW just after seven and drove straight home to his bungalow in Carrignavar, an upmarket area just a couple of miles outside the city limits. O'Brien drove up a freshly-tarmacked drive and I continued past.

A couple of hundred yards down the road was the entrance to a field where there was enough space in off the road for me to park my Fiat and still have a good view of the entrance to O'Brien's home. I kept the motor running.

A cow moseyed on over to the rusted gate to the field, seemed to give me the once over. From its expression, I thought it might be a better judge of character than I could ever be. It snorted, dripping mucus from its nostrils, and moseyed on back the way it had come. The judgement, it seemed, wasn't favourable.

My plan for the surveillance had been straightforward enough: sit in the car and see what happened, where O'Brien went. As a Guard I would have been given my orders and I would have followed them, because one slip could see everything thrown out of court. But I was my own man now.

This was a one-time deal, I had decided. I would do this one thing for Jordan. No, scratch that, it was for myself. I had to be very clear on that. O'Brien was somehow implicated in me getting a seeing to up in Churchfield and if that was the case, I would find out why and how. And when I did, well, I wouldn't have to lift a finger. I would give the evidence to Jordan and the rest would take care of itself. All quite naturally. And there's nothing more natural, in my order of things, than one crook taking out another.

I had a digital camera with a half-decent optical zoom. Something I bought in Cash Converters for the job. I would photograph O'Brien as he came and went, focus on the registration plates of any visiting motors – all with an embedded time stamp so that I could easily place the photos on the wall chart I would maintain at home.

It wasn't like what I snapped would see the inside of a courtroom – I hoped not, at any rate. If I needed a close-up, like really close up, then I would just have to get there without the power of a zoom lens. With legwork. Good old-fashioned legwork.

The Leftfield CD looped back to the beginning for what might have been the fifth or sixth time. That was OK, though. It was that kind of music. It was real music, in my estimation. The fewer words the better. Words are for books. Music is all about the melody, the lifting of the spirit. I wanted to feel the music somehow resonating with the nerve centres of my brain.

Rain started to fall. I put the wipers on and turned up the

volume. The music soothed me and I settled back into the seat.

I woke up.

"Fuck!"

"Open Up …" came one of the rare lyrics of the Leftfield CD. The wipers screeched on dry glass.

"Jesus Christ!" I said, my eyes all bleary.

I was still in a brief post-sleep phase of figuring out if it was dawn or dusk. Dawn. I had slept straight through the night. The engine was still running – that was something, at least. I checked the fuel gauge. Almost empty.

I had broken the cardinal rule of the tail: lose sight of the target for one moment and you break the chain – the chain that begins with the first moments of your shift and ends with the last. Between the beginning and the end, each blink of your eyes is a link in the chain. Close your eyes for long enough and you break the chain. And when you do, you might as well call it a day.

I engaged first gear and crept towards the entrance to the O'Brien residence. No BMW.

"Fucking Christ Jesus!"

And this is where I not only second guessed, but third guessed myself. Had O'Brien left in the BMW? Had his wife taken it? There was also the question of when the BMW had left. Everything up to this point was for nought. I didn't even know when I had fallen asleep!

And then O'Brien came out of the front door to fetch the morning paper.

He was wearing a white woolly dressing gown and I could see his hair was wet. What also caught my attention was the pair of shiny legs that glistened like they might have been oiled. I sighed with relief. True enough, I had a blank timeline between when I fell asleep – whenever that was – and now. And I didn't know if O'Brien had gone out or if anyone had visited. But I could begin to trace that line again.

I did a U-turn and parked back at the field again. Next time I would bring something with caffeine in it to help stay awake.

The long shadows shortened as the sun lifted itself above a mound at the end of the field. Rising dew steam cast an eerie pall over the countryside. I looked at the petrol gauge again. There couldn't have been more than one-sixteenth of a tank left; enough to just about get me to the nearest petrol station in Blackpool. However, this was an old Fiat and you couldn't trust it to tell you the truth any more than a priest.

I couldn't just keep the engine running. I thought about calling a halt and driving home with nothing more interesting to document than the sight of O'Brien in a fluffy gown and the useless fact that he probably waxed his legs. But that was the thing about surveillance – what seemed like something insignificant could turn out to be crucial later, so I would document it and at the very least it might give Jordan something to laugh about, maybe provide some entertainment value for the good money he was paying.

I shifted in my seat and felt a dull ache reverberate from my coccyx. The springs were prodding through the seat cover as whatever sixteen-year-old foam there had been now offered about as much support as internal affairs gets from rank and file Gardaí.

The decision is simple: get a cushion or get a new car. I breathed deeply and my nostrils, now more acute to smell since giving up the fags, registered the years of absorbed smoke and body odour. It was the smell of my life. It would be like scrapping a piece of my history. *I'll just get a cushion.*

A passing bird sent a glob of shite splattering onto the windscreen and I wondered if maybe my luck was beginning to turn. Isn't that what people said? That being shat on by a bird was a sign of good luck?

I took out the Leftfield CD – enough was enough after a dozen plays of it, good and all as it was. I had picked up a CD at a car boot sale in Kilcully that had a blurb describing it as *space music*, which I had to confess I knew nothing about. But where was the risk in spending two Euro? Or maybe there was a reason it was two Euro and at the bottom of a bin.

The player swallowed the disc and nothing happened. At least, that was how it seemed for about two minutes until I realized that it was actually playing something that sounded like an old geezer wheezing through a pillow. Five minutes later and it sounded the same, so I put the Leftfield CD back in. I made a mental note to get more chillout CDs.

A number of cars passed. Mostly expensive models – the kind that execs drive. I saw one approach in the rear-view mirror. An Avensis, maybe, but I couldn't be sure with the blinding head-lamps. It pulled into the gap behind me and my heart stepped up a few beats. I instinctively put my hand over the gear stick and moved my foot to the clutch, ready to make a move.

Someone got out of the car and I was just about to engage gear when I realized the someone had a uniform – it was a Guard.

Sneaky fucks in their unmarked car, I thought as a second Guard got out of the passenger side.

Despite the brightening dawn light, one of them was shining a torch at my car and it momentarily blinded me. I made a safe decision – I would make no move, invite no suspicion.

One of the Guards came to the window and twirled a finger. It took an age to wind down the window. It tended to wobble from back to front when I did.

"Morning, Guard," I said without making eye contact.

"What's your business around here, sir?" one of the Guards asked in a disinterested midlands voice.

"Just taking a break. My eyes were getting a bit sleepy."

"Where have you come from?"

"Limerick."

"And where are you going?"

"Gerald Griffin Street."

"You took a bit of a detour, didn't you?"

"I like the scenic route."

I could hear the Guard sniffle, but still I did not make eye con-tact. I could see just about to his shoulders.

"Up here."

"Huh?"

"I said, look up here, sir. And be quick about it."

I obliged and I could see that the Guard was young enough, maybe early thirties. I couldn't make out his rank in the dim light, but he sounded confident, maybe even a right ball breaker. I knew how this worked – the Guard was eyeing me up, making a snap judgement about my state of inebriation. A few months back and there would have been little doubt about it: I would have had a few snifters to keep warm, make the time pass quicker. I was OK now, though.

The Guard seemed to be searching for more than just the wandering eyes of a drunk. There was the glint of recognition there and I wondered if I'd been rumbled.

"Do I know you from somewhere?" the Guard said. "You look awful familiar."

"I was on *Winning Streak* a few weeks ago. Do you watch it?"

One thing anybody could say about me – those who've known me long enough – is that I'm quick on the draw. The gap between the question and the lie, even utter bullshit, is almost imperceptible.

"Now and again. On *Winning Streak*, eh? Maybe that's it."

The other Guard, a stocky woman with peering Clint Eastwood eyes, had spent her time pacing around the car, looking at the state of my lights and tyres, peeking in at the back seat for anything noteworthy. I didn't let it get to me; at least, I didn't let it show on my face. But I could feel my veins turning to wire.

The Guard on my side of the car scratched at something on his cheek. "Did you win much?"

I extended my arm out the window and patted the side of the door.

"Well, I didn't win a new fecking car, did I?" I said with an intentionally gormless grin.

Like I said, quick on the draw.

The Guard almost let a smile cross his face, but restricted it to a crease.

"Ah well, make sure you go for a decent holiday, anyway."

"Will do, Guard. I hear Iceland's nice this time of year."

He seemed to ponder that bit of touristic advice for a moment. "I'd say it would be. Not too cold, not too dark. All right then. Be on your way. I wouldn't be hanging around here."

The Guard waved at his colleague and they went back to their car. They waited a few moments, perhaps recording the registration. They hadn't asked for my licence, so I doubted there would be any follow up. It was more suspicion than I needed, though, and there would be no second chances. I'd need to go into full covert mode, not be hanging around in plain sight.

The Avensis pulled out and continued on towards Blackpool. I leaned back into the seat, stretched my arms over my head, and yawned. I would have to stick to the rules from there on. If I blew my cover, everything would be for nought and that would undoubtedly piss off Jordan. And I didn't quite know where I stood with Jordan.

I was about to drive off when an SUV approached from in front of me, then pulled into O'Brien's gaff. The windows were tinted and not even the silhouette of a driver or passenger could be discerned. I grabbed for the camera and hit the power button. It beeped a farty little beep and took a couple of seconds to boot up, or get its arse in gear, whichever is the more appropriate technical term. It took too long. The car was gone and I couldn't make out the reg. Fecking new technology. My last camera, a good old-fashioned 35 mil, would have been ready for action – a bit like an old pro. Press the button, click, job done, reg in the bag. Now I had shag all.

I thought about the next course of action. The Guards had asked me to skedaddle and there was every chance that they might double back, especially if they harboured even the slightest doubt. Or, perhaps more likely, were on the payroll of none other than my target.

My head told me to get the hell out of there, life being too short and all that, but my gut was telling me that after three fruitless days this was not an opportunity to duck out of. It was that blue blood working its way round my brain. I decided to risk it. Sure, wasn't my gut getting bigger all the time anyway – it was bound to rule my head.

I went through the rusted gate next to the car to enter the field. I could see that it directly adjoined the O'Brien site. It was just grass, probably for grazing, left to grow long for the cows to mow. The field was largely clear of livestock – just my friendly cow and a friend – and, though it had rained, the ground didn't seem too mucky.

I didn't want to be spotted for fear of someone reporting a prowler, but it was nearing ten and I guessed the majority of the morning commuters would have set off on their journeys long ago. Besides, the old, lichen-covered stone wall separating the field from the road was pretty high. I walked briskly to the hedge that demarcated the O'Brien residence from the surrounding farmland.

The hedge was quite dense. Some kind of perennial bushes with large leaves and fairly thick branches, though these were pliable enough and spaced far enough apart that I thought I might be able to squeeze through.

I looked at my sleeve. The jumper I wore was knitted from large, fuzzy strands and would surely catch on any stray twigs, but it wasn't like it was anything special – a Christmas present from Mam nearly three years ago. I'd only worn it initially to avoid hurting her feelings, but more recently because fewer and fewer clothes seemed to fit as I gained weight. I would push on, regardless.

I didn't think there was a dog around, but that would be something to be aware of, so I trod carefully to begin with. I picked my way through the branches protruding between two of the bushes that formed the hedge. As I did, a strand of wool caught and pulled out into a big loop. I cursed my mother under my breath. I grabbed it and yanked it so that it stripped the leaves from the branch it had caught on. Another branch nearly ruptured an eyeball, scratching the skin just above my left eye.

I peered out into the back garden before breaking free from the hedge and when I saw that the way ahead was clear, I stooped and awkwardly shuffled towards the gable end of the bungalow.

Another of the wool strands caught and dragged a branch behind me. I pulled free sending the branch flinging back with a swoosh, which was followed by a rustling sound that seemed to go on for an eon as if there was some animal in there doing the hokey-pokey. I glanced anxiously at the back door as I quickened my steps to the side of the house.

The SUV was parked there. Whoever it was had backed it in to maybe allow for a quick exit. There was just the one small window on the wall and I gently lifted my head up to glance into the room. In the split second I allowed myself, I could tell it was some sort of small utility room. There was a laundry basket, tumble dryer, a large fridge freezer. More importantly, though, it was unoccupied. The window was slightly ajar and for one crazy moment, I considered going in to take a look around. But that would have been suicide.

I could hear O'Brien talking. It came from the other side of the door to the utility room, so it was logical to assume that O'Brien was in the kitchen. I wondered if my hearing was beginning to go, because O'Brien's voice seemed muffled and there was a humming in my ear. Another health-related foible I could have done without. I relaxed when I realized that the hum was from the tumble dryer. If I was to eavesdrop on the conversation, I was going to have to find another window – and raise the stakes.

As I made my way around to the back of the house, continuing to stoop, I could feel the tendons in my knees getting sore. All the crouching around like a rabbit was making me stiff. But this wasn't exactly the kind of job you could bring a deck chair on, so I would just have to put up with it.

I could see a larger window at the rear of the house, where I thought maybe the kitchen would look out onto the lawn. There was a slide and a set of swings, perhaps where mammy would keep an eye on the kids as she prepared the dinner. I couldn't help but think traditionally like that.

"—valuable those boxes were," O'Brien was in the middle of saying. "It'll set us back weeks."

"I'm well aware of that," another man said, his voice muffled slightly, like he might have been in the hall. "I thought our little problem had taken care of itself, but obviously not."

Could I risk rising up a bit to take a peek? They could be staring out the window right then, and wouldn't they get a nice surprise to see my ugly mug appear from nowhere like a decrepit meerkat.

"I dunno," O'Brien said. "There's obviously some other snitch out there. Maybe our problem wasn't really the problem. Maybe he was clean."

O'Brien paused for a while, then spoke again.

"We need to plug the hole, get the fucking rat."

A moment of silence followed. Then a bird fluttered in the bushes and my heart nearly went pop. *Not now. I'm not able for that shite now.*

"It's not one of my lads," I could barely hear the stranger say. "That I can guarantee you. Can you say the same for your own?"

I was straining my ears and it was giving me a headache. There was something about the voice, something familiar. If I could just hear him a bit clearer I was sure I could identify it. I inched along below the window sill to get nearer to the part of the window that was ajar.

"You leave my lads to me," O'Brien said. "And we can't use Druid anymore. Not after the robbery. Do you have any more on that?"

I was just about to settle into some semblance of a comfortable position to earwig on the rest of the conversation when I heard a car pull up out front. I could hear a door open and a kid shouted something – a boy I would have guessed. "Who's that?" the stranger asked with some urgency.

"Shit. Karen's back early with the kids. What is she playing at? I told her you'd be visiting. You better go out the back way before the kids see you."

There was no time for ceremony. I got up on my haunches and hobbled as quickly as I could to the bushes. I pushed through at the same spot I had eased though earlier, leaving nearly half my woolly jumper in strips on the branches, and ran as fast as I could towards the car. There was blood streaming into my left eye from a cut on the eyebrow.

There was no hesitating when I reached the car. I got in, fumbled for my keys, and finally got the thing started. The stranger had not followed me through the bushes, but there was every chance he would appear on the road and drive past in his SUV. I revved the engine to fuck, engaged first, and did about the quickest U-turn in history. As I sped down the road – though that, perhaps, would be to give my Fiat too much credit – I kissed the steering wheel. *You might be old and ugly as sin*, I thought, *but you never let me down when I need you.* It was quite sad, really, but the old girl was about the closest thing I had to a dependable friend.

I took the next left down a boreen, then another left down an even narrower boreen. I had no idea where I was, but I sensed I was pointed in the direction of the city. I looked in the rear view mirror. No sign of the SUV. It looked like I was in the clear. Maybe the bird shite had worked its magic after all.

I replayed in my head what I hadn't had time to process moments earlier. The stranger had said "who's that?" and it had been loud and clear. I played it again in my mind. It sounded familiar. Was it? Was it Dave Savage? My stomach churned. I was sure it was, and that moment I thought my goose might very well have been cooked.

Later back at home I lay in the bath surrounded by Radox bubbles. The doc had said to fit in more relaxation time and there had been this bottle of stuff I had not planned on buying near the shaving cream I had actually planned on buying. It promised to take me to another world full of meditation and the smell of a woodland glade.

I thought about what to report to Jordan. It wasn't something I relished doing. For my four days of effort I'd managed about five minutes of eavesdropping. And with Jordan's history, he might send old granite face, O'Keeffe, to pay me a visit in the middle of some dark night, to pop out from one of the many narrow lanes around Blackpool and send me to meet my maker, whoever or whatever that might be. Perhaps my Dad knew the answer to that one.

I pinched my nose and submerged my head. I felt the heat on my cheeks and a sting from the scratches above my eyelids where the hedge had done its damage. I did this a couple of times to soften the four-day-old stubble that was beginning to feel like a Brillo pad every time I rested my chin in my hands, which I was doing a lot. I shaved and felt a bit cleaner.

Then I just lay there to relax. But I couldn't. I had to process what little I had heard at O'Brien's. I'd figured the boxes, what with them containing flat screen televisions, might be valuable, but enough to set him back weeks? And wasn't he just distributing for other suppliers? Sure, the insurance would sort out any monetary issues. And what problem had been sorted – a mole? I was sure O'Brien and Savage had stood there talking about a hit. Did they mean Moolah?

If that was the case, I could probably rule out Jordan as a suspect, because it had been Jordan that put me on the job in the first place. That was contrary to the rumours someone had been spreading.

When I had done washing myself I stood up in the bath. I felt light-headed and had to steady myself with a palm on the wall.

What the fuck! What's wrong with me now?

It took about ten seconds for the spell to pass and I was able to step out of the bath with some degree of confidence. I felt heavy on my feet and went to the bedroom to sit on the bed.

My arteries, my heart, and now my fucking head – I'm falling to pieces.

I dried myself as I sat and warily stood up. Again I felt light-headed, though not as badly or for as long as before.

Jesus Christ! What am I going to die of first? A heart attack or fucking Parkinson's?

I dressed myself and tottered a bit as I donned my trousers. I thought a Barry's tea with plenty of sugar was well in order. Maybe it was just low blood sugar.

Just low blood sugar? Diabetes? No hang on just a minute, I've had my bloods checked not so long ago. Doc would have called if there was anything wrong ... wouldn't he?

The sup of tea was most welcome. If it wasn't exactly a phar-macological effect that calmed me, it was at least the fondness of connecting with other tea-filled moments. Sharing tea and bis-cuits with Mam, for example.

Mam … oh God, what date was her birthday again?

I turned on the telly to double check the date on the news channel. It was her birthday. I'd remembered a couple of days ago only to forget until now. That bloody memory of mine again. What *was* happening with my head?

I took another sup of tea and tried to regulate my breath. Breath in … and out … breath in … and out. I'd learned this technique from an old cassette tape I'd bought at another car boot sale in Kilkully – a time before I bought the *space music* CD. Tapes and CDs I was comfortable with. I could hold them, stick them into some basic machinery to make the music play. Now it was something else entirely: digital downloads. I just didn't know where to begin with those.

Feeling somewhat better, I clicked my brain into a more ratio-nal gear. I had only been on the case for a few days, hadn't much, but suspicions to follow up. It was a start, enough surely to justify Jordan's retainer. I decided I would give the surveillance another twenty-four hours before calling Jordan.

I'd been parking by the post office to surveil O'Brien, but con-tinuing to do so might have drawn suspicion. Someone might have mistaken my surveillance as casing the post office. I knew a traveller by the name of John Paul Kiely in the halting site just up the road from the post office. From there I would get a good view of the lot. An even better one, in fact.

I drove into the site to the askance looks of a couple of kids who should probably have been at school. I saw JP outside his caravan tending to a lawn mower. I parked nearby and walked over to him.

"Hi—" I began.

He held up a hand to quieten me, pulled a chord to start the petrol mower. It rumbled for a few seconds and then stopped with a clank. He cursed something in an accent or language I didn't understand.

"Ah, howya boss man," he said, wiping grease from his hands with a rag. "I suppose you're to be welcomed now, not being filth and all that."

He grinned and revealed a surprisingly polished full set of teeth. My preconceived notions about the dental health of travellers was confounded.

"I'd like to think you would have made an exception for me anyway, JP. It's good to see you again."

"It's been fair time since last time. Is it four years?"

"More like five or six."

"What can I do you for?"

I pointed to the corner of the site. A car was on blocks, some of the panelling missing, the engine bay empty. Car parts was just one of the travellers' many trades.

"Do you mind if I spend some time parked over there?" I said.

I would have expected a puzzled look, but JP just spat in his rag and went to work on his hands finger by finger.

"A space like that's worth money," he finally said when all of his fingers had been cleaned – though they were still blackened by old engine oil. The space was just another commodity to be sold by a resourceful traveller, no more, no less than a piece of carpet or a settee.

"I figured it would be," I said. "What's the damage?"

"Depends," he said without elaborating. He picked up a splinter of wood from the ground and got to work on picking the dirt from under his nails.

"It always does, doesn't it."

"Sure, once a Pavee, always a Pavee."

"Will we say fifty Euro a day?"

"If we say eighty, we can call it a deal."

"Let's split the difference," I said.

I spat in my hand and offered it.

JP laughed. He spat in his hand and clasped mine.

"Deal," he said.

"And no questions," I said.
"About what?"
Enough said.

I had a perfect view from the halting site of O'Brien's BMW. The bustle of traveller life went on behind me – the comings and goings of vans, the various clattering and banging of their trades, horses neighing in the field to the back. It was a microcosm of a way of life that was under threat – from local authorities, politicians, the public, even the Guards. Ironically, it was their desire to keep to themselves, the very thing that those who despised them would want, that made them seem even more suspicious to those who sought out suspicion.

It was a crisp early afternoon. Ideal surveillance weather – no haze of any kind, a clear view for miles. I wondered how much O'Brien's car cost. I'd probably have had to pay someone to take my old Fiat Uno away. Given the choice, I'd take the Fiat, though. I've heard it all about the reliability of Fiats of that era, the tendency to rust, and so on. But there was a spirit to the Uno that O'Brien's seven-series just did not have.

O'Brien left his office at 2:15 p.m. I moved my hand towards the ignition key, but O'Brien took a pack of fags from his back pocket and proceeded to smoke two cigarettes. I hadn't seen him smoke before, maybe just overlooked it, but I thought maybe it was because he was feeling the pressure of recent events. There was time enough for him not only to inherit Jordan's old empire, but his paranoia also.

An hour later he left the building and got into his car and that cop feeling I'd felt before returned. Nostalgia, I suppose, for better days, a better purpose.

I kept my distance as O'Brien turned left from the facility down towards the northern edges of Blackpool, then left again to take the shortcut to Commons Road. This quickly became the main Limerick national route. There were a number of possible destinations along that road, Blarney and Mallow chief amongst them.

O'Brien passed the turn for Blarney. A cement lorry slowed us mid-way between Blarney and Mallow and I worried about O'Brien's view in the rear view mirror. I slowed and allowed a frustrated woman in a Fiat 500 – the new breed of Fiat that lacked spirit – to pass me, giving me a buffer to O'Brien.

The cement lorry took a right into Mallow town at the main roundabout and O'Brien continued straight. I wondered if he was heading to Limerick or, God forbid, Galway or beyond.

O'Brien stopped in a garage just before Buttevant. I pulled in around the side of the garage where the car wash was. I had more than enough petrol for Limerick and back, but if he went further I'd be in trouble. I got out to stretch my legs.

O'Brien filled up on diesel and went into the shop to pay. On the way out he was taking the plastic wrapping from a packet of Rothmans. He put one in his mouth and lit it despite the many warnings to the contrary next to the pumps. I guessed his stress levels were rising the closer he got to his destination.

Through Buttevant and on through Charleville also. Then a long stretch to the outskirts of Limerick where O'Brien took an exit for the city centre.

Limerick has a bad rep. Unfair in my estimation. Sure enough, there are areas you wouldn't want to find yourself in daylight, let alone on a dark night, but Limerick people are gas characters. Self-deprecating and with an interest in any sport that involves a ball and brutality.

After going straight through a couple of roundabouts, O'Brien took a left away from the city. He continued along a road that became more rural – a field with cows here, an animal feed plant there – until we hit a pocket of recently-built housing estates. Some of the estates looked unfinished, once freshly-laid pavement now cracked and with weeds flourishing in the cracks. Flowers and long grass grew from the edges of manhole covers. Pipes to nowhere stuck out of the ground where foundations had been laid and covered, but no house built.

O'Brien turned in to one of the estates. There were no inhabitants. Without context, one might have thought a nuclear holocaust or a mining boom-bust had cleared the estate of life. I knew better. The Celtic Tiger had ravaged the land here.

Following him into a housing estate where no one lived would have invited suspicion, so I drove into the next estate where most of the houses were occupied. I found an empty, boarded-up house that was adjacent to the ghost town, with an estate agency sign hanging at an angle by one nail from a post, a diamond swaying gently to and fro in the breeze.

I parked in the driveway. I was a prospective buyer, surely, to any of the other residents. I went into the back garden to check the wall that separated the only-a-bit-ghost estate from the fully-ghost estate. It was about eight or nine feet high, built with plain concrete cavity blocks, so there was no way to climb without something else as an interim step up.

I looked next door. Good old wheelie bins – one for general waste, another for recycling. I surveyed the back garden – clothes on the line: women's, men's and kids'; a playhouse for a boy, judging by the camouflage decoration; a doll's head, with maybe the body taken hostage in the playhouse; but no dog, no car parked out front, no sign of anyone at home.

I climbed over the wall and checked out the wheelie bins. The general waste bin was quite full, but the recycling one was nearly empty. I dragged it to the wall and was able to lift it up and lower it gently to the ground on the other side to avoid startling any of the other neighbours who, despite having no view, might get spooked and investigate a noise.

I pushed the bin to the back wall and was able to climb on, though I had to hula my waist a bit to keep steady before grabbing the top of the wall.

A quick peek: O'Brien's car a couple of hundred yards to my left, parked in front of a dilapidated shell of a semi-d. I climbed over and landed on my feet, making sure to keep the camera I was carrying safe. I cased the surroundings: no way back up over the wall. If O'Brien had left then, like if maybe he had only driven in to take a discreet piss, I would have been screwed.

The grass by the wall was high, like Savannah grass, only even wispier as it was dying off in the late Autumn. I had some cover when I crouched, so I carefully made my way to a nearby house for cover. It, too, was a shell. Walls, ceilings, a roof; but no doors, windows or drywalling. Just another skeleton left behind by a certain tiger.

I walked from the back of the house to the front room. Through a glassless window I could clearly see O'Brien's car. I couldn't see O'Brien. I would have to get closer if I could. I walked to the doorless front door frame, peeked out and … a car. A car raising dust as it approached – a jeep of some kind.

I stopped and returned to the front room. The car arrived – a Mitsubishi I believed – and parked behind O'Brien's. There were two men in the car. They looked around and I ducked. I peeked back up to double-check my cover. I was fine, for now. I had my camera at the ready, powered up, no lens cover, no chance of missing the shot – I hoped.

The driver stayed in the car and the passenger got out. I would have guessed he was about fifteen stone, which hung about right on his six-foot-plus frame. He was wearing blue jeans and a brown leather jacket. There was an air of confidence about the way he walked, something in the way he held his shoulders back and danced his head about.

I took a few snaps, zoomed in as much as the camera would allow – five-times optical zoom sounded impressive until you needed to capture the wrinkles on someone's face from a hundred yards. All I got was a side profile through the car door window and the back of his head – a full head of springy brown hair – as he walked to the house where I presumed O'Brien was waiting. I got a glimpse of O'Brien. He was waiting for the stranger in the front room, pacing about and fidgeting his hands.

This was as close as I was going to get. I kept my eye on the window through the camera's viewfinder, darting over to the door occasionally. I saw a shoulder. It was the stranger's. I caught a glimpse of something: a bag. Clear plastic, something shiny inside. O'Brien handed it to the stranger and I could not quite see what the stranger was doing with the bag, but he was definitely doing something with it.

I wasn't sure if I got a shot of the bag and the exchange in time. Another glimpse: a handshake and O'Brien's face from behind the stranger; he was smiling, but it looked forced. The stranger put the bag into his jacket pocket and went out of view. A couple of seconds later and he walked out the door. He got into the car and they left without delay, leaving a cloud of dust in their wake.

Inside, O'Brien came fully into view. He was walking around in a tight circle, kind of bouncing as he did, like he really did need to take a leak. He took the pack of cigarettes from his pocket, took one out, and lit it. He stopped circling, looked out the window, seemingly right at me for a moment, and took a long, deep drag. He closed his eyes and exhaled a long stream of smoke. I caught every bit of it on camera.

When he finished his cigarette, he flicked it out the window, red ash sparking in the air for a second. He left my sight for a moment before reappearing at the door. He paused briefly, inhaled so that I could see his chest rise, and moved towards his car.

I had a choice to make. I could tear back to my car, hope to catch up with him. Or I could believe that I had enough from whatever exchange had taken place. I remembered what I had promised myself: this was for myself, on my terms. I could run for the car and risk knackering a knee, or I could, at my leisure, walk back to the car and make the assumption that O'Brien was heading back to Churchfield. I took the easier option.

As I walked back to my car, I realized my pulse had been racing. I took some time to practice my breathing exercises. *This is pleasant, most pleasant.* An affirmation that I then believed.

Back at the car, I browsed through the thirty-seven photographs I had taken. A lot of blurred, out-of-focus stuff, but even from the two-inch screen I could see there was a gem or two among them. I'd need to get them onto a computer screen to be sure.

I drove back to Cork, drove up to Churchfield. O'Brien's car was there. He didn't move for the rest of the afternoon. At about seven o'clock he left, went home, and so did I. Sometimes things work out OK when you take the easy road.

75

5

Rope Ladders and Wrapping Paper

THE NEXT MORNING, AFTER what I must admit was an excellent night's sleep for once, I walked to the local Cash Converters to buy a laptop. Any old thing would have done, though the sales assistant – a pock-marked teenager with a bad haircut and a name tag that read OLIVER – tried to convince me that a tablet would also be a wise purchase.

I'd always thought that tablets were for headaches and commandments, but it seemed that a new computer had been invented for the saddos in society for whom a newspaper wasn't enough. The assistant did, however, convince me to buy a printer and some paper. Carrying around a laptop just to show someone a picture wasn't practical, so Acne Boy's advice was most welcome.

Much to the sales guy's annoyance, I went for the absolute cheapest second-hand laptop, case and colour printer I could see. I got him to explain how I could download the photographs from the digital camera and print them out. I forked out two-eighty in cash and walked home with the gear under my arms.

At home I looked through the photographs. Only about four

of the photos were of any use. I had a photo where the exchange of the bag was fairly clear, though what exactly was in the bag was debatable. My guess was meth, but it could have been cocaine or even bread soda. I didn't have O'Brien's face in the exchange, but I had an arm. When matched to the arm in the photo I had of a seemingly relieved O'Brien, only the most cynical would have denied it was the same person.

The stranger was an important dynamic in all of this. If he could be identified, it would answer the question about O'Brien's dealings in Limerick. The best photo I had of him was when he left the house and I could finally see his face, but there was some blurring.

Apparently the camera didn't have image stabilisation, which, as Oliver in Cash Converters explained, is a prerequisite when taking photos on the move; but how was a technophobic relic like myself, who didn't even own a computer, supposed to know.

The photo of the blurred stranger might have been enough, though. There were no distinguishing features on his face: no scars, tattoos, or moles. But given context – Limerick, drug-related dealings – a knowledgeable Guard might know. And Barry Cotter was pretty knowledgeable about these things.

The encounter with Barry a few days ago had been an uncomfortable one. He'd not taken kindly to me talking to Jordan. Showing him the photo would be a risk.

Was he still my friend? We'd had each other's backs enough in the past – admittedly him having mine more often than not – that I thought our friendship would survive anything. When a kid graffiti artist had lodged an official complaint about me slapping him around the back of the head, Barry backed me up. By the book was one thing, but the book didn't extend to those in blue.

I arranged a meet with Barry in De Agostini's cafe on Sheare Street at twelve – not too far from the Bridewell, but not exactly round the corner either, so probably no other Guards would be there.

I walked to Sheare Street, about a fifteen-minute walk from my house. I walked when I could. I might have been fat, but lazy I was not.

De Agostini's had a cheery look about it. It was one of those continental-style cafes that a previous justice minister wanted to see being licenced more for alcoholic beverages; the idea was that a French-inspired wine-drinking culture would lead to a more relaxed approach to booze, cut down on binge drinking in pubs. The vintners lobby shot the idea to pieces.

De Agostini's was an exception; it had a drinks licence. I asked the waiter to seat me at a table for two away from everyone else and asked him not to seat anyone nearby. It was a bit of an ask, but he was agreeable when I promised a large tip. I wouldn't say the waiter was dirty, but it reminded me that everyone has a price.

I ordered a Peroni while I waited. Though not a craft beer, I like the sharpness of a cold Peroni. It makes it a more than tolerable mass market beer.

Barry arrived. I didn't like his expression. I'd seen my mother wear it a few times and she could squeeze your heart with a flinch of her mouth or the wrinkle of a nose.

"Hi Barry," I said.

He just nodded, didn't speak.

"I want you to see—"

He cut me off.

"I don't want to see whatever it is you have if it puts me in a compromised position. Is that clear?"

It was. And it had been my intention to leave Jordan well out of it. That meant no photo with even so much as the arm of O'Brien in it. I just had a single picture of a blurred Limerick man.

"Don't worry, Barry. I have one photograph. If you don't know who's in it, I can just leave. Otherwise … well, otherwise maybe we can talk."

Barry nodded again, looked over his shoulder to see who was around.

I took out the printed photograph. The printing process hadn't done it any favours. Streaks ran across the page like the photo had been constructed from bits of other photographs, worse even than a photofit. I handed it to Barry.

"Fuck sake, Mick. I was expecting a photo and you give me this?"

"I'm not exactly Lord Litchfield. I'll grant you that."

Barry came close to laughing. "More like Lord Sutch."

He studied the photograph. He didn't seem to recognize him.

"I took that in Limerick," I said. "Does that make a difference?"

Barry continued examining the page. A corner of his mouth elevated. "You know, I might know who this is," he said. He didn't look up from the page.

"Who, Barry?"

He brought a thumb and forefinger up to his chin, squeezed his stubble between them.

"There's a new player in Limerick. He doesn't run with the usual families there. I think he moved into Limerick from Ennis. He's organized, if you know what I mean, in the sense that he runs a tight ship, doesn't tolerate any messing around like the families."

"A name, Barry."

"If it's this guy, he goes by Moose. His real name is Stephen Morrisroe."

"What's his poison?"

"Meth, mostly. Guns too. But he's choosy about who he sells his guns to. Deals with guys around Dublin. No one likely to turn his guns back on him."

"He's serious, so."

Barry finally looked up from the photo. He had this quizzing face on him that I knew. It was the same face he made when interrogating witnesses.

"As serious as cancer, Mick."

I believed there was nothing more serious than that, so his point was driven home. Driven home in a hearse.

"Would you mind telling me why you have a photo of him?" Barry asked.

Before I could answer – and it would have taken a while for

me to get my words in order – he answered the question himself.

"You know what, Mick? I don't want to know. If you want to dig a hole in the ground for yourself, by all means do so. But don't expect me to throw down a rope ladder when you can't get back out of it."

The waiter returned, asked if either of us wanted to order anything. I waved him away.

"I fell in that hole a few years ago, Barry. Guess what? It's raining and I'm already waist deep in water." I took a sip of Peroni. "What I need is a boat."

I don't think what I said made much sense to myself, let alone Barry. He shook his head.

"Speaking of holes in the ground … there's a hole that's going to have a new occupant in a cemetery somewhere sometime soon."

For a second I thought he meant me. But he must have meant someone new had been killed.

"Who is it, Barry?"

"A guy by the name of Alan Brick. A small time hood from Bishopstown."

I knew him. A little fart of a guy that people nicknamed Pebbles. About six years prior I had busted him for possession of ecstasy. He'd gotten off on a bullshit technicality. I'd heard he gained in confidence from the incident, thought that he was untouchable.

"Jesus. What happened to him?"

Barry seemed lost in thought, didn't answer me.

"Barry?"

He was looking down at the oak table, as if studying an imperfection in the wood. "He … em … he was strangled."

I had considered telling Barry about my connection to Brick. Now I'd leave him to figure that out for himself. Strangulation and I had history.

"That's terrible, Barry. Hell of a way for someone to … I dunno, take revenge, maybe?"

"Maybe."

I could see the waiter watching us, looking for the right moment to intervene with a menu.

"You want a drink, Barry?"

He shook his head. He took one last look at the Moose photo and handed it back to me.

"You need to give up this amateur PI stuff and try to resurrect your life." His face became strained. "For God's sake, Mick, you're almost forty. You're supposed to be in your prime."

"I'm just doing this one thing," I said. "Then I'll sort myself out."

Barry sighed. "It's always just one thing. Then another. And another. Draw a line in the sand, Mick. Walk away from whatever it is and drive into the fucking sunset."

But I couldn't. You didn't turn your back on The Gentleman. And I didn't want to. For all his faults, Jordan had given my life purpose.

"Look, Mick, I'm supposed to be on duty. If I get spotted in here, I could easily get a reprimand for drinking tea on the job — even though I'm not."

I thanked Barry for his time, for giving me his best guess at an ID. I tipped the waiter a tenner and left.

I went to the English Market on the way home. It was a detour I often made to get good quality artisan food: fresh fish, bread, organic vegetables and meats.

When I got home a man was standing at the door wearing a furry suit jacket. It was Halloran.

"A word, Bosco."

"Mohair."

"What?"

"You asked for a word. I've given you one: mohair."

"I didn't come here for your cheek, Bosco."

"Then what part of my body *did* you come for?"

"Enough with your guff. I have some more questions for you. Let's go inside."

I opened the door.

"I've nothing to say to you, Halloran."

I tried to close the door, but Halloran put his shoulder to it before I could close it all the way. He stuck his face into the gap.

"Where were you on the morning of the tenth? The morning before the robbery."

I didn't bother taking the time to consider my whereabouts. I just responded, "I'm not answering any of your questions, Halloran."

I shoved the door and it latched. Halloran thumped on the door.

"Bosco! Open up. I'm not done with you."

I ignored him.

"Bosco!"

A minute later, I heard a car drive away. I went into the kitchen.

I put an Arbutus baguette on the counter and cut it in half. I couldn't abide by the factory-produced instant bread you can find in any supermarket; it lacks the artistry of the Arbutus bread and its inner bubbles. The Arbutus keeps its form through the entire biting and chewing process and has a distinctive yeasty flavour – a talisman of the traditional baking process.

I had also bought some Gubbeen smoked cheese and Italian cured ham from the On The Pig's Back stall. I further sliced the half baguette so that I could fold it over. I had some soft butter on the counter, so I spread that on both sides and lined one side with thickly sliced Gubbeen and the other with the cured ham. This was the real ham and cheese sandwich.

I made a cup of Barry's Classic Blend and sat at the table. I took care to finish a sup of tea completely so that I would have a dry mouth to savour the sandwich. I took a bite. Irish, French and Italian in a single mouthful. It was magic.

I got my thoughts in order. What was Halloran on about with his "morning of the tenth" business? Was it something to do with planning the robbery? Seeing as I had nothing to do with it, I decided to think no more about it.

Another thought. I had to call Jordan. I'd procrastinated enough. First I'd call Jordan, then Mam. Not quite the proper order, but I wouldn't be able to relax talking to my mother knowing I had to face up to a difficult conversation with The Gentleman.

And what was I going to do about Savage? Could I tell Jordan? Was it something I could discuss with Cotter? I decided I would report the fragmentary details of the conversation I'd overheard, the movements of O'Brien in Limerick and the exchange, but hold off on the involvement of a certain Garda Sergeant and the identity of the Limerick man for now.

I needed more time to think of a strategy for dealing with Savage. For the man in Limerick, if Jordan could tell who he was from the photo, then I'd leave it at that; but if he didn't, I would follow up myself, put more meat in the sandwich, so to speak. I didn't know if Jordan was in the business of nipping things in the bud, like he used to, so I had to be circumspect for now.

I'd known there was a whiff of something from Savage, had done for years. And he'd talked about his lads. What lads? More dirty Guards?

I paused before punching the last of the digits into my mobile and again before pressing the call button. But I'd procrastinated enough. I steeled myself for an uncomfortable conversation with Jordan.

It was Grace who answered, though, completely catching me off guard. I couldn't get a word out of my mouth.

"Michael? Is that you?"

"Ye-Yes. How did you know?"

"Because you are the only person with this number. Daddy asked me to keep the phone. This is one of those – what do they call them? – burner phones?"

I might have suspected as much. He was paranoid as fuck, Jordan. They'd probably change the number frequently.

"Watch your hands, then," I said and laughed.

Silence on the other end.

"Burner phone, hands on fire?" I tried to explain.

"Hold on there, Michael. Before you say another word, Daddy insisted on no phone conversations. We meet face-to-face at a moment's notice. OK?"

"OK … em, where do we meet?"

"You know Corrigan's near White Church?"

"Sure."

Only when I'd gone there years ago to enforce the closing time, but it was a great deal more civilized a place than the dive I now called my local. It was an old man's arse pub, but there was something endearing about that.

"Meet me in twenty minutes."

I looked at my watch. I'd struggle to make it in that time with the school traffic, but I didn't feel like prolonging the conversation.

"OK, Grace."

I arrived in Corrigan's just before four and went up to the bar. I was out of breath having run from the car park. I was nearly ten minutes late. A barman seemed to recognize me and nodded towards a door at the side of the bar.

Behind the door was a stairs, narrow and steep enough that it made me a tad dizzy, and this led to a room entirely clad with pine slats – floor, walls, and pointed ceiling. A dart board was on the wall, complete with backboard, chalk scoreboard, and an oche on the floor. Three stubby darts with tricolour flights were impaled in the board. I noted the score was 135, my guess being that the final dart deflected into the treble five.

Grace was waiting at a table and gestured for me to sit opposite her.

"Sorry I'm late," I said.

Grace returned a nonchalant look. *Don't be fucking late again*, it said to me. There was something of her father in her, after all.

I brought her up to speed on the surveillance, leaving out the identities that I was fairly certain about. I also gave her the picture of the Limerick man. Like Cotter, she wasn't impressed by the quality, suggested that I email her the Jay Peg or something technical like that. She explained that a Jay Peg was a particular file format. I'd thought you just had a picture file and that was that. When I told her that I didn't have an email account she thought I was trying it on with her. She abandoned the whole email idea when my technical illiteracy became obvious.

"Daddy's not going to be too pleased when I get back. I think he was hoping for more."

"Well, I'm sorry to disappoint, but it's not like I gave any money back guarantees or anything. The way I see it, I was doing your dad a fecking favour. Pardon my French."

"Forgive me. Perhaps I'm putting words in my father's mouth. He'll be interested in this guy in the SUV and the trip to Limerick. And maybe he'll recognize the man in the picture."

She paused for a moment, for the first time betraying anything approaching emotion with a crease in her forehead. Then she spoke again.

"Where are my manners! What would you like to drink? I can get Paul to bring them up."

I opted for a Jameson – an odd one now and again wasn't so bad. Besides, rural pubs weren't really ones for craft beers. Grace went for a gin and tonic.

Hang on a minute. When was the last time I had a drink alone with a woman? The thought sent a wave of dread up from the pit of my stomach. Deborah, I remembered. 1999, Imperial Hotel restaurant. An expensive bottle of Chianti over a Valentine's dinner. I'd said the wrong thing that night and I was bollocksed if I was going to do the same thing now. What was I saying to myself? That I fancied Grace? Hadn't I been too far up my own arse these past few years to even begin to consider another relationship?

"Keep doing what you are doing. Just keep yourself out of harm's way till you hear from me again."

"So it'll be you I'll be meeting from now on?"

"Isn't that what I said, or at least intimated?"

Intimated. God, she talked nice. I was too used to the likes of Mogs and his blabbering on about this *feen* and that *beor.*

Grace took a brown envelope from her bag.

"Fifteen-hundred," she said. "The first week's payment as agreed. Keep track of any additional expenses."

I felt awkward taking the money. Maybe it was just the colour of the envelope.

"I'll await your call, then?"

"You do that."

She smiled. She fecking smiled.

Don't read too much into it. It's just the sad fantasy of a man who's gone too long without.

Without what, though? A shag? No, it was something more than that. I was lonely. I needed companionship and I wasn't going to risk that with a cheap shag. That's how Deborah had seen it. No, it was just a smile, anyway. Just politeness. No value in reading more into it than that.

I'd only planned initially to phone Mam to wish her a happy birthday. But for whatever reason, I decided it was important to visit her, to tell her in person. I stopped at a Texaco garage on the way back from Corrigan's and picked up some flowers. My mind drifted back to the anniversary visit to the cemetery. The same kind of tired-looking flowers had adorned the wreath. It was the thought that counted, though, wasn't it?

She doesn't live far from me. I'd always dreamed as a teenager of moving somewhere exciting like New York or Argentina. I can't remember why Argentina. Maybe Maradona had something to do with it.

The house where I grew up is deceptively large. From the outside it looks like a standard terraced two-up two-down like my own, but it is very deep and has a big living room to the rear that opens onto a large yard. I'm an only child, so I always had plenty of private space upstairs. Maradona posters on the wall, of course – Mexico '86, Italia '90. They're still there.

It was a rather haggard-looking Mam that answered the door. I'd not seen her looking so bad since, well, since I could remember.

"Everything OK, Mam?"

"I'm fine."

We walked into the kitchen and she put a kettle on the gas.

"Happy birthday, Mam," I said and planted a kiss on her cheek.

She reacted uncomfortably.

"I got some nice jam off the farmer today," she said. "Blackberry and apple. It's very—"

"What's wrong? Did something happen?"

"Oh no. You don't need to be worrying about me." She pointed to the bread basket. "Get the soda bread over there. I baked it yesterday."

I obliged and put it on a chopping block. I took a bread knife from a drawer and cut four slices. I put one up to my nose and sniffed. It smelled wonderful. It was the smell of happier times.

"Ah Jesus, Michael! Will ya get yer snout out of that bread. You'll spread germs all over it!"

I quickly dropped the slice to the chopping block. She had a way of making me reflex like that with a snap of her tongue. She gave me an unlabelled jar and I spread jam on the slices. She handed me a mug of tea and, with a slice of bread and jam clenched delicately between my teeth, I brought the tea in one hand and a plate of bread and jam in the other to the table.

I slurped from my mug and mashed up the thickly-sliced bread and jam with the tea to make a kind of porridge in my gob. My mother sighed as a little bit drooled at the side of my mouth. I tidied it up with a wipe of my finger and sucked it clean. She frowned.

I looked at her tired face. I wondered what was troubling her and what I could do to lighten the load. Then I remembered the flowers. Hadn't I only gone and left the fecking things in the car.

"Just a minute, Mam," I mumbled through a full mouth.

I ran to the car and retrieved the flowers. Water had seeped from the bulb at the end of the wrapping and left a damp patch on the seat. Nobody had sat in the back for years, anyway, so I didn't pay a blind bit of notice to it.

"Ta da!" I said as I returned and revealed the bouquet from behind my back.

"Oh thanks, Michael. Grab a vase, will you?"

She pointed to one on top of a cabinet. I filled it with water and put the flowers in it, emptying the flower food sachet that had been provided. I returned to my minor feast.

"How's the job hunting going, Michael?"

"Ah, so-so. It's not too good out there at the moment."

I didn't dare tell her about my current job. It was strictly a freelance deal, but it wouldn't have sat well with her.

There was a look on her face that I had never seen before. Or was that actually the case? Hadn't I seen it as a kid, when Dad was alive? Those late nights when she would sit at the same table, dragging her fingers down her face until she left white trails on her red cheeks. And the vodka. Always the vodka. She drank it with a dash of white lemonade in the pub, but at the table, waiting for Dad, she drank it neat. There was no vodka at the table now, just the same face, aged by the emptiness of a life lost to devoted widowhood.

"You know, you can tell me what's wrong," I said. "Whatever it is. I know there's something up."

I thought about moving my hand to hers to comfort her, but I didn't. We didn't have that kind of intimacy. Our love was understood, kept at a distance, because getting too close meant the loss would be greater. And it was the fear of loss that paralysed us both. Was that what had pushed Deborah away? Was that why I left home so soon after turning eighteen?

"I can't, Michael. I'm sorry. I'm tired now. I'd like to go to my bed."

I sighed. She didn't look like she could take an inquisition right then.

"OK, Mam. Happy birthday."

I couldn't think of anything better to say. I felt like a bit of a tool.

"And Michael … don't do anything stupid or dangerous. Just … just …"

She left it there, unable to find the right words.

The woman I helped upstairs to her bedroom was like a stranger. Distant. Very much troubled. And I felt wholly inadequate and ill-equipped to deal with it.

I dropped into Dunne's Stores to buy some craft beer before heading home after my mam's. I'm a sucker for beers with strange names. I picked up a couple of bottles of Twisted Hop and Headless Dog, both from the Hilden brewery in Lisburn up North. I'd pop one of them into the freezer to chill quickly so that I could crack open a bottle soon enough after getting home. I'd settle in and watch the Premier League highlights later, followed by a good read before falling asleep. Hopefully in bed, but it often happened in my armchair.

I was making a ham and cheese sandwich when my mobile rang. It was Grace. No doubt a quick, sharp instruction on where to meet to discuss the next assignment in the hunt for O'Brien's wider network.

"Michael?" her gentle voice at the end of the line asked.

"Call me Mickey. Everyone does."

"Like Mickey Mouse."

"Em, yeah, I suppose. It's just, there was one Guard, Mick, and another, Mike, and there was Mikey. They were senior to me and got first refusal on their choice of, well, whatever version of Michael they wanted."

"And what was wrong with plain old Michael?"

"Ah come on … Michael? What kind of name is that for a Guard?"

"I'm not going to go around calling you Mickey. Michael is more … dignified. I'm going to call you Michael."

"Or …"

"Or no date."

"Date?"

"Isn't that what I said?"

I went silent. I hadn't seen that coming. Was my radar so out of whack that I hadn't seen the come on? I hadn't picked up on anything at Corrigan's and yet here was Grace, free and direct as you like, doing what I thought was unfathomable – a girl asking a guy out on a date.

"A date," I said.

"Dinner and a tape that self-destructs in five seconds. Just dinner, mind."

"Of course, just dinner, I mean, of course."

I was beginning to be embarrassed by my phone manner, which had deteriorated to the level of the Bozo the clown school of telephone technique. Just dinner. No sex, just dinner. Just plain old meat and two veg, thank you very much, kiss on the cheek, call me, nighty night, see you at school tomorrow. Just dinner and business, see how it goes. Just dinner. Christ, I was a mess.

"I'll drop by your place tomorrow at eight," she said. "Is that OK?"

"That's … em, that's just fine." I'd have agreed to anything. "Where are we going?"

"Surprise me."

She laughed softly, almost giddily, and hung up.

For the remainder of the evening, I floated around my house whistling Lemon Jelly tunes. I was in a state of euphoria.

The next morning reality started to set in. I had my reservations about a date with Grace. Not that it had anything to do with Grace, particularly. She was pleasant to be around. If I was honest, though, I could not quite fathom what she saw in me. I may have cut a dashing figure at one point, a few years back. The uniform might have had something to do with that, though. Like fancy wrapping paper around a pair of Christmas socks. I groomed myself better back then – gelled my hair, moisturized after a shave, wore respectable clothes. Now I was beginning to look like a tramp. That was what living alone and with too little human contact did for you. If you had low esteem, then you didn't care how you looked in the mirror. As long as you had a clean pair of jocks and washed under your arms regular enough, then that was good enough. It would do around the house during my all too many episodes of moping. I'd put on a few pounds in just the last year too, maybe as many as twenty. I didn't have a weighing scales, but it only took the first two popped trouser buttons to tell the story. That meant that anything decent I had to wear would no longer fit. A trip to the shops was well in order.

"Surprise me," she'd said.

But I didn't know anywhere *fancy*. And it wasn't like I could phone anyone for advice.

I'd invited Mogs over once for a full Irish. "Better than any hotel," he'd said, his face smeared with so much ketchup that he resembled a clown. *How could anyone ruin my full Irish?* I had thought. Sure, anything smathered in ketchup just tastes like ketchup – Clonakilty, Denny, it was all the same with so much sugar mixing with the salt of the cured rashers. As for advice on restaurants? – you'd get better from the travellers' horses tethered in the field up the road. If I'd asked my mother, she would have become nosey. And when it came to nosiness, Mam had few equals, her beak sticking into things like a crossbill finch prising open a seed. I wanted to keep my *date* to myself for now.

I walked into Patrick's Street – only about ten minutes from where I lived – and went into Gentleman's Quarters. I supposed a nice shirt – light blue maybe? – would be appropriate, a pair of navy slacks too. A plain navy tie would set off nicely against the shirt. I thought about shoes too. A pair of black shoes, leather heels.

Christ, what am I doing? I'll end up looking like a fecking Guard!

I spotted a pair of what looked like a cross between trainers and walking shoes. Isn't that what the *hip* people were wearing these days? A plain pair of jeans – no faux vintage treatment, thank you very much – and a check shirt and I was in business, maybe even *the* business, but I was probably getting ahead of myself. Not until I got my hair trimmed, anyway. And if only Grace knew what an ordeal getting a haircut was for me.

I flicked my fringe back with a nervous twitch of my head. Between stress and the sheer habit of clearing hair from my vision, the twitch had become almost a permanent fixture in my long list of undesirable mannerisms. I wondered if I would still be twitching like that after I got my hair cut. It might not be long, I thought, before I ended up looking like an epileptic.

I gathered up my new glad rags and paid for them with cash.

Maybe this was some kind of a fresh start for me. Maybe I was now, finally, about to get some kind of a break. Didn't I deserve a turn in my luck like this? Or were the new clothes just a mask – a bandage over a gaping wound that was still festering?

92

6

The Devil's Snot

I STOOD IN FRONT of the mirror in my bedroom with my new clothes on. A good fit, even if I had to admit I was looking a bit portly. I was on edge, though.

If I just sit here in this house waiting for tomorrow's date, I'll explode. Like Jaws. Chunks of blubber everywhere. God, I need a drink!

And when I needed a drink, there was one man I could count on. There wasn't much else you could count on him for, but going for a pint was where he was world class. I punched Mogs's number into my new mobile.

"You fancy meeting up for a pint in an hour?" I said.

"Does the Pope molest choir boys in the woods?"

Thank God for Mogs's irreverence. Exactly what I needed just then.

Once again I found Mogs without a pint.

"The usual?" I said with a wry smile.

I went to the bar and came back, as I had before, with a pint of Howling Gale and a pint of Bud.

"Jaysus, I'm gaspin," Mogs said.

He took such a gulp that I wondered how his throat could cope with the deluge. Not one for savouring was Mogs. I took a more leisurely sip. The Howling Gale had a tang to it, kind of citrusy – worth giving the taste buds the time to enjoy the experience.

"Story, feen?" Mogs asked.

"Ah, I'm OK. Sorry for not hanging around too long the last night."

I didn't want to mention the date with Grace. I'd only get the full wind-up merchant treatment from Mogs.

"Ah, you're grand, boy. Sure, didn't I get two free pints of Bud and half a Howling Gale."

He winked at me with a withered eyelid. He was getting on in years. What was he now? At least sixty?

"Anyway," he went on, "was it something I said, like? The Moolah – was that it? I thought you barely knew him."

I took another sip. I felt the cold beer soothe my throat.

"Nah. I just remembered I needed to be somewhere."

Mogs looked like he bought my guff. He wasn't exactly the brightest button in the haberdashery.

"Don't worry about it, boy," he said. "Happens to me all the time. Memory like a sieve, me."

Mogs took another gulp of Bud. About a quarter of his pint left and we'd only been talking for a couple of minutes. He went through beer faster than a gas bubble.

"What do you think about the Cork team in the league, boy?" he asked, directing the conversation into comfortable territory.

"Hurling or football?"

"Does it matter? Like, we'll be lucky if the players don't all go on strike. Dozy muppets."

"There's two sides to every dispute, Mogs."

I knew first hand about sides. There was the media version of me giving Chambers a right flaking, and there was the version that my Garda *friends* should have held up on. Now, it didn't matter a tuppenny fuck that the media was on the money – that wasn't the point – the point was that a plausible story wasn't offered in my defence. A little white lie would have done: Chambers resisted arrest – which he did – and required ultimate force in restraining him. But I could have cuffed him easy enough and didn't. One fist flew, then another, and another. It was the picture of the boy under those twigs, burnt into my memory like staring at the sun for too long does to the eyes. And I could have sworn Chambers had smirked even as the fists flew. The more I'd laced into Chambers, the wider the smirk appeared to become – or had his brain gone by that stage?

Mogs's lips were flapping vigorously as he was saying something undoubtedly unimportant, but I could not hear him. Instead, I was picturing both Chambers's pulped visage and the stark image of *Little* Robbie O'Meara's corpse, so white that the bruising around its neck was clearly visible – a necklace of knuckles like the one I had given Chambers to cut off the blood supply to his brain and send him into that coma.

"I said," Mogs repeated forcefully, "they can get in all the minor and B squad players, get guys with some pride in the jersey, boy. Like, maybe show up the senior panel for the jumped up pricks that—"

"Ah hang on, Mogs. I think you'll find they're on strike precisely *because* they have pride in the jersey. They're sick of all this amateur crap from the county board. They just … ah for feck sake, I don't want to have another Roy Keane-style argument where we both lose – even if we think we win."

"Too right, boy" Mogs said. "Those feens can go and take a running jump into the River Lee for all I care. Not worth the steam off me piss talking about them."

Mogs finished the last of the beer and fumbled in his pocket for a non-existent – at least that would be his excuse – wallet. He tisked loudly and said, with the most exaggerated exasperation: "Sure, didn't I only go and leave me wallet in me dirty jeans."

I half coughed, half grunted. "Let's hope Maude doesn't put that dirty jeans into the washing machine with your wallet still in it, eh?"

I raised up my eyebrows to indicate my disbelief. But this was just a game we played. I had my part to play and so did Mogs. I would nearly have been disappointed had Mogs actually had the temerity to pay for his own pint, let alone mine.

"Mam's not so thick as to not check the pockets," Mogs said without a hint of irony.

"What is she now? Ninety?"

"Eighty-eight."

"Shame on you," I said, laughing. "Getting your old mam to wash your clothes."

"Jesus Christ, Mickey," Mogs said, a serious look in his eyes. "Be sure to never let her hear you call her old. She'll come after you with her blackthorn stick and give you a right flake."

Mogs cupped his hand around his upper arm as if covering a sore spot. He appeared quite unaware of what he had just done and rather than feel amused, I imagined how distressing a childhood Mogs had had. There had been other clues to this. Little mannerisms here and there.

"Anyway, about this Moolah fella," I said with such apparent disinterest that it must have appeared to Mogs that I was just filling an awkward silence.

But this was partly why I was here. The eavesdropping at O'Brien's house had suggested Moolah was O'Brien's handiwork. But if there was a link to Jordan, then I needed to know for sure. I needed to know if Jordan was as retired as he claimed. I needed to know because I was about to date his only daughter.

"What about him?"

"You said he was shipping in some stuff on a yacht?"

"That's right."

"From Spain or somewhere?"

"Couldn't tell ya. Maybe."

"How did you hear about this?"

Mogs looked incredulously at me. "And if some feen – oh, I dunno, let's just say some porky fecking pig … no offence—" I offered up my hand to indicate none had been taken. "—were to ask you where you heard the skinny from?"

I gave Mogs a few sharp nods of my head.

"Exactly," Mogs said. "You got your sources, boy …" He placed the fingertips of both hands, their knuckles standing proud like a mountain range, on his chest. "… and I got mine."

I felt like there was a colony of ants crawling all over my arms and the back of my neck. There was honour among thieves, even retired bagmen, for sure. I couldn't push this line of questioning any further and the frustration was agonizing.

A lifetime deal, Doc O'Reilly had said about the kind of meds I would need should I not mend my ways. And here I was inviting stress into my life when I should probably have booked into a fecking spa – not that I was into that kind of girly shite, just that that was what they usually did on TV shows like *How Long Will You Live?*

I felt like leaving early again, perhaps more abruptly this time, but I realized I enjoyed the kind of banter we had engaged in prior to hitting that brick wall. It took my mind off the serious stuff – Jordan, O'Brien, Dad.

Mogs and I drank a few more, laughed loudly more than once, and decided, ultimately, that hunger would call a halt to our drinking rather than the barman flashing the lights for closing time, not that the clientele of An Capall Bán – an assorted rabble of sham-feens and flah-bags if ever there was one – were ones for such limp gestures.

I felt like I could murder my own mother for a battered sausage and so Mogs and I decided to head for Phelan's chipper, a short walk down Blarney Street.

"You're some gimp, you," Mogs said with a grin, about halfway to the chipper.

"What?"

"You were onto a good wan there, boy. In da shades, like. Pension, overtime. Then you go and mangle that kiddie rapist big time. Like, nearly bate him to death, like."

"I know, but—"

I felt and heard a swish in my right ear. And then Mogs wasn't there anymore. I looked around. He was down on the ground, back to the wall of a house, holding his stomach. He looked up at me pleadingly, blood pouring between his fingers. His mouth opened, but no words came.

My police training kicked in. Even as langers as I was, I managed to duck behind the nearest car. Then the sound of a shot registered. A shotgun blast. Then another blast sent pellets clattering into steel and smashing through the car window.

"Mogs! Mogs?"

I looked to him. He was out in the open, easy prey for whatever gunman had opened up on us.

I didn't carry a piece. I'd been stripped of my side-arm when I was thrown out of the Guards and I'd not bothered applying for a private security or a gun licence. I'd always thought the butt of a torch, like the one I used to carry on my rounds in Churchfield, would have been enough.

I stayed crouched by the front wheel arch of the car. The pause in the action seemed interminable. Another shot rang out and I could immediately feel something dig into my shin. I tried to suppress my voice, but I let out a strained cry. Again it seemed like time forgot its business and everything froze. And in that moment of temporal frigidity, I experienced several things that my usually suspect memory would later recall as clearly as the seven, exactly seven, twigs I knew had protruded over Robbie O'Meara's body: the warmth of the blood trickling down from my shin onto my calf; the rumbling growl of a high-cc motor cycle; a man shouting, "forget him, he's not important,"; some girl in some house screaming; Mogs looking at me desperately, piss streaming along the ground from beneath him. And then, mercifully, there was the screeching of tyre rubber as a bike sped away up the hill.

I continued to stoop, petrified almost. My friend was lying on the ground, his life quickly draining away and I could not move. Then I could stoop no more and fell onto my arse with my back to the tyre of the car that had saved my life.

"Are you OK?" some girl was asking.

It barely registered. I looked up to see a freckly red-headed girl, no older than fifteen, staring down at me.

"Your leg looks pretty bad."

"I'm … I'm fine."

I tried to get up, but couldn't. I climbed to my feet using the car for leverage and felt fine – for about ten seconds. Then the endorphins wore off and the pain was like someone had stuck a bread knife through my calf muscle. The girl – with that red hair of hers, like a river of blood, oh Christ! – she pleaded with me to sit back down and wait for the ambulance her mother had called, but I was having none of it. Mogs. I had to check Mogs.

"Dad!" the girl cried in the direction of what must have been her home. "Get a coat!"

I hobbled towards Mogs. It was a horrific sight, one that I – what with my tendency towards obsessive thoughts – would never be able to banish from my memory, in much the same way I had never been able to clear my mind's eye of that crime scene with the dead boy whose name I would rather have forgotten. I had to look away for a moment and felt ashamed for doing so.

I noticed a light in the corner of my eye and looked across the street to see an old woman, maybe in her eighties, peering out from between some tattered old curtains and netting. She looked for all the world like Mogs's mother. What was her name again? Christ Jesus, what was her fucking name? Mogs's mother with the blackthorn stick, with all those knobbles eager to make contact with muscle and bone. She'd not hit him again; the bitch would see her son go into the ground before her.

And then a weak voice said, "Ya fecking gobshite, help me!"

Mogs was alive. I bent down to look at the damage. I pulled up his shirt and could see that blood was draining from at least two holes. There was nothing gaping, though – that was something positive to hold onto. Probably a couple of pellets had lodged in his gut. With some luck, he'd make it through. I looked into his eyes. I saw enough pain in them that I believed he was going to be able to cling on by those filthy fingernails of his.

Hang on a minute. I'm standing here waiting for an ambulance. For the Guards. Detectives. Savage. That cunt could be out there somewhere monitoring the radio, might even be the first responder. Could be that the dirty fuck was behind the hit.

I had to get away from there, get some medical attention, and think things through. Then maybe call Cotter. If I thought he could be trusted.

"I'm sorry, Mogs, I've got to make a run for it," I said and put my hand reassuringly on his shoulder. "You're going to make it." I said it like I meant it.

The girl's father came from the house with a coat. "Hey, where are you going?"

"I'm grand. It's just a nick. I'll look after it myself. He needs help more than me."

"Are you mad? The ambulance will be here in two minutes."

"I'm grand!"

"Stop him, Dad!" the red head called out.

"I'm not getting involved," her Dad said.

That's right … look after your daughter. Be a good father. Take her inside and keep her safe.

I shuffled off dragging one leg behind me in the direction of Doc O'Reilly's home.

You better be in, you fucking sadistic cretin, I thought as I approached the door to Doc O'Reilly's home, the pain crawling up my leg like some kind of demon spawn was gleefully burrowing its way around inside my thigh.

The doc lived in a new apartment just around the corner from his practice. I thought maybe he owned some of the other apartments too, had maybe lost a good deal of his pension on the ill-advised investment when the boom became bust. I buzzed the intercom and prayed the old man was in.

"Yes?"

"It's me, Doc. Mickey."

"Mickey?"

"Fecking Bosco, you … just let me in, please."

There was a pause. No buzz.

"I'm hurt, you bastard," I called into the microphone, my lips pressed up to it such that I left a trail of spittle behind me.

There was the buzz and the door released. I went into the main hall. I tottered over to the lift. OUT OF ORDER, a sign read. I looked up at the ceiling as if I could see through it to the heavens above.

"You langer," I said. "You good-for-nothing langer."

In all my life, I resolved, I had never experienced such pain. I began to climb the stairs. Each step seemed worse than the last, to the point where I considered just stopping and lying there. And if I bled out, then all well and good as far as I was concerned. I'd had a good run of it for a while. But the last few years had been shite and it wasn't as if the next few offered anything different. I'd bleed out on the nice shiny marble stairs and crawl right on into the boot of that rusting car with my father.

"What the fuck?" Doc said as he stood at the top of the stairs. "What a mess."

I looked behind myself as if I were a child who'd soiled himself. A trail of blood snaked its way up the steps to meet me. My blood? Of course it was. Maybe it was the mess on the stairs the doc was more worried about than the undoubted mess that I had become.

"Sorry, Doc. I kind of had an accident."

"Never mind that, you poor fecker."

He ran down the last six or seven steps – I had climbed at least fifteen – grabbed my arm and put it around his shoulder. The doc was twig-thin, but showed surprising strength in supporting me as we awkwardly bundled our way up the remaining steps.

"What kind of shite have you heaped upon yourself now, Mickey?"

I grunted as much out of non-committal as from the pain. The less I told the doc, the better. We stopped at the third door along the corridor. A rubber plant was in a pot to one side of it – real or not, I couldn't tell, or give two shites about.

"Mind yourself," O'Reilly said as he dipped his hand into his pocket to fetch the key. I whelped as some of the weight transferred onto my injured leg.

"Sorry, Mickey."

He helped me to a couch once we got inside and fetched a towel to put under the bleeding leg. Some blood smeared on the leather and I apologized, but the Doc said it would wash off easily.

"You can start by telling me what happened and then I'll tell you whether we need to amputate or not."

My eyes bulged. *Ampu-what?*

O'Reilly let out a throaty laugh.

"Relax, Mickey. It's just a flesh wound. You wouldn't have made it this far if the bone had been shattered."

He fetched a scissors and cut my trouser leg to reveal the extent of the damage.

"Shite," he said.

"What?" I said, suspecting the doc may have reevaluated the need to cut my leg off.

"Got some blood on my jumper. My son got it for my birthday."

I didn't think the guy had ever been married. Couldn't even imagine the guy being married. But quite frankly, I couldn't have given a rat's ass about the doc's geansaí.

"Are you going to tell me what happened, or am I going to have to drug you to get some answers?"

"I've been shot."

Doc O'Reilly examined the wound, cleaned it off with a wet cloth.

"No shit, Sherlock. But it doesn't look like much of a gunshot wound to me."

He got another cloth and poured some foul-smelling liquid on it, probably some kind of disinfectant, and wiped the wound again.

"Wait here a minute," he said as if I could even consider moving from the settee.

He returned a minute later from another room with some forceps.

"There's something in there all right, but I'll be fucked if it's a bullet. Brace yourself."

The pain was at a level that I couldn't put a number on. I simply couldn't count that far.

"Jesus Christ, Doc! You going to plant a fucking tree down there, or what?"

The doc kept on digging.

"Just a second … shite."

Darkness. The pain. Too much.

"Got it!"

A few seconds passed and I was unclear about whether I was awake or not. I opened an eye. The doc was there holding something with the forceps. Something black. *Like the Devil's snot.*

"You know what this is, Mickey?"

"Drink."

"Huh?"

"Get me a fucking drink. Whiskey … just get me a fucking bottle."

I couldn't have cared less about whatever the piece of crap in the forceps was. I'd doused my mental pain with drink before, so maybe it would take away my physical pain.

"No, Mickey. I'll have to give you some painkillers. Can't mix those with drink."

The doc dropped the black thing into his palm and picked at it with a finger nail.

"Tarmac," he said.

"What?" I said, some of the pain finally subsiding.

"A piece of fucking road."

"What in the name of God do mean *a piece of road?*"

I took a hard look at it. Maybe the doc was right.

"Bullet missed you, hit the road, sent a piece of it into your leg. Lucky."

Rage mixed with the pain until the pressure built inside my head. *Lucky?* Mogs was half-dead on the road, maybe all-the-way dead by now, and I'd crawled halfway across Cork to get to the doc's door, and I was *lucky?*

Breathe, I told myself. *Just breathe.*

O'Reilly fetched some pills and I, without question, swallowed four of them with the help of a glass of water.

"Get some rest, Mickey."

I grabbed the doc's jumper.

"No Guards. I'm not here. No Guards come in without a warrant."

O'Reilly's face didn't flinch. He was an old-timer, had seen pretty much everything. I didn't expect anything less of him.

"Thanks, Doc. I'll make this up to you."

Then the painkillers started getting to work on me. Less than a minute later and I was asleep or just plain passed-out, this time without the usual images to haunt my dreams. And without the picture of Mogs sitting there pleading with me, his blood gushing, an image that would, without doubt, be tormenting my sleep in the days and years to come. If I lived that long.

I woke to the smell of frying rashers. I was ravenous. I'd not eaten since ... well, since the fan had been peppered with shite the evening before. I'd never gotten to Phelan's for that battered sausage. I felt like cutting my tongue out for even thinking about my stomach after what had happened.

"Ah, you're awake," Doc O'Reilly said holding a sizzling frying pan.

He went back to the alcove where the kitchenette was. I watched him slice a tomato and put the two halves into the pan.

"I thought you might want a bit of comfort food, after ... you know."

"Yeah."

"I put on some black pudding and all."

I didn't reply. Cutting down on the black pudding didn't seem important to me, or him, then.

Doc pointed to the other side of the living area. "There's a couple of bits of clothing on the armchair. You know it's funny, Mickey. Your father came to me one night much like you have. I was a young fella then, no older than thirty. I didn't ask questions back then either."

I looked at the doc. I didn't know what to say to him.

"Nothing to do with being shot, or anything," he continued. "He took a pretty bad beating. I had to reset his nose, patch him up, make sure he didn't have a concussion." O'Reilly scooped the contents of the pan onto two plates. "You wouldn't have remembered. You were probably still in nappies."

I pulled myself off the settee and got a sudden reminder about what part of my body was injured as pain tore up my leg. I removed the trousers that Doc had cut to ribbons on the left leg. I went to the armchair and changed into the jog pants and sweat shirt Doc had put there.

"Careful there, Mickey. You'll need to watch the stitching on the wound. I'll talk to you after breakfast about changing the dressing."

I limped to the kitchenette where O'Reilly had put the plates on the breakfast counter.

"Get your chops around that," he said.

Whatever about my leg, there was nothing wrong with my appetite. I dispensed with the use of a knife and fork and snapped a sausage in half with my two hands. I didn't bother swallowing before moving onto the rashers and crumbly pieces of black pudding.

"Easy, Mickey. You'll give yourself indigestion."

I waved him off. Where was the sense in maintaining my humanity after what I'd seen? I thought about Mogs. I'd just left him there, skulked off and left him to die. Then I thought about Grace.

Dinner at eight. Tonight. Disaster. It's all falling apart!

"I heard the news this morning on the radio," O'Reilly said. "About a guy being shot up Blarney Street. The Guards were asking for information about a man leaving the scene. Kind of matched your description."

I didn't respond. The less I involved the doc in things the better. Plausible deniability. A way for the doc to only tell white lies instead of dirty great big black ones should he be questioned by the Guards.

"I called the hospital this morning. The guy is stable by all accounts, should pull through."

I couldn't hide my relief. He'd at least nine lives, the fecker. He'd survived TB, cancer, and a car crash. Now it looked like he could add another badge of honour to his collection.

O'Reilly went to the fridge for some orange juice and put the kettle on.

"Did you find out who beat up my father?"

"No." He paused for a moment, got a couple of mugs from a cupboard. "But I had an inkling."

"Go on."

"Well, at that time there was one guy you didn't want to mess with. A guy you didn't want to be asking too many questions about, like your father would have."

The kettle boiled. He took two teabags from an airtight container, put them in the mugs, and poured the water.

"Can you guess who that might have been?" he asked.

"Jordan." The answer came like a reflex.

"In one. Back at that time he was just a thug who pissed on every street corner to mark his territory. I always imagined the guy would burn brightly for a while before some other nut put a bullet in him. Now look at him."

I grunted. I took a mug of tea and sipped. It could have been watered down mud right then and I would still have been refreshed by it. It triggered something in my brain, because I thought about the note that had fallen out of the *Billy Budd* novel. The one that had Starman written on it. It was a long shot, but I decided to test the doc with it.

"Does the word Starman mean anything to you? My father would have known what it meant."

"Starman?" he said. "I remember a film, was it? With Beau … no Jeff Bridges. But in relation to your father … no, I can't say it rings a bell."

I thought I would never figure out who or what this Starman was. But I wouldn't stop trying.

I looked out the window and could see people busily go about their business. The Guards would no doubt be out canvassing the area, might get a tip-off from some Samaritan who'd seen a dodgy-looking bloke with a limp. I might even have left a blood trail behind me.

"I'm not going to be able to hang around for long more, Doc."

"You need to rest that leg. We need to keep an eye on it in case infection sets in."

"I'll be grand. Just give me a box of painkillers and some anti-biotics and I'll look after myself."

Doc sighed and looked at me, probably gauging my lucidity and strength. "OK, Mickey. But you never got the fecking stuff from me. That clear? I don't want to end up suspended from practising. I have it up to my tits with mortgage repayments, so I need the income."

I nodded. Doc went and got two cartons of pills. Pain shot up from my leg despite the painkillers I had taken the night before, but I suppressed the grimace. I'd pop some more pills as soon as I got out the door.

I shook Doc's hand and told him I'd see him in three months for our scheduled follow-up. It's easy to make promises when you don't believe you'll be around to fulfil them. I made my way gingerly down the stairs.

It wasn't far to my house, but I knew there was every chance someone was there waiting. Could be just a Guard with a few questions, or could be someone waiting behind the shower cur-tain with a garotte. Parking wasn't possible down the narrow side lane off Farren Street where my house was, so I had parked a good bit away. I hoped no one would be watching the car.

I got to the top of Great William O'Brien Street and looked up to where my car was parked on Gerald Griffin Street. I could see nothing of note. That wasn't to say there wasn't someone lurking in the shadow of a doorway. But with the state my leg was in, I needed wheels.

I walked as upright as I could and passed Farren Street. I glanced to the side and could see a Garda car parked near my home. I quickened my step until I was out of view. Still I could see no one near the car.

I got to the car and got in. Because of the way I was parked, perpendicular to the kerb and between two other cars, I half expected a car – Garda or otherwise – to pull a box manoeuvre and stop me in my tracks, but none did. I simply turned the key, pulled out of my parking spot, and drove away.

As I drove, I thought about what I'd been through over the past week: I'd been beaten, practically kidnapped, and then shot at. I didn't have the time or the energy to feel sorry for myself, though. But there was no question in my mind about it: I needed a gun. And I knew just the guy to get one for me.

7

Damn and be Damned

THE EEL WAS A legend. Jimmy the Eel. The Fixer from Farranree. If you needed a piece, a whore, a quick score, he was your only man. He was well known to the Guards, but so slippery he'd squirm through their grasp every time they had heat on him. At least, that was the legend. The truth is that he had so many dirty cops on his payroll and snitched so much grade-A skinny to clean cops to fund that payroll that all the other Guards just kept well shot of him.

The last time I'd checked, when investigating the murder of an underage Lithuanian prostitute more than five years ago, the Eel hung out in The Steamship pub on Albert Quay. A popular haunt in the seventies, the Steamship became a graveyard for young men in the mid to late eighties when, after the closures of the Dunlop and Ford factories, they spent their redundancies on drink. Some were still there now, somehow with the aid of medical science, their livers seemingly impervious to the gallons of alcohol they consumed each week. Add to that the influx of East European and West African sailors, and the place was never more than a sneeze away from an all-out brawl.

It was almost lunchtime. There'd be no hot food served in the Steamship, though. The only lunches were of the liquid variety. I parked in a disabled slot and put my dead Granddad's wheelchair sticker on the windscreen. The parking wardens rarely looked closely enough to see it had expired. Sure, with the wound in my leg I *was* disabled.

I shuffled into the pub as naturally as I could. It was busy, even for a Tuesday lunchtime. It seemed alcohol was recession-proof. People had their priorities, I supposed. I looked around for the Eel. No sign of him. I went to the bar and ordered a Jameson. I'd have ordered beer if they had some decent continental stuff, but all they served was the usual weak-tasting piss water – the stuff that goes down the neck the fastest, mere delivery systems for alcohol. Not like the quality stuff, such as Howling Gale, that you had to sip and savour.

"You seen Jimmy today?" I asked of the barman.

There was a noticeable scar on the bridge of the guy's nose, another on the hand he used to pour the whiskey. Collateral damage, no doubt, from stepping in to break up a glass fight.

"There's a lot of Jimmys in this world, boy. A lot that come in here. How the feck would I know what Jimmy you're talking about?"

Several missing teeth gave his voice a heavy lisp.

"Well, there's the Jimmy that likes to migrate to the Sargasso Sea, if you catch my drift."

The barman gave me a gormless look. Obviously, the meaning had drifted right on by his jug ears. *Too much to expect, I suppose, that this Muppet might actually watch the Discovery Channel.*

"The fecking Eel!" I said.

There was a mixture of revelation and recognition on the barman's ugly mug. He wiped it off his face as fast as he wiped the bar with his filthy rag. "What the fuck are you on, boy, with yer fecking Eel?" He shook his head and moved on to serve another customer.

I waited for the customer to move away before re-engaging. My old Garda credentials would have been all the leverage I needed in a place that had so many health and safety violations it made a building site look like a playground. But all I had now was the gift of my gab and the threat of my fists. The thing was, I wanted to upgrade those fists to a gun.

"I just want to talk to him." I took out a twenty and slapped it on the counter. "I know we're not in New York," I said, "but here's a tip for your *exemplary* service and your *warm* hospitality."

The barman went for the note. I grabbed him by the wrist and squeezed hard.

"The fucking Eel. Where is he?"

A muscled guy at the end of the counter, West African probably, looked up from his pint, then just as quickly looked back down at it. The barman winced, but kept his gob tightly shut. I gave his wrist another squeeze.

"He's … oh God … he's …"

"Over here." A voice off to the right from behind a bead curtain. Then someone came through the beads like an eel through seaweed. It was Jimmy the fixer. I relinquished my grip. The barman shamelessly took the twenty and stuffed it in his pocket.

"I wasn't gonna blab, Jimmy. I swear to God."

Jimmy said nothing to the barman. His stature said enough. You didn't fuck around with the Eel.

"Mickey the Mangler," he said, looking to me. "What an honour this is. Why don't you come into my …" He gave the barman a throat-slitting look. "*Private* card room."

For a man of about sixty-five, Jimmy had aged well since I last saw him despite the addition of a purple scar on his left cheek. It only made him more distinguished-looking when added to the now entirely grey head of hair. He was wearing a dark brown shirt with white vertical pin stripes. He wore the shirt out over stonewashed black jeans. On his feet were what looked like green snakeskin boat shoes complete with tassels.

I grabbed my whiskey and followed him into the card room, which was surprisingly plush with a felt-topped table and several leather-bound chairs. It had an executive look that was entirely at odds with the ramshackle nature of the outer bar. A picture of dogs playing poker hung on the back wall. Pictures of Steve McQueen and James Dean adorned the walls also. But there was no doubt in my mind that there was more than just poker being played out in this room. Some pretty uncomfortable stuff, I imagined.

I sat on the nearest chair when Jimmy beckoned me to. There was a bloodstain on the felt. Jimmy caught me looking at it.

"This guy thinks he can sneak an ace up his sleeve," he said, his eyes fixed on the stain. "I'm very black and white when it comes to justice. People in this country think we're civilized, law-abiding. That's a load of shite. You rob a guy with a hammer, they let you out after two weeks so you can go back and rob him with a gun. Now, Saudi Arabia ... that's a civilized country. Steal a loaf, you lose a hand. No more stealing. I take a more moderate approach. You steal from me, you lose a finger."

He laughed from the corner of his mouth and sat opposite me. He took a pack of John Player Blue from his shirt pocket, pulled out a cigarette, and lit it. He offered me one, but I refused. He inhaled deeply and suppressed a cough.

"You wanna hear a good one, Mickey?" he squeezed out of his throat.

I shrugged my shoulders, said nothing.

"What's the definition of a compulsive gambler?"

I was in no mood for jokes, but played along. "Tell me, Jimmy ... what's the definition of a compulsive gambler?"

A boyish grin lit up his face. "The guy who turns up here with two fingers missing." He took another long drag, let out a combined cough-laugh. "I shit you not, boy." He jabbed the cigarette back and forth towards the bloodstain. "Three fingers missing now. Can you believe that?"

I'm not sure I did, but it sounded like a good story. A good deterrent. I gave nothing in reply. I'd seen it before. From Jimmy, from many's the street thug and chancer. It was best to let them ramble, to run out of steam. Only when they'd shed themselves of so much bullshit could you get down to the serious business. And there was nothing more serious than my urgent need of a gun.

Jimmy was still in full flow. "But you wouldn't be impressed by all that now, would you?"

Another pull on the cigarette. I sipped my whiskey. Jimmy kept talking.

"You're a fucking superstar amongst us scum. Did you know that? A fucking legend. If there's one thing we hate more than the filth, it's kiddie rapists. And the way you did it, boy … genius. Was it like this?"

He put his hands into a choke position, writhed them around, throttling thin air, grimacing maniacally.

This wasn't what I had signed up for. I was there as a customer, not as a circus freak for Jimmy's sick entertainment.

"Come on, Mickey … show me how you did it. What's the best way to snuff out a nonce? Did you grab a hold of him like this?"

He widened his fingers so that his hands were spread out like spider crabs, stood up, and this time moved his arms and shoulders up and down vigorously until his entire body was shaking. After a few seconds he sat down again, wheezing, his cigarette broken and extinguished from his exertion. He was grinning like a loon. He breathed deeply. A chance for me to finally get down to brass tacks.

"I'm in the market for something that offers protection."

Jimmy chuckled. "I could offer you a rubber johnny if it's one of those skanks round the corner you're looking for. I could even get you a special discount. Fuck it, for you, for a legend like yourself, I can get you the first hour for free. They love you long time, boy!"

He opened his mouth wide and lolled his tongue quickly from side to side. It was a hideous sight.

As good a reason as any to nickname you the Eel.

"You know exactly what I'm talking about, Jimmy. I need a piece."

Jimmy took a few seconds to gather himself.

"A fucking gun? The Mangler looking for a gun? Are you trying to erase your legacy, boy? You're the feen that can take out guys with a single hand to the throat. You're like the Bruce Lee of Cork."

The platitudes weren't working on me. The reputation I was building was becoming a mill stone.

"Let's just say I need to be in a position to fight fire with fire."

Jimmy frowned. "Still up to your eyes in it, boy. It's always the same with the shades: you lie down with dogs, wake up with fleas."

He pulled another cigarette from the pack and sighed before putting it in his mouth. "I'll give you a mobile number."

He tore the flap off the pack of Player's, took a pencil from the middle of the table, and began to write. I drained the last of my whiskey.

"Call this number after eight. The guy's name is Sham. You'll meet up where he says and he'll have your piece for you. I hope you're not fussy – it'll be a regular nine-mil hand gun, clean, no record."

"How much?"

"For you, boy, a special price. Eight-hundred."

I'd come with a grand. I didn't know what I'd have done if it had been more. Jimmy was the kind of guy you didn't want to owe money to. I counted out eight-hundred and slid the bundle of notes across the table. Jimmy put it in his pocket without counting. It was grubby business – there was no mistaking that – but I would be ready now, I hoped, for any eventuality.

I needed a place to hole up. Going home wasn't going to be an option. Neither would I be dragging my troubles to my mother's door, putting her in harm's way.

I got the number of a hotel about five miles to the east of Cork City from directory enquiries and asked the operator to connect me. I asked if they had a cheap smoking room with a view of the car park. I also confirmed that they did room service dinners – I'd need a full stomach before going to get my gun. Best to keep up the sugar levels when walking into situations of stress.

The receptionist said they had and they did, but she asked for a credit card number, which I declined to give her. She explained that for a cash customer, I would have to pay in advance at the desk. I knew it was best to stay low-profile, to not use a credit card that could very easily be traced by the Guards, maybe even a particular bent one affiliated with O'Brien.

I stopped off at the bank and drew out another two-grand. At least they could trace me no further than my local neighbourhood. I wondered how long, if ever, it would be before I could safely return.

As I drove to the hotel, I felt the car lurching a bit any time I changed up a gear and accelerated. The old girl was feeling her age, misfiring a bit. Probably just a dirty spark plug or a dodgy lead. I'd bring it to a mechanic I knew down a back road in the back of beyond when things calmed down. If I made it through.

The hotel was one of those dreary generic chain hotels that you could probably assemble from a flat pack. Far from giving the building any character, the red brick used in construction just made the building look cheap, like an institution.

As I drove into the parking area there was a pop. For a split second my blood pressure zeroed out and I thought my time was up for sure this time. Then I realized that my old Fiat had just backfired and that my head was still intact. Maybe it was more than just dirty plugs, after all.

I parked the car and it was a few seconds before I could peel my hands from the steering wheel. When I looked at them, I could see the white imprint of the wheel across them. I just knew, then, that all the stress that was being dumped on me was doing permanent damage to my heart, literally taking years off me.

Inside, the receptionist was cheery enough, wished me a good day, but in a MacDonald's kind of way. I was glad of the pleasantries, though. At least she wasn't shooting at me. She explained that breakfast was extra, that the price I had been quoted was a room-only rate. It was an additional ten Euro and I felt like asking if the full Irish included Clonakilty pudding, but I resisted. I told her I'd play it by ear and decide in the morning.

I paid enough cash to cover the room for two nights and gave an extra fifty as deposit against phone calls made from the room. Needless to say, I used a false name: Jerry O'Leary – a combo of my middle name and Mam's maiden name. She gave me a key card for a room on the fourth floor without asking for identification.

I looked around. The lobby was full of suits. Sales people, corporate types meeting up to talk their corporate shite. They were so oblivious to the side of the city I saw. They had no idea just how much trouble was close to their doorsteps – the tweakers, the pushers, the street walkers, the homeless, people on the edges of society. I was envious of them and their shallow preoccupations, up to a point.

I got into the lift and pushed the button for the fourth floor – the smoking floor. Only then did I remember that I'd given up the cancer sticks. I closed my eyes and dropped my head down. Of all the times to give up, I had to choose the time when someone starts firing bullets at me.

The room was every bit as bland as the exterior, but I didn't care. It was safe, for now. I could smell the smoke of previous occupants. The first thing I did was to grab the ash tray and put it in a drawer. It would only have sat there laughing at me otherwise, mocking me for being such a weak-willed quitter.

I sat on the end of the bed. I took a painkiller – just the one to smooth the way until my proper dose in a few hours. It was the first time in quite a while that I had time to think clearly. And God knows, there was plenty of thinking required.

I had to decide on who to call, if anyone. I had to phone Sham at eight; that much at least I knew. That gave me about five hours to kill. Could I trust Cotter? I could probably trust Grace. It would have made no sense Jordan having anything to do with the attempted hit. There wasn't much I would have put past him, but wacking me within hours of talking to me would have been suicide. Surely it had to be O'Brien and Savage. I was sure I hadn't been spotted when I beat a hasty retreat from the house in Carrignavar, so they must have run my number plate, which the two Guards had recorded. They could have been Savage's *lads*. Two of them, anyway. Christ knew how many more of them there were.

I decided I could trust Grace. I needed to trust Grace. I dialled the number of the burner mobile into the room phone.

"Michael?"

"Hi Grace. It's me. I'm just—"

"Are you OK? Are you hurt?"

How could she know? But she was Jordan's daughter, after all. O'Brien had Savage, but Jordan probably had an army of Guards, some ranked even higher. Not necessarily on his payroll, but former *employees* of his in much the same way I had become.

"I'm OK. I'm safe."

I could hear her exhale loudly.

"Honestly, I just got a scratch," I said. "I got the hell out of there before …"

I almost said Savage, but restrained myself just in time.

"… before they could come back."

"Daddy was furious. I'm not sure if he was mad at you or whoever sent those men, maybe both. The last thing he wants is a war."

A war? I hadn't considered anything beyond myself ending up dumped in a field somewhere. Like a piece of rubbish. Like Robbie.

"The bastards got my friend. Shot him in the gut."

"I'm sorry, Mickey. I didn't realize he was a friend."

I guessed he really was, then. What I felt for him, despite leaving him to bleed out, was something a friend would feel. I moved my leg a little and then all I could feel was agony. I moaned into the phone.

"What, Mickey?"

"Nothing. Just clearing my throat." I gritted my teeth, nearly bit off my tongue. "Look, I'm just going to lay low for a bit, see what way the wind blows." *Get a gun, maybe seek revenge.*

"Where are you now?"

I hesitated. Could I trust her not to bring an entire barrack of

Gardaí along behind her, maybe a side order of hoodlums? I had to trust her judgement, her discretion.

"I'm in Shanley's hotel, to the east of the city."

"I know it."

I remembered our original plans for the dinner date.

"We can order room service."

I felt like a right bollocks.

"That would be … nice."

I imagined her squirming wherever she was.

"Six o'clock OK? Ask for Jerry O'Leary. That's the name I'm under."

"Six is good. I'll see you then, Michael, Jerry, or whatever. And for God's sake, stay out of trouble."

I could try. But somehow, I thought, it would eventually seek me out. It had a habit of it. I said goodbye and hung up.

"Fuck!" I said to myself, cursing my lack of foresight. I didn't have any proper clothes. And after all my effort picking out a new rigout in Genteman's Quarters. I looked like a homeless guy with the sweat pants and top. I looked in the wardrobe mirror. I was shocking – hair matted from sweat, stubble poking out like badger bristle, and a pallor like I'd just crawled out of a body bag. Plus I smelled terrible.

I decided the least I could do was take a shower, but the dressing was going to be a problem. If that got wet, I'd have to redo the whole thing again. I looked in a desk drawer and found a plastic laundry bag. I wrapped it around my leg and used my shoe laces to get it good and tight, as waterproof as I could. I felt like MacGyver; a couple of lollipop sticks, an empty toilet roll, some Sellotape and the world could be mine.

The warm water negated the pain somewhat as it drained over my temples. I turned the heat up to just below lobster-cooking temperature and savoured the therapeutic effect of hot water on tight, sore muscle. I whistled Leftfield's 'Melt', spitting water from my mouth when it put a stop to the whistling. Steam got in my chest and I coughed, stripping something away from the lining of my lungs. Probably tar or some other toxic shite the fags had coated them with. I'd heard of smoker's cough, had had it myself for years, but nobody talked about post-smoker's cough.

There was no light-headedness when I stepped out of the bath. I guessed that only happened when you got up from a sitting position and had the blood rushing to your feet. Now, despite the hammering I had taken, despite all the drugs, I felt strong. But more mentally than physically. I felt I had entered a new state of mind, one where I didn't care what happened to me. I could take it, had taken it. Steel strengthens steel, they say, and I had been strengthened for sure. Emboldened too. And with that gun in my hands, nobody would be tougher.

Fuck it, I'll call Barry. I'll call his bluff. But later, in town where my mobile can't be triangulated back to here. And only after I have my gun.

I had little doubt that Cotter wasn't one of Savages lads, but what I wasn't sure about was whether Cotter was a company man, would try to cover his ass. I hoped not, because with Mogs in intensive care, I was short on friends to turn to, and as fractious as our recent dealings had been, I needed him. If push came to shove, I'd need someone to call on, to watch my back, as he put it.

I dried myself and climbed under the duvet butt naked. I set an alarm on the room phone for half-five, which I was able to do despite my technophobia, and laid down for a power nap.

I woke to a tinny rendition of *William Tell* the room phone was chirping by way of an alarm. I beat my fist down on the phone and the receiver flew to the ground. I hated that fucking tune. Far from any refreshment from the sleep, I had a pounding headache. Just another chore for the painkillers. I popped three of the opioid tablets without any regard for the recommendations on the leaflet within the carton.

I rang the reception desk to check on room service arrangements. Cash on delivery, the girl said, which was fair enough. She said she'd have a menu dropped up and ten minutes later there was a knock on the door.

I'd been sitting watching the RTE news, waiting for any update on the shooting, maybe catch some statement by the Gardaí. It was only mentioned in passing. Mogs, it seemed, didn't warrant the time of day when there was a potential heave on the leader of a major political party. The rap on the door sent a cold chill through me. I quickly put on my track garb.

I looked through the peep hole. Guy in smart-enough dress, maroon-coloured formal jacket that seemed genuine, a respectable, inoffensive haircut – he would have made a convincing croupier.

I opened the door and he handed me the menu. I wondered if this was how things were going to be with me from then on, questioning every motive, suspicious of every identity. I wondered where it would stop. Would I start doubting my friends? I'd already started doubting Cotter – maybe not deeply, but enough that I was uncomfortable with him knowing where I was hiding out. Could I start doubting my own mother? She had been evasive last time we met. Fuck it, maybe I'd even start doubting my loyalty to myself if I got paranoid enough.

I looked at my watch. Ten to six. Grace seemed like the punctual type, had looked at me with scorn when I'd been late arriving at Corrigan's for our last meet. Sure enough, five minutes later the phone rang and the receptionist, who it seemed I was building quite the rapport with, told me that a Ms Jordan was waiting for me in the lobby.

I wasn't one bit satisfied with my attire, but I suppose it was better than turning up in shredded trousers like some guy marooned on a desert island. I was nervous about leaving the room, about being somewhat out in the open. And there was that fraction of a percent of doubt in my mind about Grace and her father, about their potential involvement in the hit or any other intentions towards me. These fractions were being magnified in my mind, blowing themselves up from mere possibilities to probabilities. Like suspecting that a simple, easily-explained bout of light-headedness might be Parkinson's or some other neurological disease. No, I could trust her. I was sure of it.

The lift opened into the lobby and I felt as if everyone's attention had been interrupted by the lift's electronic beep when the doors opened, that somehow, in unison, everyone was probing me. In truth, only Grace was looking at me. But she wasn't alone. I stopped in my tracks. I didn't recognize the person who stood next to her, his back to me, his eyes fixed firmly on the front door.

Grace must have noticed my reaction. She smiled reassuringly at me. She tapped the man next to her and whispered in his ear, then walked alone towards me. I began to walk slowly to meet her.

"Sorry about Mr Geary. Daddy insisted. He's just got a bit more worried about things after that shooting."

A bit more worried? More paranoid more like. Was that even possible?

"Can't say I blame him. Who's this Geary?"

"He works for my father. He fills in for O'Keeffe when he's not working. Usually he's head of security for one of our companies. A banana importer, in case you're interested."

Yeah, because crimes against bananas have been on the rise.

I wondered for a moment why O'Keeffe wasn't working right then, but didn't pursue it.

"I hope you're not expecting Geary to accompany us for dinner."

She smiled awkwardly. "No, it'll just be you and me. He's going to wait in the bar."

"OK, then, let's go up to my room." It didn't sound right, sounded seedy. That Catholic upbringing of mine, I suppose. "I mean, let's go up for dinner."

Grace put a hand to her mouth. I could see she was suppressing a laugh.

Her reaction to the room was different. She couldn't hide the fact that she had become accustomed to better surroundings.

"It's not the Ritz, that's for sure," I said. "But it's off the beaten track, which suits."

She nodded. "It is that. It's got a certain … charm."

That rules out a drink in An Capall Bán, then.

121

I handed her the menu. I'd already decided on chicken supreme, with chips instead of vegetables. My health-improvement endeavours were well and truly on hold at that stage. Grace decided on pork steak with a chestnut stuffing.

"Chestnuts roasting on an open fire," I began to sing, then stopped, embarrassed at myself. Christmas was more than two months away. Then a brief moment of clarity. Had I lost the run of myself? It was the fecking opium drugs, or whatever they were. I must have been high as a kite, maybe as high as a satellite.

"You're in a cheery mood for someone who's just been shot at."

"If you can't sing, you can't laugh," I said.

It made no sense. Or maybe in some twisted way it did. I was *definitely* beginning to lose the run of myself. But that could get me killed. It was going to be a fine balancing act between pain and lucidity. The thing about pain, though, was that it kept you sharp, alert to danger. A natural reaction, perhaps, to the possibility of a killer blow that could arrive at any time.

Grace cocked up an eyebrow, said nothing. I concentrated on my behaviour, did my best not to embarrass myself. If I was lucky, maybe the effect of the drugs would taper quickly enough. But for now the drugs had chipped away at my sense of inhibition. I felt I could open up to Grace. As disastrous as it sounds, I did.

"Does it ever bother you that your father can, at his whim, assign you a bodyguard? Do you even worry about why you are in that position – needing one in the first place?"

She didn't seem taken aback in the slightest. She was unflappable.

"I won't deny my father has made a few enemies over the years—" I noticed she dropped the *Daddy* business when the conversation became more serious, maybe when the talk became more grown up. "—but I suppose you don't get anywhere in business without making a few enemies."

Business? Was that what they called it? Extortion, drugs, money laundering, an occasional punishment beating and worse, and she legitimized it as *business*? I suppose he was in the business of crime – that much I could grant him.

"I've made a few enemies myself," I said after my brief contemplation. "Last night's a prime example. But I've never courted friendship either, so I suppose I can't be surprised."

She pulled her lips inside her mouth, an expression that suggested to me her resignation to life's vagaries. Even when pulling such a face I could see her beauty, even more so a kind of inner beauty. She had a gentle manner that I was unaccustomed to. I realized that mine was a harsh upbringing surrounded by harsh people. Her father, despite unforgivable brutality to others, had obviously done right by his daughter, had seen to it that she was shielded from it. He didn't deserve credit for that, though. There was no balancing out when it came to murder, however far removed he was from the vile act itself.

There was another knock on the door. The dinner, surely. I checked the peep hole. It was the same guy who had brought the menu. I opened the door and he took the tray to the little round table by the window that had a premium view overlooking the car park. I gave him a fiver for his trouble and he left without so much as an acknowledgement of my generosity.

"You can see everything here," she said, looking out the window. "All the comings and goings."

She was sharp. I couldn't imagine much getting past her.

"Can't be too careful," I said. "Can't be too sure who's tipped them off, ratted you out."

I wasn't specific about who *them* was. I was beginning to lose count, if I was to be honest. Grace said nothing for a moment. I hoped she hadn't taken my comment as some kind of warning.

"Jesus, here I am," I said, "bleating on like an old sheep and the dinner's going cold."

We tucked in. I'd not eaten a thing since the doc's fry-up for fear of being spotted by some blabber mouth, so it was everything I could do not to use my hands to eat with – to shovel everything into my mouth like a mole burrowing in the earth.

I let Grace take the first bite, then I took the next one, and the next two or three after that before Grace had daintily cut the second piece of her pork steak, dipped it in her red wine gravy, and carefully placed it in her mouth – it was like a feat of precision engineering.

"Geary doesn't know what he's missing," I said, barely perceptible through my vociferous chewing. "Treat em mean, keep em mean, I suppose." I laughed and some gravy dribbled down the side of my mouth.

"You know," she said, a puzzled expression on her face, "I don't believe I've ever seen him eat. Maybe he's an automaton."

Automaton. A fancy word when *robot* would have done just fine. Maybe she had to find that word that was a cut above just to rise above her beginnings in life. Or maybe she was just better educated than I was.

"We all are, I suppose, until something slaps us in the face to wake us up."

She nodded sagely. Maybe the drugs had heightened my consciousness, made me reach a new level of philosophical contemplation. Or maybe I was just blowing out of my hole. Whatever it was seemed to impress her.

We finished our meals. Neither of us left anything worth talking of in terms of scraps.

"Nothing to trouble our consciences there," I said. "You know – with the starving in Africa."

It was something my mother always carped on about, as if the scraps on my plate could somehow be airlifted all the way to the dark continent.

"You haven't heard about the foundation, have you?"

I shot her a sceptical look. "The foundation of what?"

"Daddy's charitable foundation for the orphanages in Botswana."

Jesus Christ, I thought, *is there no end to the man's barefaced attempts at redemption. He might as well hang a sign around his neck saying: 'Forgive me for I have sinned, but here's my credit card number.'*

She burst out laughing. "I had you there. You should see the look on your face."

I'd just seen a new side to her, the wind-up side I never knew existed. I liked it.

"I'll talk to the management of the hotel for you," I said. "See if maybe we can book a function room for your comedy tour."

She snorted. It was the first time I'd seen anything undignified from her. She put a hand to her mouth, then turned it around in apology. Christ, she'd only gone and left her guard down. Wasn't that what happened when people became comfortable with each other?

I was still feeling a bit more forward than usual. The half-life of the drugs was longer than I had anticipated.

"Is there some reason other than just being your bodyguard that your father sent Geary with you?"

That puzzled look was back.

"What I mean is," I continued, "perhaps your father doesn't like you in the company of other men, particularly one such as myself, a bit of a rough diamond."

"Diamond?" She chuckled. "You've a very high opinion of yourself. The fact is, my father has no idea where I am. For all he knows, I've gone to the supermarket to buy milk."

"What about Geary? Won't he spill the beans?"

"Not on your nelly. He knows better than to cross me. He fears me more than my father."

I could see, even from our limited time together, that she was easily underestimated. I guessed that many had to their cost.

"I did talk to my father, though, about what to do next. He has another job for you."

I stopped chewing the morsel in my mouth. The conversation had detoured away from our dalliance to what, after all, was our primary business, date or no date. I was still in the employ of The Gentleman, no matter how many bullets I had dodged.

"Go on."

I swallowed and held off on attacking the next forkful.

"O'Brien had an associate that came to an unfortunate end. A man by the name of Fitzmaurice."

I couldn't believe Moolah had entered our discussion.

"For some stupid reason," she continued, "the Gardaí think it was my father who sanctioned it. I mean, can you believe they would think something like that?"

I cleared my throat. "God, no." I meant it, too, though it had been a very recent revelation.

"Which brings me to Daddy's job. More of a favour, actually. You must have a friend or two left in the Gardaí, right?"

Here we go. This just joins up the dots: me being assigned to Churchfield, getting the subsequent job offer.

But the bang on my head, how that fuelled my subsequent quest for retribution under Jordan's pay – was that just a coincidence?

"I might have, but I don't see what that—"

"Daddy knows what O'Brien is into. What he doesn't know is how a two-penny bully boy, someone my father used to turn to in times of crisis, can carry off an operation the size of his."

So that was it – O'Brien was a former heavy of Jordan's, probably dished out some punishment beatings, maybe even worse than that. Now the apprentice had stepped in when his master had retired. Either the audacity of his unsanctioned enterprise just got up The Gentleman's nose, or the attention it was drawing on Jordan, what with O'Brien using his premises to ship drugs, was drawing The Gentleman once more into the gaze of the Criminal Assets Bureau.

"And you want me to tap up my buddies in the Guards for the inside track, is that it?"

"My father is willing to add a bonus to what you've already agreed. A substantial bonus."

"Like a reward."

"Exactly like a reward. If you get us the name or names, and it turns out to be sound information, the bonus is yours."

I didn't like the way our conversation had shifted. I had thought she was maybe one step removed from Jordan's dealings, but here she was as a broker, speaking the words of The Gentleman as if he were in the room himself. I sighed.

"But that isn't the main reason I came here this evening," she said.

"No?"

She put her hand on mine. For a moment I was uncomfortable. I wasn't sure if it was because it was a man's place to make the first move or if it had been so long since I'd experienced a woman's intimacy.

"No," she said and squeezed my fingers.

I smiled and she smiled back.

"It suits you … the smile," she said. "I haven't seen enough of them from you."

We went on talking for about thirty minutes after we finished our meals. I told her about my family, about my father, my mother. I told her a couple of things I'd never told anyone – and that was after the effects of the drugs had worn off for sure. I told her about my childhood friend, Declan, and his suicide, for instance. She told me about her childhood, about her mother's death at the hands of one of her father's rivals when she was just twelve; about how she rejoiced when the rival's body was fished out of Atlantic Pond near Páirc Uí Caoimh in several pieces. She spoke of her new love of horses, about how devastated she was when her favourite was put down after falling and becoming lame during a race.

I could have gone on talking to her all night. I felt very much myself in her presence. There was a connection there that went beyond chemistry; it was something deeper, a more innate compatibility. But it was getting on for eight and I needed my gun, so I had to politely bring our little soiree to an end.

"I'm glad we still had the chance," I said, "you know, to have our …"

"Date?"

"Yeah, date. If room service in a grotty hotel can be called a date."

She smiled. "It was lovely. We must do it again some time. Maybe somewhere a bit nicer, though."

So it hadn't been a complete disaster. I was relieved. Guys like me weren't supposed to have a chance with the likes of Grace. I walked her the ten feet to the door.

"Goodbye, Grace."

She kissed me lightly on the lips and I swear I could have fainted right there and then. Like I was a love-sick little girl.

"Goodbye, Michael."

Sham hadn't taken kindly to waiting. He'd been waiting in his car since seven-thirty, he said, freezing his hole off. That was what he said on the phone. Now it was time to meet the man face-to-face, to pick up my gun. Eight-thirty we'd agreed and I didn't want to be one minute too late or too early. In and out, no hanging around.

I could see a man standing in the doorway of Leahy's clothes shop on Oliver Plunkett Street. There was a glow by his face. Not a cigarette, though. A mobile phone display had lit him up like a ghost in the night. It was an eerie scene. I approached gingerly, taking care not to startle him. A guy with a gun to hand off probably had a gun of his own, maybe in his pocket, the safety off, trigger sensitive to any touch. I nodded at the man when he looked up at me. He couldn't have been more than twenty-one, twenty-two.

"Howya," he said.

"Sham?"

"I am meself. What can I do ya for, boy?"

"Jimmy sent me. I was on the phone to you a few minutes ago."

A smile crossed his face. "Jimmy told me about you. Fecking Jet Li of Cork, he said."

"Bruce Lee."

A quizzical look. "Whatever. Follow me."

We walked for a bit and Sham was jumpy, looking all around him. He couldn't have been more conspicuous. He turned down a lane and we came to a building site and pulled back some loose chain-link fencing.

"In here, boy. Just over there."

I looked around. I could see no one in the lane, no light from any window. If there was a place to wack someone in the city, this would have been it. I made sure to follow behind Sham, to not give him my back. He took me to a cement mixer and put his arm inside. He pulled out something wrapped in cloth.

"Clean as a whistle, boy" he said. "You could eat your breakfast with it."

I'd seen a guy eat his gun once before. Seen him leave his brain matter on the walls and ceiling of his kitchen. Guns were for mugs. Until you needed one.

I unwrapped some of the cloth and could see the piece inside. A Walther P99 nine-millimetre. I felt a strange awkwardness. I'd fired countless weapons, practised to improve my aim, but I'd never shot a living thing. It didn't give me the slightest thrill holding the dead weight of the pistol.

"What about ammo?"

"Only what's in the clip. It takes ten bullets."

"I'll only need one," I said, trying to cover my nerves with cockiness.

"That's what they all say, boy," the youngster said as he began to walk away. "Still, a feen like yourself probably won't need one. What with you being the Jet Li … sorry, Bruce Lee of Cork, like."

The kid was right, though; I was much more comfortable using my bare hands. But if I encountered a certain brand of trouble, the kind that put little value on life, I wouldn't hesitate for a second. I'd pull that trigger, damn and be damned, and let others be guided by their own moral compasses when judging me.

8

You're On Your Own

I STOOD IN THE side street for a while holding the gun in my hand, mesmerized by it, by the power I now yielded. What cretin was going to mess with me now? Who was going to take their chances with Michael fucking Jeremiah Bosco? Bruce Lee with a gun – that was a combination and a half!

The bravado lasted all of two seconds. Some woman passed by the end of the side street with a child in a buggy and I quickly put the gun in the pocket of my anorak. Jesus Christ, what havoc was I about to unleash? Maybe I should have just waited for the damned ambulance with Mogs.

It was time to call Cotter. I'd keep my cards close to my chest for now, not mention the gun or what shite I was going to stir with it. I'd taken to carrying the burner phone with the battery removed. I was no forensic tech, but I did know that they could track your movements once they knew what phone you were using. But only if it had the battery in it. I put the battery in the phone and dialled Barry's number. I didn't even get an opportunity to say hello.

"Mickey? Mickey? What the fuck are you up to now?"

Barry's words were running into each other, such was the urgency in his voice.

"I'm glad you're OK, too, Barry. I could be dog food right now, but you go ahead and be like that."

"Well, you're fucking talking anyway, that's something." There was a sigh. "Where are you?"

"Right now … right now I'm in town. Seeing a man about a dog."

"Ah Jesus Christ, Mick." It was a strained voice, one that told a story in its own right; Barry was taking it from all directions and here I was taking a shite on his head some more. "Would that dog be a steel one? You know … one that doesn't go bark, but goes bang? Because if that's the direction you're going, I have to tell you—"

"Easy, Barry. I'm not going in any direction. I'm just laying low, waiting for when it's safe to come up for air."

"I know you. I know when you're lying."

"Look, I've got to ask about Mogs. I mean Colin McCarthy. How's he doing? There's shag all on the radio about it other than he's still sucking in air."

There was an unexpected laugh from Barry. "You know, I didn't give him an ass's roar of a chance, but the old git is going to make it. It was touch and go for a while – fifty-fifty I think one guy in the hospital said. But somehow the pellets missed every major organ in his gut. They yanked them out, sowed him up good and tight, pumped a few litres of blood into him and he's sleeping like a baby. They say he might even open his eyes tomorrow, but you can never be sure."

I was speechless. Things had been moving so fast that I'd hardly had time to think about Mogs. And yet subconsciously it must have been weighing heavily, because it was as if a sack of spuds had been lifted from my shoulders.

"Mickey? You still there?"

"Eh … yeah. Eh … thanks for the update. I'm glad he's going to pull through. Or likely to, anyway. You don't know how … em—"

"Relieved you are? Fuck it, Mickey, were you even going to visit him in the hospital? Were you just going to bury your head in the sand and hope everything bad went away? That's not the Mickey I know. The Mickey I know would have stood his ground, given the two fingers to whatever was coming his way. I mean, is there some particular reason you've been underground until now?"

"You fishing again, Barry? I've got feck all to hide. Some nut job shot at me and I got the feck out of there. I wasn't going to hang around like a duck at the funfair waiting to get plugged."

Barry sighed again. "But why the wait until now before you call? You know how it looks, right? You were a decent enough Guard, maybe one of the best, so you know it makes you look dirty."

"And I didn't look dirty before?"

"Point taken, Mick, point taken. But it's not too late. You meet up with me somewhere. I take you in for a statement. I'll be your buffer. I mean, you've nothing to hide, right?" He asked probably more in hope than expectation.

I was standing there with a gun in my pocket, in the employ of a retired, or not retired, gang lord, with nothing but an inclination towards retribution; in Mogs's name, yes, but mostly in my own. I'd taken a lot of shit sitting down for too long. But I had no intention of hiding. It was time to stand up and fight.

"Not just yet, Barry. I've got a few things to sort out first."

I pressed the call end button before Barry could reply.

Back at the hotel I could only pace around the room. I didn't know where to even begin organizing my thoughts. I took the gun from my pocket, took out the clip, and cupped it in my hands, pointing it at my reflection in the mirror.

"Do you feel lucky?" I half whispered, embarrassed at how predictable the utterance was.

What was I? Some American high school kid with a gun fetish and a thirst for vengeance? Well, a thirst for vengeance for sure. I wasn't so certain about the fetish.

Cotter wanted me to come in for a statement, to tie up the loose ends that would keep me on the Gardaí's radar. But I had never been as straight laced as Cotter. Cotter's approach to street thugs was a stern lecture, mine a rabbit punch to the gut. Besides, we were too far down the road for Cotter's niceties anyway – everything by the book, read them their rights, give them their day in court, innocent until proven guilty.

No, I decided, *the time for that shite has passed. I need to shake the streets. I need to shake them so that whatever falls out won't have the time to play the law card.*

I'd crossed the line before, taken the law into my own hands. And the sad thing was, each time I crossed it made the next time that bit easier. Made it self-justifying. Mogs was in a hospital bed with a hole through him, so what better justification did I need than that?

I looked back at the gun in the mirror and feathered the trigger.

"Fuck them," I said and pulled the trigger.

There was a loud click.

"Damn them all to hell."

The next time I pulled that trigger there would be a bullet in the chamber and someone would be paying for what they did.

I rang reception and ordered a double whiskey. I took a couple of painkillers and downed the whiskey in four or five gulps and shortly after passed out on the bed before I could take my shoes off.

A loud knock on the door woke me. Opening my eyes was agony and it felt like the late morning light was piercing them with shards of glass.

"Mickey!"

It was a woman's whispered shout.

I tried to open my mouth to reply, but it was like it was sealed with glue. Dried saliva parted like a spider's web and I finally got an utterance out.

"Hah?"

"It's me, Mickey. Grace."

I got up and opened the door. Grace stood there with a bag under her arm.

"They took O'Keeffe," she said and rushed in. She looked at me and wrinkled up her nose. "Did you sleep in your clothes? You need a shower." She threw the bag to me. "Here's a change of clothes. I overestimated the size just in case."

I cocked up an eyebrow, said nothing.

"Didn't you hear me? They took O'Keeffe. You need to get dressed and come with me."

"Wait. Who took O'Keeffe?"

"The Guards." She put a hand on top of her head. "They came right up to the house just after dawn. I thought … I thought …"

She didn't need to finish. She thought they were coming for Jordan. Finally.

"OK," I said. "Let me get freshened up."

I showered with deodorant rather than soap and water. She looked disapprovingly at me as I flattened the hair on my head only to have it spring back into its previous bed-ruffled bird's nest. In the bag was a pair of tan-coloured chinos and a check shirt. They actually fit perfectly, which meant I was fatter than Grace thought.

"Where exactly are we going?" I asked.

"Somewhere safe. Somewhere for us to regroup."

Suddenly it seemed like not only was I under siege, but everyone around me was too. I checked out at reception and got some change back out of my room phone deposit. I smiled at the receptionist and she smiled falsely back at me. Grace gave me a *hurry up* look and we went to the parking area around the back where she had parked next to my old banger.

"You need to ditch the car," she said.

"You mean hide it."

"I mean ditch the piece of junk. Burn it out, leave no trace."

The thought of burning the old chariot hit me like a bag of old boots.

"Jesus, Mickey, it's just a car. And a noisy one to boot. It's …"

She took my hand and squeezed it. "It's her time."

I looked at her face. Maybe she understood.

"Follow me for a couple of miles. I know a good spot to do it."

The good spot was a few miles to the east of the city. I didn't set my Fiat alight, though. Didn't see the point in it. We left it in a field off the lane to an abandoned farm, one of Jordan's speculative property investments, and drove away in Grace's Volvo.

Not long after, we arrived at a fairly nondescript bungalow somewhere just past Killeagh. High hedges surrounded the property, keeping it nicely secluded from the main road. A curtain peeled back a bit as we drove in. I thought I might have seen the nozzle of a gun doing the peeling. I thought about the gun in my pocket and panicked for a second. They'd search me for sure. And what would they make of me then?

I took the gun out while Grace was focusing intently on the wing mirror as she parked next to a Land Rover. I placed it under my seat. I would surely get the opportunity to retrieve it later.

We got out of Grace's Volvo and went to the front door. She paused.

"Tensions are up a bit." She sighed. "Just bear in mind the pressure my father is under and make allowances for it."

I nodded. The door opened and Geary was standing there. We went inside and aside from Jordan, I recognized another man.

"Jesus," I said, looking at Jordan, "you go and hide out with him?" I pointed at the man on the couch. "He'll have paparazzi swarming on this place in no time."

The man was celebrity lawyer and socialite, Terence Goulding. He only represented the highest profile clients in the highest profile cases. If he was around, Jordan can only have been expecting the worst.

"I can be discreet when I need to be," Goulding said when I was expecting a reply from Jordan.

Jordan, it turned out, was in pretty subdued form. The guy who was prone to repeating his words for emphasis, couldn't seem to utter a single one.

I took a look around the room. Geary and two other heavies. All wearing suits, insides of their jackets bulging with submachine guns. It didn't make me feel any safer. Geary came over to me and patted me down. Thank Christ for my quick-wittedness in the car.

"What do you take me for?" I said. "If there's one bastard you can trust, it's me."

Grace gave her father a reproachful look. I was surprised by how much that look meant to me.

Jordan finally spoke. "Please, Michael."

He gestured to a chair next to Goulding. I sat.

There was no whiskey this time. It was probably low on the list of priorities when they had no doubt made a hasty retreat from the mansion. But it raised a question in my mind: how did they escape the Garda surveillance? Had they escaped it at all?

"Why have you brought me here?" I asked. "If it's heat you're trying to avoid, I'm sorry to burst your bubble, but I'm practically melting."

Jordan sniffed. He sat next to Goulding. "I take it Grace told you that O'Keeffe was taken for questioning?"

"Not arrested, then?"

I had assumed wrong, perhaps.

"No. But we weren't going to wait for the Gardaí to come back with a warrant. I told O'Keeffe to co-operate and he accompanied them to the Bridewell. We didn't hang around for long after that."

"Questioning about what?"

"That's where we are in the dark, I'm afraid." Jordan sank back into the settee. "It's where I'm hoping you might be able to help us out."

I laughed sardonically. "I've come up pretty dry so far. What makes you think I'll fare better now?"

I looked at Goulding. The guy was all over radio and television, yet here he was in the company of the biggest crook of them all – the guy who had put the organised in organised crime in Munster. How much of a bulwark had he been between Jordan and the CAB? How much credit could he take for decriminalizing The Gentleman? Was Goulding the artist who had painted the portrait of Jordan as legitimate businessman?

"You've taken some knocks, Michael," Jordan said. "You're a canny man. A canny man. Get out there and make it happen. Find out what they have on O'Keeffe."

"And on the Moolah hit?"

Jordan tried to force a smile.

"And the Fitzmaurice hit. Two birds with one stone, as I like to say."

I had to ask now. If I was going to go back out in the open, I had to know if the Guards were out there with their telephoto lenses.

"You know the Guards are watching, right?" I said, testing them.

I looked up at Grace, who was standing at the door to the dining room, then back at Jordan. Neither expression changed.

"We're OK," Jordan said. "We sent out a decoy vehicle. Drove it out of the garage. Blacked-out windows. No way they could tell who was in it. No way. We also have an escape plan for just such a situation – a tunnel leading from a safe room to an out building where a Land Rover took us cross country. So unless they had eyes in the sky, I'd say we were good."

Paranoid as fuck. Of course he had an escape tunnel.

"Why can't you send Goulding? Or one of his associates?"

A most serious look came over Jordan's face. It sent a chill down my neck.

"We have an unwritten rule. And by *we* I mean anyone who works for me." He leaned forward to emphasize his next sentence. "And I include you in that." He relaxed back into the couch. "If the Guards have you, you're on your own."

Besides, even if Goulding was there, the Guards weren't going to show their cards up front. They'd fish for information to hang you with. Seemingly irrelevant stuff they could use to contradict you later. The only strategy was silence and O'Keeffe didn't need

Goulding to remind him of that.

Goulding took something from his pocket. A mobile phone. He tossed it to me. Jordan spoke for him.

"Use this to call me. There's a single contact saved on it. That's how you contact me."

I keyed into the contacts list. Sure enough, there was a single contact by the name of A.

"I'll need a car."

Jordan nodded to Geary. Geary took keys from a trouser pocket and threw them to me. Now I had a problem: my gun was in Grace's Volvo. But I'd been resourceful – I'd left my bag on the back seat of the car. I explained that I had to retrieve it and prayed that they didn't look out the window as I retrieved the bag – and my gun.

As I opened the front passenger door, Grace came out the front door. I very quickly reached under the seat, took the gun and bent into the back to grab my bag. I just had time to slip the gun into a side pocket on the bag when Grace arrived.

"I don't want you to take any risks," she said quietly. "It's in my father's nature to look out for himself and his family, but I don't want that to happen at your expense."

I got out of the car and nodded. I checked the windows to make sure no one was looking. When I was sure, I took Grace's hand.

"Your father is getting on in years now. He's had his day, had a good run of it. You have so many years ahead. I wouldn't …" A lump formed in my throat and I cleared it quickly. "I wouldn't want you to get dragged down with him."

She squeezed my hand as if in reassurance. "He's changed. Nobody's going anywhere."

I forced a smile. He hadn't changed. That was more clear than ever now.

"Till the next time, then," I said.

She waved to me as I drove away in Geary's Volkswagen.

I stopped in Castlemartyr and got out the old burner phone. I keyed in Cotter's number and hit the green key.

"Mickey," Barry droned like a tape player on low battery.

"Yeah."

"I'm not even going to ask what you're up to." He was barely audible, like he was talking through a pillow. "Are you going to come in and make a statement?"

"I am. Sooner the better."

"Get your hole down to the Bridewell. Thirty minutes?"

"Thirty minutes works for me, Barry."

"Meet me inside the One Euro shop on North Main Street."

"Got it."

 I almost hung up there and then.

"Eh … it's going to be just you taking the statement, right?"

There was a pause.

"That's the plan, Mick."

The response didn't reassure me.

"It's just a statement, right? I'm not coming in for questioning or anything."

"Understood, Mick. You make your statement and get the shag out of Dodge."

"Because it's a fucking rat's nest in there. Savage will no doubt be sniffing around, his buddies ready to tip him off at the first sight of me. And yer man Halloran with the hairy suit will be trying to join up the dots with a line straight through me. I'll fucking hold you to it, Barry – statement only."

Barry sighed again, said nothing.

"And maybe a couple of pints later when your shift is finished. Like old times."

"Why not, Mick. Maybe I could do with it."

Barry was looking at the underside of a toilet roll holder when I arrived at the One Euro shop.

"Expecting more shit than usual?" I said.

Barry looked up without changing expression. He looked stressed.

"What do you think?" He put the holder back on the shelf. "Are you ready for this, Mick?"

I nodded. But could I ever be ready for a parade through the very institution I'd betrayed? Being a Guard had, for a large part of my life, defined who I was. I had defiled that, disrespected the notion of An Garda Síochána as the guardians of peace. But my intentions, if not my methods, had been true. I think most Guards would understand, if not condone, that. I had to go through this because there were others in blue who were staining the force, blackening it, poisoning it from the inside out.

I followed Barry the short distance to the Bridewell. There are Bridewells throughout the UK and Ireland. The first was established as a place for harlots and the homeless in the London of the sixteenth century. The site of the current Bridewell in Cork dates back to early in the eighteenth century, though the building itself is more modern, having been built after the original building was sacked and burned during the civil war of the 1920s.

Barry led me through the side entrance. My chest tightened and the pain in my leg worsened, but I was damned if I was going to limp in the door. I would hold my head up high.

Barry whispered muted greetings to a couple of Guards, one in uniform, the other plain clothes. My head dropped, dispelling the idea that I could handle their gaze, almost welcome it. He led me to a corridor where I knew there were a number of interview rooms.

I wondered if O'Keeffe was in one of the rooms. For all I knew, O'Keeffe might have been questioned and released, done a runner already. I would need to dangle some bait out there, hope for Barry to bite, divulge something of use to me and The Gentleman. Although our goals were different – mine revenge for Mogs, Jordan's the lowdown on O'Brien – they intersected through Savage. I was quite confident of that.

We went into a small interview room in the middle of the corridor. It was well lit and private. No false mirror, no surveillance that I could see. Barry gestured to a chair and I sat. He leaned against the table.

"I don't even know where to begin, Mick. Fuck it, let's just start with what happened on Blarney Street, take it from there."

And so I did. I took him from the moment Mogs and I left An Capall Bán to the moment I hobbled away with the wound in my leg. Barry took notes. He looked up from them when I stopped talking, as if he expected me to continue beyond that point.

"You wanted a statement, you got a statement," I said. "Anything more and you are questioning me."

Barry raised an eyebrow.

"And your leg … miraculously healed did it?"

"I've been saying my prayers," I said.

Barry sunk his head into his hands.

"Do we have to play this game again, Mick?"

"I told you what happened when I was with Mogs. Beyond that and you are showing a lack of trust."

Barry grunted. How could he have trusted me, anyway.

"It's OK, is it?" Barry nodded downwards.

"The leg? Yeah, patched up OK. I'll be fine."

"Well, I'm quite confident that McCarthy was the target and you were just collateral damage. I know with all the goings on in Churchfield, your dealings with Jordan, that seems a stretch, but it's what we've heard from …" He paused then, perhaps for dramatic effect. "The street."

"Mogs was the target?"

I didn't understand it. Mogs's bagman duties had ended at least four years earlier. Now he was just marking time, spending his remaining days in a drunken stupor.

"McCarthy didn't co-operate. Our information … you know I can't say anything on that."

I understood. A CI – a confidential informant – was likely the source.

Barry stayed silent for a moment. He seemed deep in concentration. Then he snapped out of it.

"I'm not stupid, Mick. I know you're in bed with Jordan. What's the arrangement?"

"What did I say about the questions, Barry?"

"Some old associates of his have been – how should I put it? – active. Guys who had gone to ground for a while. Have you seen or heard anything?"

"I saw a busker on the way in, heard him play the theme tune to *Game of Thrones* on a tin whistle."

Barry sighed deeply, ran a hand through his hair. "I'm not going to get any more out of you, am I?"

"Unless you are looking for a tip on the hounds, no."

Barry muttered under his breath, "For fuck sake."

He looked down at the paper he had written on.

"This isn't exactly an immunity agreement, Mick. I'll use it to get the others off your back for a bit. Try to, anyway. I'll say you are a co-operating witness."

He forwarded the pen to me so that I could sign the statement.

"Thanks, Barry," I said. "I'll be laying low for a bit. They'd have a job finding me."

It was time to cast out the line, try to get the skinny on O'Keeffe and the Moolah hit. But how could I broach that subject without betraying my allegiance to Jordan?

"You look a bit under the kosh, Barry. Things been happening around here?"

He opened his mouth to say something, but held off saying anything.

"Cat got your tongue?" I said.

"Rat, more like."

The door opened and Halloran walked in. Barry closed his eyes in a grimace.

"What's this?" Halloran asked, looking first at me, then Barry.

"Witness statement, Dick," Barry said. "Mick's been helpful, very generous with his time."

Halloran turned back to me and took some time to size me up.

"Very good of you, Michael. To help out your old pals. Let's mint you a nice big medal, shall we? Michael J Bosco, good Samaritan, an example to be held up for society." He turned back to Barry. "Is this some kind of fucking joke? Witness?"

Barry held up the statement.

"Says so right here, Dick."

Halloran grabbed the paper, crumpling the top half of it. He straightened it out and began to read.

After a few seconds he said: "Best read since *The Da Vinci Code*. A right fucking page turner." He handed the sheet back to Barry. "What's next? A pop-up book, a happy meal toy?"

I looked at Barry. I caught his glance. He looked away instantly.

"Listen, Dick," he said, "if you want to make more of this, we can talk privately. I invited Mick in for a statement and I'm satisfied with it."

Halloran took a step towards me.

"I said you were a bad seed. Rotten to the core. You waltz in here, the saviour of us all … it's enough … it's enough to make me puke. Thirty years I'm a Guard and the likes of you—"

I got out of the chair and rose so that my face was inches from his. It put a halt to his ramblings.

"I'm a co-operating witness. Unless you have any more questions, I think, no, I know, I'm free to leave."

Halloran said nothing.

"That's what I thought," I said.

"I think we should call it a day," Barry said. "Let everyone cool off."

"Not so fast," Halloran said and took a file from under his armpit.

He opened it and thumbed to a page he searched for. He handed the open file to Barry. I noticed the letters *Fitz* with some more letters covered by Halloran's thumb. Fuck! Moolah. Jordan had asked me to keep my eyes and ears open for intel on the Fitzmaurice hit.

Barry studied the page for a minute, briefly thumbed through the rest of the file.

"What the fuck, Barry?" I said. "A statement. Remember?"

Halloran reached for the file and turned the page over to reveal a photograph. He pointed to it. I had a good look to see if I could get something worthy of Jordan's interest.

"There," he said.

"Barry?" I said.

Barry didn't shift his gaze.

"Same MO," Halloran said.

He seemed smug.

"As?" Barry said.

Halloran held out his arm in my direction.

"As the fucking hillside strangler here."

I was all at sea. Why was he connecting me to Moolah?

"Barry?"

"Say nothing, Mick. Just keep your trap shut." He turned back to Halloran. "You've got nothing here. No transfer of alleles – nothing. Any judge would laugh at this." Without looking at me, he said: "Mick … walk out the door and keep walking."

"Not so fast," Halloran said. "There's more."

He took a sheet of paper from his pocket and unfolded it. He handed it to Barry.

"I've saved the best for last," Halloran said.

Barry gave it a once over. Then a twice over.

"Purely circumstantial," he said.

Halloran seemed to pick up on something. "Did you know about this? That he was the arresting officer?"

Barry shrugged his shoulders and said nothing.

"Jesus Christ," Halloran said. "You're covering for him, aren't you?"

"What is it, Barry?" I asked.

Halloran intercepted the conversation. "An old pal of yours … Brick. You caught him with a jar full of X, but he got off. That must have got on your goat. I mean, he must have laughed when you fucked up the chain of evidence and the guy walked. I'll bet you wanted to wrap those big hands of yours around his neck and—"

"Walk, Mick!" Barry shouted. "Out that door now."

"What—" I began to say.

"Walk. Now."

"Sit back down, Bosco. I'm not finished with you. The law's not good enough for you, eh? You literally have to take it into your own hands? Who do you think you are … Batman?"

"Walk, Mick. He's got nothing. Dick … you'll fuck up the case if you go through with an arrest."

"Bosco!" Halloran shouted.

I decided to take Barry's advice. I would walk. I would test the strength of whatever case Halloran thought he had against me. If he thought he had enough, he could arrest me, read me my rights.

"OK, Barry," I said. "Do your worst, Halloran."

I walked through the door and could hear the argument continue behind. Halloran didn't come after me.

I wondered what Halloran's story was. What case was he building against me and why? Was he bent like Savage? Was he in cahoots with Savage? And what could this mean for my relationship with Jordan. He'd asked me to get the inside track on the Moolah case, and there I was at the centre of it and another murder, seemingly the prime suspect for both in Halloran's estimation.

I was walking along the corridor when a Guard walked from another interview room in front of me. I couldn't tell who it was from behind, but it seemed like a greenhorn.

"Two sugars in mine, Dom," a voice boomed.

Savage.

I came to the door and just had time to glance in. O'Keeffe was sitting there, bruising around his left eye. No one else other than Savage was in the room. No solicitor. I assumed the situation hadn't escalated beyond just questioning.

"I hear you are good with your hands, Bill," Savage said, holding his hands in a choke position.

Like the Eel had. Christ, how many suspects did they have? And how many were linked to Jordan?

Savage never took his gaze off O'Keeffe, didn't seem to notice I was there. I picked up the pace until I reached the car park to the rear.

Savage came thundering out the back door.

"Bosco! Bosco!"

I turned to face him. I was already shell-shocked from my encounter with Halloran, so I was in no position to fend off the barrage from Savage.

Savage scrunched up his nose, breathed in deeply through his nostrils.

"We'll have to get in the cleaners after you stinking the place out, Bosco."

Savage pushed my shoulder, goading me.

"What are you doing here, Bosco?"

He pushed my shoulder again and continued his tirade.

"Haven't done enough damage to the reputation of the Guards – you have to come back for more? You're not wanted round here, Bosco. You were a disgrace when you wore the uniform and you're an even bigger one now."

Again he pushed my shoulder and I could take no more. I rushed Savage, sending him sprawling to the ground. Before I could get a kick in, someone grabbed my hair from behind, then pinned my arms like chicken wings behind my back.

"Good man, Dom. You hold him there for me."

I was in no shape to resist the young buck that was Dominic. As much as I tried, I could not free my arms from his.

Savage got up and his eyes seemed to glow with relish at the sight of my exposed body. He delivered a punch to my gut. I bent over, but Dominic pulled me back up. Savage sent another fist into my right ribs and this time the pain nearly made me pass out. A liver punch.

"You're not much without your hands, are you, Bosco?" Savage said with a sick leer.

He hooked a punch to my jaw. The cheek inside my mouth cut and I spat blood on the ground.

Other Guards had begun to gather at the back door. I couldn't tell if they were enjoying the beat down or just too afraid to be the first to break it up, to appear weak in front of the others. Savage just had time to get off a final punch to my belly when Barry ran out to intercept him, restraining him in a bear hug.

Dominic released me and backed away. I doubled over, my

vision blurry, my legs barely able to support me.

"Go, Mick, just go," Barry said, struggling to keep Savage at bay.

It was the final nail in the coffin. I was a disgraced ex-Guard. Now I was a total embarrassment, a shambles. I scurried away, shuffling Quasimodo-like until the blue mob could see me no more.

9

Rum and Reasons

BACK AT THE CAR I gave serious consideration to going back to the Bridewell with my gun. I thought I might gladly spend the rest of my life in jail in order to plug one in Savage's skull. I thought of Grace and the deluded thought dissipated.

I let out a roar, which hurt my ribs. I gripped the steering wheel hard. I strangled it. For a moment, I pretended it was Savage's neck. Was that my basest of all reactions? To choke something … someone? Was it any wonder Halloran was all over me for the Moolah murder?

It was hard to call that a hit now. A hit was something planned, something clinical, detached. A bullet to the back of the head with a pistol or a spraying of shotgun pellets from a motorcycle. Strangulation was more personal. I knew that from experience.

As my breathing calmed, I began to think more clearly. I decomposed what had happened into chunks that I could process. I started with Savage.

Why had he rushed me like that? If he had something to do

with the hit, why get his hands dirty? Why make himself a suspect if down the road a hit did eventually work on me? I'd heard the bastard in the house in Carrignavar. Heard him … or had I? I replayed in my mind the few sentences I did hear. How sure could I be that it was Savage, or even a Guard? The gist of the conversation suggested it, but what level of certainty did I have? I had jumped to conclusions with Savage, perhaps tainted by my encounter with him in Churchfield. No, it *was* Savage; I couldn't start second guessing myself on that score.

Next up was Halloran. Why go after me with nothing? So the Moolah and Brick murders and my seeing to Chambers all involved strangulation. Weren't there other incidents involving strangulation that would have revealed other suspects? It's not like I had patented the technique. It seemed too personal with Halloran.

It felt like the more I got involved, the further away from the truth I was getting. Dancing around the edges had gotten me nowhere other than Hurtsville – a beating here, a shooting there. It was time to turn the tables, dish out some hurt of my own, invite a few others to a little town I called Retribution.

It was past time I paid a visit to Mogs. The rumour about a Moolah hit and The Gentleman's involvement was looking ever more suspicious and I needed to get to the bottom of it.

After a quick trip to an off-licence, I parked around the corner from Holy Cross Hospital. I made sure to park facing out into the traffic in a location where I was unlikely to be boxed in should I need to make a quick escape.

Would Mogs be under Garda protection? There was every chance. Could I just ask at reception which ward Mogs was on? I guessed it was OK. I'd been to the Bridewell, given a statement, put it up to Halloran to arrest me. If Mogs wanted to see me, then Mogs had every right.

Mogs was on St Therese's ward and a nurse at the nurses' station directed me to a room where there was, indeed, a Guard on duty outside. He was vaguely familiar. I thought his name might have been Hartigan or Halligan. He was old as Guards go, looked like he might have been put out to grass with this assignment. He got up. He clearly recognized me.

"Are you out of your mind, Bosco?" he said.

I peered into the room. Mogs seemed to be asleep. Or was he in a coma? Not another fucking coma!

"Mogs," I shouted.

"Be on your way, Bosco."

"I've every right … Mogs!"

"I'll have you removed for making a disturbance."

Then a whispering voice: "Mickey."

I put a finger up to my mouth to try and shush the Guard.

"Mickey, you dirty sham-feen. Get in here, boy."

Mogs's voice was a bit clearer.

I stared down the Guard for a few seconds. Eventually he relented. He patted me down – obviously I had left the gun in the car – and allowed me into Mogs's room.

Outside I could see the Guard was on a mobile phone. I didn't have long before Savage or Halloran, or both, would arrive.

Mogs pointed a bony finger at a chair and I sat down. I couldn't say he looked any worse than he usually did, as close to death's door as he perennially seemed.

"How are you, Mogs?"

He looked up at me, a bitter look on his face.

"You left me, you cunt. To die on the road. Like a dog, boy. Like a fecking dog."

I couldn't deny I'd run. I had good reason, though. But this wasn't the time to enter into a debate. I needed information on the Moolah murder.

"I can see how it might look that way. But if you knew what I knew, you'd understand."

Mogs looked away, looked right out the window at a view of the River Lee.

"I need you to tell me something, Mogs. My life might depend on it."

Mogs said nothing, kept staring out the window. A flock of

seagulls was picking away at whatever tasty morsels were being flushed into the Lee.

"Mogs, I need you. I need … my friend."

Mogs sighed. Kept staring the other way. But if there was one way to win him back, it was free drink. I looked to the door; the Guard was busy with his smart phone.

"Hey, Mogs," I whispered. I took out a naggin of Captain Morgan and shook it so that Mogs would hear the familiar slosh. "I got something to perk you up, get some heat back in your bones."

Mogs turned quickly and I could see there was a glimmer in his eyes. Mogs was a dependent drinker, of that I was sure. I doubted he'd gone more than twelve hours without drink in the last twenty years.

"Don't fuck up again, Mickey." He held out his hand, swiped the bottle when I offered it, and immediately opened it, taking a long swig. "I swear to ya, boy, I'll get my mother's blackthorn stick and make you wish you'd never heard my name." He took another sip. "Jaysus, that's class, like. Can you come and visit again tomorrow?"

I was relieved that Mogs was somewhere approaching his old self. The one that was determined to curse life all the way to that six-foot-deep hole in the ground.

"I'll see what I can do, Mogs. But I need to know where you heard about the Moolah hit."

Mogs thought for a bit. "You won't be mad if I tell you, boy, will ya? I know you've said to avoid the place, like."

"Not a chance," I said.

And I meant it. He was due a break.

"I heard it at a card game in the Steamship, boy. Some feen I didn't know said it. Mad red hair he had. Could've been about fifty. A demon at the cards he was. Like he could see what I had in the hole. I'd have thought he was cheating, only the Eel—"

"Doesn't take too kindly to cheating," I finished. I wondered about that, though. Maybe he was selective in that regard. Like he'd snitch to one Guard, pay off another.

Mogs grinned. "You hear the one about the blood stain on the table?"

I smiled back. "Yeah."

"Two Fingers Terry the feen's called. At least, that's what the Eel calls him, like. I nearly believe the sham too."

I'd done business with the Eel, gotten a piece I had yet to use. I didn't really have an excuse for a return journey. But Jimmy had been there when someone talked about a hit by Jordan on Moolah. I didn't have much choice but to go back to swim with the Eel.

I'd be keeping Mogs's information from Jordan for now, like I had kept silent about Savage and the Limerick man. I didn't want to go in head first with that particular accusation when I had yet to see if the rumour had any substance.

Mogs gave me a few other details about the red-haired poker player. Height, weight, his tendency to bully with his chip stack.

"One other thing that might help," Mogs said. "The guy only plays in the weekly tournament. High stakes stuff, eight players max, winner takes all. Goes on all night, boy. A bit rich for most, like, so it's usually the same five or six guys."

"That's good, Mogs. Really good. Rich for most? How much we talking?"

Mogs paused. Usually he blurted the first thing that entered his mind. Now he was scheming, it seemed.

"Five thousand. Usually I play in the cash game, but I chanced my arm at the tourney."

I nearly swallowed my tonsils.

"Five grand!"

"Ah, I had a bit of money coming to me. Inheritance, like."

I was sceptical. Was there some rich uncle of his I didn't know about?

"Who died?"

Mogs squirmed in the bed. Not from pain, though. A natural reaction to being trapped in bed when all he wanted to do was run.

"Eh, no one. You see, me mam's getting a bit dotty, like. She leaves cash in drawers, in tins up in cupboards. Doesn't spend much of her pension. So it'll be mine soon, anyway."

I brought a hand up to cover my forehead.

"Mogs … doesn't she have the right to a will, to decide what to do with her estate *after* she dies?"

He winked at me. "Sure, won't I write her will for her anyway, make sure she does what's right, boy."

I just grunted in response. I didn't want to interfere. He'd suffered at his mother's hands long enough to deserve the cash. He didn't deserve her giving it all away to the dogs' home.

I had to broach something else before I left. The hit had been intended for Mogs. He hadn't co-operated with the shades, but he might tell me something. Maybe I could help in some way.

"Guards say you didn't co-operate with them. They seem happy … no, that's not the right word … they seem sure that you were the target and not me."

Mogs laughed. "It took my retirement before I became important to someone. I know things, Mickey. I know enough to put some people away for a long time, like."

I wondered if Mogs was talking to the Guards. Was he a CI? Is that why he was on someone's hit list? But there was another possibility.

"How much of a problem is the cards?" I asked. "How much are you in the hole to the Eel?"

Mogs swiped a hand.

"Ah, I can handle it, boy."

The holes in his belly said otherwise. His possible need for Garda cash also.

"You don't think the Eel had anything to do with it?"

Mogs snorted.

"Nah, boy. I'm worth more to him above ground. It's got to be something I know about some sham or other."

I wasn't so sure I agreed with him. If there was even a grain of truth in what the Eel said he did to card cheats, what might he do if you welshed on a debt? But I kept my counsel. I had enough scumbags to sort out without adding Jimmy the fixer to the list.

At that point I'd heard enough. Enough to last me a lifetime. I rose from my seat.

"I would love to stay longer, Mogs, but there's a couple of dodgy shades that have a hard on for me."

Mogs nodded. When it came to the Guards, Mogs was all in favour of getting one over on them.

"Hey, Mickey," he said as I exited the door. "You owe me a pint, boy."

Didn't I always.

Mogs wasn't the only patient I knew in Holy Cross. There was also Chambers. The last time I'd laid my eyes on him was when I had almost choked the life out of his. Now he was in a coma, barely a flicker left in his brain. Enough maybe for a next of kin to deny he was brain dead, but in truth not enough to justify his undoubted continual suffering. And maybe it was the one flicker left that was enough for Chambers to be aware of the suffering, perhaps God's or whatever vengeful higher power's last laugh.

I had a ridiculous thought. Chambers was the seed of all my troubles. Maybe if I could just see him for a moment, maybe say … say what? Sorry? Damn you? Maybe choke him until his life's flame was finally snuffed out? Wouldn't I be doing us both a favour if I did?

I knew which ward he was on, had heard it more than once from an acquaintance or overheard it in a bar. It couldn't hurt, surely, to take a look.

I went into the lift, punched the button for the fourth floor. The lift stopped at the third. A burly man, his head bald, a tattoo on his pate, got on. He was wearing a white tunic, white pants. A nurse. A male nurse. It was Scoobs.

I turned my head slightly to avoid my face being seen, but the lift was all mirrors and I could see Scoobs had identified me. I said nothing. Scoobs said nothing, initially. But he looked at the display panel on the lift when we stopped at the fourth floor, knew I meant to get off there. And there could only have been one reason for that.

"Mickey, isn't it? We met ... we bumped into each other in the Horse."

"Yeah," I said. "Nice to see you again."

I moved towards the door. Scoobs put an arm out to block me. He hit the close door button.

"I don't think that's a good idea," he said. "Do you?"

I probably looked a dishevelled mess, maybe looked desperate enough to try anything.

"I just want to see him." I almost called him Scoobs, tried to remember his real name. "I just want to ..." I tried to find something to say, hoped something would come from the heart. Instead I just made up some bullshit I'd heard all too often from victims on the news. "I just want to find some closure."

"Jesus Christ," he said. "Look, you might just come back if I turn you away, so I'd better do the decent thing and make sure there's no family there first."

Make sure I don't cup my hands around his throat, you mean.

He pressed the open door button.

"Wait here by the lift," he said. "I'll check."

I had an anxious wait. Were there grounds for security to eject me? Probably. I had no proper business on the fourth floor. But Scoobs returned alone and he led me to a room where I saw Chambers for the first time in nearly two years. I didn't recognize the man I saw.

"He's been stable a while," Scoobs said. "I've heard there's even been some sign of improvement in his brain function."

The man I beat to a pulp had been a monstrous man in both size and behaviour. What I saw before me was a thin man with saggy skin. He looked ... no, I didn't want to think it. He looked angelic. Like Robbie had.

I had a revelation then, one that I was glad to have, relieved almost. What if this idea that there was a heaven and a hell was a load of crap? What if there was only one gaff in the sky teeming with the best and worst of humanity. Like down here on Earth. No, Chambers was better off in his purgatory right there in the room where he was of no harm to anyone.

"Enough improvement for him to ever wake up?"

I counted the numerous tubes and wires poking out of his body. Were there seven? Like those twigs poking out over Robbie's body?

"Doubtful," Scoobs said. "Improvement is one thing. Maybe he'll piss on his own one day. But he'll never have any quality of life, probably never another conscious thought."

Scoobs looked down at Chambers. I didn't like the look of pity on his face. Chambers didn't deserve it.

I'd seen enough.

"Thanks," I said. I remembered the name. "Geoff."

Should I touch Chambers, say goodbye in some way? Like the last touch of a loved one in the funeral home. No. God, no.

Scoobs walked me to the lift.

"So did you get it?" he said.

I was puzzled.

"Closure," he clarified.

I pondered. Had I? Would the dreams stop? The visions of things in dark corners? No. There would never be closure. But I knew the boogie man would never boogie again.

"In a way," I said. "In a way."

I got out on the ground floor and walked to the exit.

I saw someone walk in. Someone wearing a suit jacket that looked like it might have been scalped from an animal's back. It was Halloran. Either he was there to question Mogs, or the Guard at his room had phoned him.

I turned. I'd find another way out or wait for him to walk past.

"Bosco?"

I picked up my pace.

"Bosco!"

I ran down a corridor in the opposite direction to the front entrance. I saw an empty trolley bed. I pulled it and it turned sideways to block the corridor. It slowed Halloran.

"You can't dodge my questions forever, Bosco."

I took a left at the end of the corridor and ran a bit more, though it was more of a hurried shuffle by that point as I ran out of steam. To the right I saw a back entrance – a service entrance where dirty linen was being loaded onto a truck. I left Holy Cross hospital and looked back. No sign of Halloran.

Why had I run? I had nothing to hide, did I? But I did. I had a gun in my car and I had every intention of discharging it.

I couldn't claim that Blackpool is the most glamorous of neighbourhoods. But it's full of what southerners in the United States call *good people*. I think in the round I'm good people. My Mam's definitely good people.

It seemed I wasn't on anyone's hit list. I was on Halloran's radar, though. But he'd had his chance to arrest me and he'd blown it. All things considered, I decided it was OK to return home. Before I did, I retrieved my Fiat Uno and left a message on Grace's phone that I had left Geary's VW in the field.

When I arrived home, the kitchen smelled terrible. The bread on the counter top was mouldy, bananas had turned black, and the fridge smelled like a horse rendering plant. I opened the windows and hoped a good breeze would freshen up the gaff.

Could I dare sit down, enjoy a stiff drink and get back to my book? Surely I deserved one relaxing evening having circled a whirlpool of destruction.

I rummaged through the box for a new book. Or should I say, an old book I hadn't read before. I'd enjoyed Melville's *Billy Budd*, still had some of it to read, but I knew I wouldn't be able to concentrate on it anymore after finding the Starman note.

I found an old favourite, *Slaughterhouse-Five*, by Kurt Vonnegut. It made me reconsider my search for something I hadn't read before. Vonnegut's writing style was uncomplicated, unpretentious, the cadence carrying the reader along. For probably the fourth or fifth time, I settled in for a night with Billy Pilgrim. It was a sufficiently intoxicating read that I didn't lament the absence of alcohol in the house.

Sitting in my old armchair, my stomach was hurting. Worse was the pain pulsing metronomically up the ribs on my right side with each laboured breath. I found it difficult to find a comfortable reading position. I still had some painkillers left and downed a couple with a bottle of Diet Coke.

As I read, I thought about how it would have been nice to be Billy Pilgrim. To travel back in time and make some changes. But when I thought deeper about it, I realized that Billy was just a passenger, that he had no control over events, that no matter what he did, things never changed. It was exactly how I felt.

I slept terribly that night. For once it was the pain in my body rather than the pain in my mind that kept me awake.

The next morning I planned to go to the shops in town to get some food. Healthy food. A ring of Clonakilty, though, to have with my dinner. If you didn't have some kind of treat, you were liable to fall off the waggon completely. Low-fat milk, porridge – Organic Odlums – and fruit muesli to mix with it for the breakfast. Maybe a newspaper too. It was time enough that I started connecting with the world again.

After some changeable days weatherwise, the morning was cold, but bright and the good people of Blackpool seemed to have a spring in their step. I put on a light jacket, donned a pair of sunglasses and opened the door.

My house is just off a little *cul de sac* hill-lane called Farren Street. How it became known as a street is anyone's guess. I took a right onto Gerald Griffin Street.

Gerald Griffin was a Limerick man, but joined the Christian Brothers congregation in the North Monastery just around the corner from where I live. I was educated in *The Mon*, went some way to becoming a man there – one might well call it a school of hard knocks, and I received a few there. Griffin, one of Ireland's lesser known literary figures who had been a newspaper reporter in London in the early nineteenth century, died a young man. Young like my Dad. A newspaperman like my Dad. But I felt like I had a few years left in me yet, might even see old age. I hadn't thought like that for a while. Maybe I had found some new reasons to live. Like Grace, for instance.

Some kids were on their way to the North Presentation school.

A little one, probably still four years old and no more than a few weeks in *big boy* school, was clinging on to his father's trouser leg. I vaguely remembered doing the same more than three decades ago. It was sights like that made me feel my age, feel pressure to find a woman, settle down, have a kid or two. I'd found a woman. I think I wanted to get serious with her. And she was of good child-bearing age. Jesus, that was reductionist of me, but pragmatic all the same – no point pussyfooting and dying alone and childless.

The new burner phone rang. I recognized Grace's number.

"I was just thinking about you," I said.

"O'Keeffe's at home," she said, getting right down to business. "He was released without charge this morning."

"That's good, Grace. I saw one of the Guards in there laying it on thick. But I guess he was just putting the frighteners on O'Keeffe."

"I think O'Keeffe's pretty immune to the frighteners, Michael."

"True that," I said.

It didn't sound right to my own ears when I said it. I sounded frivolous. I took a left onto Cathedral Walk in the shadow of the North Cathedral.

"Daddy would like to meet you in person. He's in a funny mood. I'm not sure whether I like it or not."

I was surprised by this development. Grace had been the intermediary to this point, but now The Gentleman wanted to talk to me directly. I could be sure it wasn't something to like.

"There's a small warehouse unit near Blarney Street that he's having converted to some sports hall or something. He wants to meet you there."

Grace gave me the address on Glen Ryan Road. Told me to be there at six. I agreed to the meet, albeit reluctantly. I'd gone a long way towards trusting Jordan, but for me trust was always over the next hill, never quite in sight.

"We must meet up again, Grace. I enjoyed our meal at Shanley's. Maybe we can go somewhere fancier?"

Again I had to remind myself that when it came to fancy places to frequent, I was about as knowledgeable as I was about the inner workings of a computer.

"That sounds nice." She paused for a while and I could hear her breathing more heavily than normal. "But let's see what Daddy has to say at the meeting."

I didn't see how the two were linked – what Jordan would say and another date with Grace – but I didn't follow up to clarify. Instead, I wished her a pleasant day and continued my journey to the shops in town; there was the pressing matter of sourcing gourmet black pudding for my dinner.

I called to my mother's house on the way home from the shops.

The last time I had seen her, I had been concerned. She'd been distant. She'd been worried about what I was up to. I hoped she was in better form.

She didn't look so bedraggled when she answered the door, but she had a stern look. I hadn't called around, not made a phone call for a couple of days.

"In the name of Saint Padre Pio, Michael, I was worried sick."

Invoking the name of Padre Pio was probably apt enough. I had my own stigmata of sorts: the wound to my leg, the bruising to my ribs. But I was no saint.

"There was no need, Mam. I'm grand."

I held out a bag, which she took. She went to the kitchen and I followed.

"Arbutus bread and a jar of Folláin strawberry jam," I explained. "Not from the farmers, but not far off either."

She smiled. "Well, it's the next best thing to the farm, I suppose."

I never fully understood her obsession with farm produce. She was an inner city girl from Barrack Street, but I assumed in her day that the farmers brought their produce to the markets on the Coal Quay.

She peered into the bag I kept for myself.

"Is that what I think it is?" I shrugged my shoulders, but knew what she meant. "The black pudding. I thought you said the doctor had warned you off the stuff?"

I blundered over a few words: "I, uh, em …"

She laughed. "I see it's Clonakilty too. I prefer the Denny myself. A bit more bite to it. The stuff hasn't done me any harm in all these years."

The last time I saw her I might have disagreed. Now her spirits were higher, her pallor soft and warm.

"I'll keep myself to the two slices," I said.

I meant it. They'd even be thinner than normal. Down to about fifty-percent of my usual helping. Tapering was the best approach. Like I had tried with the fags before going cold turkey.

"You seem in good form today," I said. "The last day I was worried about you. You looked like you'd seen a ghost."

Her smile melted away. Some colour drained from her cheeks.

"Jesus, Mam. What did I say?"

She sat at the table.

"Sit down, Michael. There's something I need to tell you."

I didn't like the sound of it. With my tendency for hypochondria, my first thought was cancer. It's my first thought for many things. I didn't sit down.

"I had a visitor an hour before you called over the last time. Someone who knew your dad."

For some reason I thought about the note. Starman. I had yet to ask my mother about the name. But I'd get to that later. People who knew Dad were at a premium.

"Who was it?"

"He seemed to know you, too, Michael."

"Who, Mam?"

"A detective. He had on this mohair suit jacket. The kind he wore back then too."

I knew the answer before I asked the question.

"His name, Mam?"

"Richard."

First name basis. I wondered why.

"Halloran?" I asked.

She looked puzzled.

"How could you know that, Michael?"

"Dick Halloran and his hairy suit," I said. "We've met more than once. But he has business with *me*. Why did he call here? Why didn't you tell me? Was he harassing you? Because if he was, I'll—"

"No, Michael. That's not a road I want you going down. Richard and your father had history."

At that point I sat down, couldn't bear my weight anymore.

"What kind of history?"

"You remember when the IRA kidnapped that horse trainer? Harkin, I think it was."

I did. The ransom demand. The botched Special Branch operation. I nodded.

"Richard was one of those Special Branch officers. Your father did that exposé in the Standard. He would probably have had to retract it if …"

I saved her the pain. "He hadn't died."

She nodded. She got up and went over to the cupboard with the drawbridge.

"No, Mam," I said. "That stuff doesn't do you any good."

"Pah!" she said and opened the cupboard. A full bottle of Huzzar was in the back. "It helps me think."

I'd thought that about the Jameson. Thought wrong, though. Nothing made you think more clearly than a clear head.

Mam poured herself a standard measure. Left it neat. She sat back down.

"It explains a lot," I said. "Halloran's had it in for me. Was getting up close and personal. Didn't seem rational."

Mam took a little sip. She was more measured in her approach to drink than I had been.

"Richard was asking about your whereabouts on the morning of the tenth."

He'd asked the same question when he doorstepped me a few days earlier. I'd pleaded the fifth, dared him to return with a warrant. That was before he revealed his suspicions in the Bridewell.

"And?" I prodded.

"What do you mean *and*?" She was offended for some reason. "And nothing. I said you spent the morning here."

I hadn't. I'd woken in a stupor, crawled to the doc, gone home and drunk some more before falling asleep. I was offended she thought she might need to alibi me.

"Jesus, Mam. That wasn't clever. Do you know what kind of trouble you could get yourself into lying like that? And how suspicious I would look if they proved you were wrong?"

That bitter look painted her face. "The fact that I feel like I have to lie about your whereabouts should tell you all you need to know. Moping about at home, on the drink, no doubt."

She looked into her glass. "Like father like son," she said and took another sip.

I felt like replying that like mother like son was apt also. I didn't want to stick the needle in, so I left it. I took my mother's hand.

"I've changed," I said.

I wanted to tell her about Grace, but didn't. I wanted to explain that I was on a new path, that it was paved with gold and not briers. There was something biblical in it that she would have understood.

"I want to believe that, Michael."

She squeezed my hand.

"Halloran's just a bitter old man," I said. "If it comes to it, I'll put him straight."

Mam sighed. Maybe she'd heard my father's bluster one time too many. I meant it, though. If this Halloran guy was going to besmirch my father's name, I'd see he paid for it. An image of my gun flashed into my mind, but I banished it.

"Trust me, Mam. Things are going to be different from here on."

She smiled warmly and the tears that formed in her eyes were not really sad ones. They glistened with hope, I believed.

"I know, son. I believe you."

I had an opportunity to ask about Starman. I'd ducked it for long enough.

"Does the word or the name Starman mean anything to you?"

"You mean like in the David Bowie song?"

She didn't know. I blew her off.

"That's the one. It was driving me mad trying to remember who sang it. Anyway, enough of the past. Let's look to the future."

Mam held the glass of vodka in her hand and for a moment I thought she would knock it back in a single gulp. Instead, she rose from the table, went to the sink and poured it down the plughole. I'd done something similar some time back with a bottle of Jameson. However, there was something more symbolic about what my mother did.

She opened up the bag with my milk, porridge and muesli.

"There's always tomorrow for that," she said. "Get the cast iron frying pan for me. Let's cook some of that black pudding instead."

10

Boxing and Bagging

THE GENTLEMAN WANTED TO see me in person. That worried me. I'd given him some useful information from my three days of surveilling O'Brien. But I'd held vital pieces of information back.

I walked to Glen Ryan Road. Who this Glen Ryan guy was is anyone's guess, though he must have been a someone if there was also a pub named after him in Gurranabraher. Maybe he was a movie star with a name like that.

The warehouse unit looked small from the outside – too small to house a regular gym, I thought. A grey corrugated frontage had a large sliding door that allowed space for a van to drive through. The door was slightly open so I walked through.

Jordan was standing with O'Keeffe in what I could only describe as an animal pen. A six-sided cage with chain-linked fencing and padding on the corner posts. Behind the cage was something I was more familiar with: the squared circle – a boxing ring. That Jordan was out in the open, relatively, and standing next to O'Keeffe told me that Savage had nothing on them. O'Keeffe had walked into the Bridewell with Jordan fearing the worst, but walked out of there with the certainty that not only was O'Keeffe in the clear, but that the CAB wasn't on Savage's coattails.

I walked closer and could see boxing gloves hanging around Jordan's neck. O'Keeffe was wearing what seemed like smaller boxing gloves with the fingers cut off. They could have been mistaken for weightlifting gloves, but the padding on the knuckles said otherwise. I could see the black eye that Savage must have given him and it looked darker now. Jordan wore a grey singlet and baggy blue shorts and had already worked up quite a sweat judging by the patches on his singlet.

"Come on in, Michael," Jordan said.

I didn't like the enclosed space. Not with Granite Hands and The Gentleman to keep me company. With no little trepidation, I walked through the gate into the cage.

"What is this place?" I asked.

Jordan looked around and I followed his gaze. The boxing ring, the cage, a number of different-sized punch bags hanging from the ceiling, things that looked like punch bags with handles lying on the floor – like little children, dead children. There was also the usual stuff I'd seen in a gym: dumbbells, barbells, exercise bikes and the like. Everything unblemished, smelling like a new car. It was a compact space and I could imagine it bustling with fighters exercising and sparring.

"This is the future of gyms. The future of gyms. MMA training is the future for serious gym-goers. Wouldn't you agree?"

I didn't know what MMA was, didn't want to appear not to.

"Can't disagree with you there, Jim," I said.

"You see, the key word in the acronym is *mixed*. People have a tendency to see results quite fast in the early days of their gym membership. Quite fast. But then they plateau and lose spirit. The problem is they don't mix up their training. Their bodies adapt and they think: hey, this is easy, I must be really fit."

He took a step towards O'Keeffe.

"But then the lack of improvement. In cold business terms, a dispirited client is not going to be a repeat client. You understand what I mean by dispirited, right?"

I did. With knobs on. I just nodded. Jordan had run his eyes up and down my body. My pallor, my gait spoke volumes. It was obvious that word of my beat down by Savage had reached his ear.

"White collar boxing is on the rise. Executive types, all pent up with stress from having it shoved up their arse from whoever they report to – and doesn't everyone report to someone bar the Man Upstairs?" Jordan pointed to the ceiling. "Guys and gals fighting their line managers, desk mates duking it out. It's like that film I saw recently – *The Purge*. For one night only, you can unleash mayhem, go to work the next day like nothing ever happened."

Jordan went to the edge of the cage, picked up a bottle of water, took a sip. He offered it to both myself and O'Keeffe, but we refused. I understood the sip to mean that Jordan was far from finished conveying his grand vision.

"I see a gap in the leisure market," said Jordan. "White collar MMA. These executive types like their punishment. You can trust me on that."

I wondered if he meant the services of a dominatrix. Or maybe he'd ordered some punishment beatings on these executives he spoke of. I wasn't going to probe. He took another sip. I was getting fidgety. O'Keeffe stood tall, unwavering. Like a secret service agent.

"But that's not the best part." I dreaded how many parts there were. "I'm going to make it affordable – free for some, in fact – for some of the more disadvantaged kids to train here. Get them off the streets. Off the streets. Teach them discipline. Show them another way." Jordan sighed. "It worked out for me. So far anyway. But I've seen more than my fair share fly high and then fall to ground."

Jordan seemed genuinely proud. Like it was possible to redeem oneself by building a cage and then filling it with the rabble that lived around Cork City's Northside. It was like a Guard's dream. Only Jordan would let them out. Maybe even make them contributors instead of offenders.

"O'Keeffe here," Jordan said, taking the gloves from around

his neck, "is a prime example. He won't mind me saying that I found him down a rat hole of his own digging." O'Keeffe didn't flinch, wouldn't have no matter what Jordan said. "He's what you might call a proponent of the fine arts of combat. Quite the artist he is. Quite the artist. I challenge you to tell me he's any less talented than a Jackson Pollack or a John Lennon."

I wouldn't have challenged Jordan on anything.

Jordan tightened the Velcro around his wrists to secure the gloves. O'Keeffe held up his hands in a tight guard and Jordan began to dance around in front of him. Jordan landed a combination of body shots to O'Keeffe's mid section. Rat-a-tat-tat they went and I could almost feel Savage whaling on me again. The combination matched the pattern of Savage's blows and I could not consider that to be just a coincidence. O'Keeffe did not even flinch – granite hands, granite abs. O'Keeffe parried a right cross aimed for his head and Jordan danced back a few steps.

I was impressed with the speed of Jordan's fists for a guy his age, how light he was on his feet. He seemed to have lost little of the speed and agility he must have had in his early twenties when he had progressed as far as the Irish amateur boxing championships semi-final.

What happened next surprised me, though. O'Keeffe lunged, almost superman-like, for Jordan's legs, wrapping his arms around them and taking Jordan to the mat. I stood like the statue I had been in Churchfield, unable to comprehend what was happening.

Within about two seconds O'Keeffe had crawled onto Jordan and trapped his neck and an arm with an embrace of his own arms. I still couldn't move. The pair were between me and the cage door. I felt that tingling in my groin again.

Then I could see Jordan tapping his free hand against O'Keeffe's thigh. Was that some kind of ridiculous attempt at a fight back? And then the bulging tension I had felt deflated with a laugh from Jordan. O'Keeffe had released him and was immediately helping him back to his feet.

Jordan held up O'Keeffe's arm.

"And the winner … the winner is Billy *Bad News* O'Keeffe by way of a head and arm choke."

Jordan rubbed his shoulder, then the back of his neck. He turned to me.

"I'll bet you thought my hands were fast until you saw the speed of O'Keeffe's double leg takedown." Jordan's face was purple, his breath laboured. "And his BJJ is up to a brown belt now. A brown belt."

Enough with the acronyms.

Jordan obviously saw my puzzlement.

"Brazillian jiu-jitsu," he clarified, a quizzical look on his face, as if a hard case like myself was bound to know.

I'd assumed jiu-jitsu, which I had heard of, was some kind of kicking and punching martial art. Like kung fu. Like Bruce Lee. But wasn't I the Bruce Lee of Cork? Shouldn't I have known about this stuff, the takedown, the choke? Then I realized I did. I'd taken down Chambers, mounted him, choked him out. Not as quickly or as skillfully as O'Keeffe, though – he'd pounced like a tiger before morphing into a bear; I'd had all the artistry of a rhinoceros.

Had Chambers tapped like Jordan had? A sign of submission to a superior force? No. I'd felt nothing, seen nothing. He could have tapped, so to speak, with his eyes, shown a pitiable suffering. But there had been nothing in them, no submission I could see. And would I have released my hands anyway? I knew I had gone too far beyond myself to stop.

O'Keeffe grabbed a towel from atop the cage and tossed it to Jordan. O'Keeffe seemed bone dry, without the need of a towel. Jordan dried his arms and legs, then rubbed his hair.

"You know why things didn't work out before, Michael?"

Because I was a disaster zone, a magnet for trouble.

"It's not your body. Not your body. Though, that's been out of shape for a while. It's your mind. That's as plain as the nose on my face, as I often say."

He threw the towel back to O'Keeffe.

"You like my daughter, don't you, Michael."

I didn't want to draw suspicion. I gave a standard answer, a platitude.

"She's a decent woman. A credit to you, Jim."

Jordan squeezed one eye almost shut, widened the other. "She's more than decent. Out of the league of most men, I'd say. Would you agree with that, Michael?"

I did and I wasn't afraid to say so. "I couldn't agree more."

Jordan's expression changed, became serious, like he was staring down an opponent in the centre of the ring.

"I'm not a fool, Michael. Not a fool. I see the signs, the looks, the way she talks about you. Are you going to deny I'm wrong?"

I knew what he was talking about. I could own up right there and then, or I could drag it out to its inevitable conclusion. I went with the latter despite the futility.

"I'm not sure what I'm supposed to deny, Jim."

Jordan peeled the gloves from his hands, flexed his knuckles.

"You know, when I started out I didn't wear gloves. Bare knuckle it was. Kicks, bites and gouges – all fair game. Fair game. Like dogs. I was inside a ring of men fighting all sorts – itinerants, alcoholics, members of other gangs."

He paused to examine his knuckles as if he were surveying the damage caused by one of those bare-knuckle brawls.

"Now, I'm going to ask you again, Michael, and I think you should reconsider your strategy. Are you involved with my daughter?"

I can't say I was stunned. Jordan didn't get where he was – having survived gang wars, attempted hits, the CAB – without being a cute hoor. Could I ever have expected it to evade his notice?

I took a few seconds to gather my thoughts, plan my words. Because the wrong word could be fatal. Retired or not from the thuggery business, when it came to his precious daughter Jordan would not maintain perspective.

"We've talked a few times. Shared a dinner and a drink. Nothing more."

Jordan walked over to me. Again with the tingling in my groin.

"Michael, Michael. Would you say you were in her league?"

I looked down at my shoes. "I … I … "

"I, I, I," Jordan mocked. "Look at me like a man. You are one, aren't you? A man?"

I looked up. Jordan's face was stony.

"Yes."

Jordan brought a hand in front of his chest, made a fist, tensed it. His face became a grimace. "Then fucking act like one. I mean, look at you. You're a mess. A mess."

Jordan began to pace around me. When he was behind me I waited for a choke hold that never came. It would have been ironic to go out the same way Chambers had.

When Jordan returned to face me, he said: "You're a good man, Michael. A good man. But you're damaged goods. Let me tell you a story about a horse."

When he mentioned *story*, I just knew there would never be an end to my suffering.

"A fine horse it was, probably the best I've ever owned. Unbeatable on the flat anywhere up to a mile and two furlongs. Unbeatable."

Jordan's expression changed to one of sadness.

"Then against my trainer's advice, we entered her in the Oaks in Cork. A mile and four furlongs."

O'Keeffe had stood diligently by. Jordan stretched his arm back to him.

"Tell him, Bill. I can't bring myself to say it."

"Horse fractured his leg a hundred yards from home. Got it stuck in a hollow or something."

"Thanks, Bill. The vets put him down on the spot, put some kind of tarpaulin around the scene to spare the crowd from seeing the procedure. To see ... Gracey Aphrodite ... die in her prime."

It looked like Jordan's eyes were welling up. I'd heard the story before. During the room service dinner with Grace. When we'd begun to open up to each other.

"I'm sorry," I said. "You were obviously close to that horse."

Anger took over Jordan's face. "I couldn't have cared less about that horse. Grace never forgave me. Never forgave me."

Jordan composed himself. Attempted to control his breathing. Like a boxer between rounds.

"You can see the parallel, can't you, Michael. The lame horse being put down, my daughter's sorrow?"

I could only sigh and then nod. I understood fully. As much as Jordan had shielded her from his world of mayhem, I would have dragged her into the murk of my own life. There couldn't be a future for myself and Grace.

"Then that's settled. But like I said, Michael, you are a good man. And you deserve a second chance. Like I've had."

Jordan tossed me his gloves.

"Do your worst on O'Keeffe. Don't worry – he won't fight back."

I put the gloves on, fastened them. I'd only boxed a couple of times, fancied myself at it, truth be known. I wondered how I would have fared had Dominic not come to Savage's aid.

O'Keeffe once again put up a tight guard. The little gloves on his hands didn't offer the protection traditional boxing gloves would. I feinted a left hook to the body, instead landing a right jab to O'Keeffe's shoulder. A little off target, but a hit none-the-less. My confidence grew. I'd go for the kill, I resolved, show Jordan there was man enough in me still. I feinted the same right jab, but instead went for a left hook to the head. O'Keeffe arced back and I missed his jaw by inches. The momentum of my attempted punch put me off balance and I spun around almost three-sixty.

Jordan laughed. "Exercise control, Michael. You can't expect to load up on every punch."

I gathered myself, but my breathing was already laboured. I tried to dance on my toes, but it felt like my feet were rooted. I was a fat bastard, of that there was no doubt. For your average street goon, the weight might have been imposing, the impression of additional force behind one of my favoured sucker punches persuasive. But for O'Keeffe, with all of his agility and speed, my lumbering mass could only have looked pathetic to him. Easy.

I tried a combo. The old one-two. A light left jab was parried and I put my hips into a right cross. O'Keeffe moved his head to the side like something from *The Matrix*. Like I had boarded a plane in a different time zone and he was waiting patiently, newspaper in hand, for my flight to land.

Again Jordan laughed. "Nice try, Michael. Bit predictable, though, don't you think?"

Predictable? It was as good as I had. As much as I'd learned in training. Anything else I'd learned to do with my fists had been done on the job. Those rabbit punches I had doled out to many's the corner boy; the repeated hooks to Chambers's face.

By this point I could feel the sweat dribbling down my back. I could barely breathe. I held up my hands to Jordan.

"You've made your point, Jim," I said. "I'm a lame horse. And I assume you are dispensing with my services too. Couldn't blame you if you did."

Jordan nodded to O'Keeffe. O'Keeffe walked out of the cage and headed towards the changing area. I took off the gloves and threw them to Jordan.

"I'm going to say this a third time, Michael. And I don't like to repeat myself, so listen carefully. You are a good man. The kind that'll take a beating and come back for more. I can always do with men like that. Besides, no one walks away from me till I say so."

Many had found that out to their cost. I was drenched with sweat. Jordan retrieved the towel from the cage wall and walked over to me.

"Dry yourself off, Michael. Better yet, dust yourself down. Take a few days off to recover. Then report back here on Monday at six. The grand opening is at eight and I'm in need of an extra body. I've had to let one of my guys go. Turned out he kept things from me."

Geary. It had to be. Grace had to be pissed off about that.

"You won't keep things from me, Michael, will you?"

"No, Mr Jordan, I won't."

But I had. Savage, for instance. No, Savage was going to be mine. After the car park in the Bridewell, it would have to be me.

Jordan smiled. It was a warm one.

"You're catching on, Michael."

He turned to leave the cage, but turned back before he reached the cage door.

"I'll get O'Keeffe to work with you on your combat skills. General cardio too. It's time for you to get yourself in shape, Michael. I've a feeling you'll need to be."

He left the cage. I left the cage. In more ways than one. I'd been caged up long before I'd walked into Jordan's gym, had felt the walls of that inner cage slowly creep inward so that they had become suffocating. The images of Robbie O'Meara; the laughing mob of Guards from the Bridewell; the fear of The Gentleman finding out about the growing relationship with Grace. But I felt then like I might be able to find the door to that inner cage, to walk right through it.

Outside the unit a van had arrived. A man was taking a sign out of the back of it. I asked if I could take a look. The man obliged and I read the words: JORDAN ACADEMY. I could see then that Jordan was ready to face the public, to stop hiding behind his holding company. Was this his way of giving two fingers to the CAB? I thought there was something more sincere to it, though. He intended to give something back to a community he had helped destroy.

On the way back to the car I had conflicting emotions. On the one hand I'd connected with a woman for the first time in more than a decade; on the other the weight of having to hide that relationship from a psychopath had lifted. It was high time I became a glass half full person, so I decided I'd adopt the latter perspective.

But perspective isn't emotion and I was missing Grace already.

Jordan seemed to have dispensed with me as a sleuth, seeing me more as hired muscle judging by my assignment as a bodyguard at the grand opening of his gym. Keeping things to myself that I might well have shared with him no doubt fuelled his revision of me.

I had time before the opening to continue my crusade. If there was one thing Savage wasn't going to beat out of me it was the detective.

The card game was on Tuesday nights. To get into the game, I would need to visit the Eel, make him see a genuine interest in gambling, and skill enough with the cards. I bet frequently on the dogs – and I'll admit I had an irrational tendency to go with the number three dog. Cards, though, was another thing.

You didn't make appointments to see the Eel. He didn't exactly have office hours. But if there was one place I was likely to find him slithering, it was the Steamship. I figured that if there was a time he'd be there, after nine would be it.

I walked in to see the same barman as before. A couple of sinewy old timers were sitting on stools at the bar, neat whiskeys in hand. When all they ate was drink, I suppose it was no wonder their tendons were standing proud from their skin like concentration camp survivors.

The barman just nodded to the bead curtain separating the bar from the Eel's private rooms. I took that to mean the Eel was in. When I parted the bead strings, I could see that there was a game going on in the card room. I sized up the five guys at the table. None was Mogs's red-haired card sharp.

Jimmy's office door was open – enough that he could see the game, make sure there was no funny stuff going on. He looked up to see me, took his legs off his desk. He beckoned me to enter. He didn't seem too pleased to see me.

"The Mangler returneth," he said. "To what do I owe the pleasure? And before you answer, I don't do customer service, don't do returns."

I hadn't shot the gun, couldn't say whether it was in good working order. I would shoot it soon, though. No good thinking about the money back guarantee when it misfires as some cretin closes in for the kill. But I was here on other business.

I waved a hand. "Nah," I said. "All good on that score."

Jimmy invited me to sit, so I did. I eased back in the chair, wanted to appear relaxed, like I belonged in the sordid setting.

"I liked what you said the last day about the game," I said. "About how you kept things clean."

Jimmy took a bottle of Jameson from a desk drawer, slid a glass to me. It seemed the upper echelons of Cork's scum lived on the stuff. I gladly accepted, raised it and gave the Eel a silent toast.

"You wouldn't see the pot sizes in my games if there was a doubt about the games' integrity."

He poured himself a glass, took a sip.

"They know the consequences," he said, nodding towards the players at the table. I noticed an empty chair at the table. "Why the interest, Mickey?"

"I've got a few Gs put away for a rainy day. And guess what? It's raining."

Metaphorically, of course; it was actually quite pleasant outside. I took a sip from the glass, gestured with it towards the game outside.

"Besides, I've got to find new ways to use my hands."

Best to play Jimmy's game, send myself up a little bit.

Jimmy's grin, which had been conspicuously absent, lit up his face.

"Until some wise ass insults your card skills and ..." He rose from his chair suddenly, reached halfway across the desk towards my head, his hands in a choke position. "You ring his neck!"

He howled like a hyena. Heads turned at the card table, quickly turned back again to their cards.

"I'm just pulling your langer, boy," he said, no hint of shame in his voice or demeanour. In the Eel's lair, he acted with abandon. You just had to go with it. Water off a duck's back and all that.

"I'm more ... disciplined these days, Jimmy," I said.

Maybe there was some truth in that. Would be soon enough, if not.

Jimmy turned the dial down to a snigger.

"The threat of a strangling would put it up to a bluffer, that's for sure," he said.

"Not if I bluff them first."

Jimmy pointed at me.

"At first, I took you for a hooligan. A legend, but a hooligan. I mean, the Mangler, for fuck's sake. But maybe there's more to you than meets the eye."

He topped up both of our glasses.

"You play a bit? Poker, I mean."

"Now and again," I said.

"Well, I couldn't give a tit about that. As long as you know the rules and you bring enough cash to cover your losses."

The last time I had played poker – and this was five card draw, not any of this new hold 'em shite – the minimum stake was twenty pence.

"I'm only interested in tournament play, though," I said. "All in or all out kind of stuff."

Jimmy nodded.

"That figures. You seem the all or nothing type. No half measures." A sick grin twisted his lips. "Maybe that's why you use both hands to strangle instead of one."

I was getting tired of Jimmy's choke references – and the more he belaboured the point, the worse his jokes got. It portrayed me as one-dimensional, kind of made me wish I'd taken out a few more guys with various techniques – a shooting here, a billy clubbing to the back of the head there.

"There's a game Tuesday nights," he said. "Winner takes all, house takes a twenty-percent cut. Starts at eleven. The games rotate – next Tuesday is Omaha Hi-Lo night. Buy-in is five grand."

Jimmy examined my response, perhaps looking for a flinch that would betray my financial limit. I didn't flinch.

"There's a seat available at the table. Six or seven players with you included."

Tuesday night. The night after the grand opening. Three nights to get hold of the five thousand and brush up on my Omaha Hi-Lo – four cards in the hole, two pots to play for, but I was short on strategy.

"Sounds good," I said. "And the other players?"

No harm in asking.

Jimmy had a sly grin.

"You'll find out on the night. But you better bring your A game. These guys don't mess around. Good sports, though."

For a high stakes game in a seedy pub where the house takes twenty-percent, I doubted they were *good sports*. The kinds of guys that played in these back street, back room games were doing so with ill-gotten gains. Not that the sizable cash payments I'd received from Jordan were any less ill-gotten. Maybe that's why the size of the buy-in didn't bother me – it wasn't any more my money than the brown envelope backhanders that found their way from property developers to the councillors on planning committees right around Ireland.

"Tuesday night at eleven? Count me in, Jimmy."

He smiled.

"Bruce Lee has a good ring to it as a poker nickname, don't you think, Mickey?"

I didn't know whether a nickname like that would buy me any more table cred, but where was the harm?

"Knock yourself out, Jimmy."

"You'll go by that so. The others will have their nicknames as well. There's no real names in my games. The reasons should be obvious."

They were. But I needed a name for my red-haired fellow. I started to get up.

"Fancy playing a hand or two in the cash game before you go?" Jimmy asked. "There's a seat open."

I didn't have much cash on me, didn't want to waste time at a table without my red-haired rumour spreader.

"Not tonight, Jimmy. I'll keep my powder dry for Tuesday night."

As I left Jimmy's office, I noticed one of the players at the table was wearing a grey hoodie and earphones. Before I left the game room, he got up, flicked back his hood, pulled out his earphones, and started pulling at his hair.

"Fucking runner, runner," he shouted. "The odds must be two-hundred to one."

I left him to despair his bad beat.

The grand opening of Jordan Academy was a flashy affair. A who's who of Cork's sporting elite were there, along with a number of councillors and reporters. Terence Goulding was there also.

A grotesque-looking man in his fifties, Goulding had to rely a lot on his considerable charm and deep pockets. On his arm hung his latest twenty-something. I'd heard she was an aspiring actress of some kind. I guessed Terence was her casting couch. Once established, I had no doubt she'd move on and Goulding would replace her with another twenty-something.

I recognized another man. He had the most distinctive head — it was Scoobs. I made eye contact with him and he waited while I made my way to him. I grabbed two glasses of Prosecco on the way.

"Fancy meeting you here, Geoff" I said. "I had you pegged for the type, alright. Muscles like you have."

I took a sip of the Prosecco and worried I sounded like I was coming on to him.

"Ah, call me Scoobs. Everyone does. Funny, isn't it?"

"What?"

"The two of us being called after cartoon characters."

Scoobs. Scooby Doo. Fair enough. But me called after a cartoon character?

"You know," he said, "like the red-haired guy that used to be on TV years ago."

First of all, Bosco was a puppet who lived in a jack-in-the-box, not a cartoon. Secondly, apart from sharing my surname with a saint, the name Bosco was of Italian origin. Six generations removed, my mother said, from a sailor who had settled in Kinsale.

"You hear what I said?" Scoobs said, snapping me back into the moment. "The red-haired guy."

"Yeah, yeah. The guy who lived in a box. I know what you mean."

"Class," he said, rather annoyingly I found.

"So the MMA," I said. "You try it out yourself?"

"Try it out? I've fought in CWFC."

I was getting tired of all the fight-related acronyms.

"Cage Warriors," he clarified. "It's an MMA promotion in Ireland and the UK. I'm top-ten ranked in the light heavyweight division."

"That's impressive," I said.

I didn't know the promotion, didn't know if it was respectable or whether it was staged in barns and car parks.

"I'm fighting in two weeks time in Neptune Stadium."

A legit outfit if it was being staged there, I assumed.

"I might just come along."

"Hey … I'll get you a ticket. If I see you around here, I'll see what I can do."

I thanked him. But I was supposed to be minding Jordan, so I looked around to find him. He was talking to a mountaineer I was familiar with, Eddie Cushnahan. Cushnahan had scaled Everest twice, survived the impossible on K2 when an avalanche took out most of his companions.

I nodded to Jordan, didn't expect to speak to Cushnahan when I assumed my duties as a bodyguard. But Jordan introduced me to Cushnahan. I was glad to shake his hand.

"Eddie here is a survivor," Jordan said. "Isn't that right, Eddie?"

Eddie laughed, but there was regret behind the laugh. Survived at what cost?

"I just did what anyone is programmed to do," Cushnahan said. "When you're hanging from a rope at twenty-thousand feet, you don't really have time to think things through. You do what it takes."

Jordan seemed impressed. "I know exactly what you mean. You do what it takes."

A waiter came by and Jordan took a glass of orange. I still had my Prosecco.

"Enjoy the rest of the evening," Jordan said to Cushnahan.

He began to walk towards someone else I knew. Someone

who'd knocked on my door a number of times in the past, but now had an army of people to do it for him.

On the way, Jordan said: "People don't know the full story about Cushnahan. If they did, they might take back the freedom of the city. But I respect him even more for leaving his friend behind. The friend's leg was shattered, no chance of making it. You have to make difficult choices when you are at the top – mountain, gang, it makes no difference."

He turned suddenly and a plastic grin formed on his face.

"Ah, Niall. Very good of you to accept the invite."

They shook hands vigorously. I wasn't introduced so I stepped back a step and put on my best secret service blank face.

"Follow me," Jordan said to Niall O'Donnell, TD for the Cork North Central ward.

Though there was a strict limit on political donations in Ireland, there were ways and means of buying political favour. Jordan was skilled in this regard and with Goulding at his ear there was always a legitimate stroke he could pull. The grand opening was no exception.

O'Donnell was on hand to cut the ribbon and stand next to Jordan for photographs. When it came to politics, the past was the past. Jordan was legit now, accounts and everything. Being linked to the opening of an academy for disadvantaged kids was like manna from heaven and ne'er a shilling exchanged. Jordan would cash in the favour at some later date.

O'Donnell cut the ribbon across the sliding door to rapturous and somewhat drunken cheers.

A little later, when Jordan had a quiet moment, he said to me: "He's in my pocket now, that one." He was looking at O'Donnell. "And it didn't cost me a penny. That's the difference now. Back in the day I'd have stuffed a brown envelope in his handkerchief pocket. Now I understand that a photo opportunity is more powerful than a bundle of readies."

All in all, I thought the grand opening had gone very smoothly. I'd discreetly ushered away a couple of drunken camogie players before things got sloppy. And I think I might have looked the part as well. Maybe being in the employ of The Gentleman wasn't going to be so bad after all.

I slept late the next morning and spent the rest of the day relaxing, listening to chillout music and reading a collection of short stories by Ray Bradbury. The card game was on my mind, though. I imagined scenarios, played through entire poker hands. I imagined myself scooping up huge piles of cash, wearing a ridiculous fur coat, diamond rings on my fingers, a gold chain around my neck, a Cuban cigar in my mouth. I imagined the red-haired man opening up to me over a large whiskey. *You'd like Savage if you got to know him better*, I imagined him say before I put an imaginary fist in his face.

I was the first to arrive for the Eel's card game. I didn't know the routine, didn't know if it was a sin to arrive late or whether it was a more casual arrangement.

I hated looking so eager. But I was buzzing. I was my own man now. Jordan wasn't pulling my strings; I simply clocked in and out as his bodyguard. I wore the rigout I bought for the date with Grace that never happened. I looked sharp.

The Eel shook my hand. I offered him my bundle of cash, but he refused.

"The others need to see you lodge it with the bank."

The Eel, of course, was the bank.

"Otherwise they'll wonder if the game is rigged."

My red-haired man arrived a couple of minutes later. As Mogs had described, he was about late forties, five-tenish and slim. He had a wild look about him that matched his hair. He looked reckless, like he'd bet on whether he could spit into a tin of beans across the road.

Three others arrived over the next three or four minutes. They all seemed to know each other, some probably by their real names. But rules were rules. Jimmy was a stickler for them. A look at the bloodstain on the table was always there as a reminder.

Jimmy introduced me as Bruce Lee, couldn't help giggling as

the words left his lips. The others were The Professor, Quick Hands, Four Fingers and the red-haired man was The Jackdaw.

The only moniker that made immediate sense was Four Fingers; on his left hand, the middle finger was missing and I thought about Jimmy's story of the compulsive gambler. But one finger missing could be explained in any number of plausible ways. And I wasn't going to enquire in the company of men of this ilk.

We were just about to take our seats when a fifth opponent arrived. The looks on the other players' faces suggested they had never seen the guy before.

The first thing I examine in a person is the eyes. The eyes tell you all you need to know. For me, they are more of a barometer than any polygraph machine could be. There was no doubt in my mind when the man walked in. He was the balaclava-wearing Doc Martins from the robbery in Churchfield. The man with the steel toe-capped boots. The man who'd prodded me all too eagerly with those boots.

Though his expression did not change much, his eyes gave him away. He knew who I was, didn't know if I knew who he was. I'm not sure if there was a perceptible change in my expression, but if there was it didn't appear to bother Doc Martins.

This was quite the coincidence. Me, Doc Martins and the red-haired man who went by the poker moniker The Jackdaw.

"Let me introduce another new player," Jimmy said, gesturing to the latest arrival. "This is Airforce One."

We nodded in acknowledgement, though the others looked wary. Seemed even more wary about him than me. Did I not have the same presence as Airforce One?

About six-foot tall and in his mid-forties, he was wearing a plain tan-coloured sweatshirt that was tight enough to show a muscular physique. Hardly an ounce of body fat, I guessed. The others had every right to be more wary. My reputation, on the other hand, didn't match up to my own physique.

The seven of us, the Eel included, shared a drink. Jameson, of course. I could tell right off that three of my five opponents, including Red Hair and Doc Martins, knew who I was. I thought one of them I might have crossed paths with before, but I wasn't sure where from – probably down some back alley or other. The other two, who were obviously the youngest of the five, maybe mid-twenties, didn't appear to recognize me.

When we had lodged our five-thousand Euro bundles with Jimmy, who placed them in a safe in his office, we got down to the business of poker. Jimmy clarified the rules and introduced the dealer he called from the bar, whom he simply called Heeney. Heeney, with his prison tats and shaved head, seemed to be the hardest man at the table, which invited a strict adherence to the rules.

Heeney took out a fresh deck of cards, discarded the jokers and shuffled the cards with no little skill. With the cash in the safe, the betting would be done with chips. I found this to be a bit of a letdown; I'd had this romantic idea of the game being played out with real cash – old, grubby notes that would have been a reminder of how serious the game was.

As the game wore on, the names used were shortened. Jack, Prof, Quick, Fingers and Airforce. I became Bruce. I studied Airforce and Jack, but I gave them no more time than the other three. I didn't want to open up even the smallest chance of spooking either out of the game. But it was an all in, all out game. They wouldn't be able to cash out until they lost their entire stack or held all the chips at the end of the game.

I played it safe early, didn't get too involved. The two young guys were more active and found their stacks being chipped away by the more experienced players.

Prof's nickname was well-earned; he studied the patterns, took his time working out the odds. He made steady progress with his stack.

Jack – my Red Hair – was opportunistic, would steal pots with obvious bluffs.

Quick, one of the young ones, liked to push the pace early in a hand and would either push you off with a big bet or be scared away by a bigger bet of your own.

The other youngster, Fingers, didn't seem to have much clue

of the game, was fast and loose chasing straights and flushes that never came. He lost over half of his stack in the first five hands and slowed down after that.

Airforce was more difficult to read. What Mogs had said about Jack, I would have said about Airforce. It was like he knew what cards you had in the hole. But I didn't see any way he could see them. His stack quickly grew to twice its original size and he began to use it like a battering ram, scaring others off hands they were probably strong in with the sheer height of his stack.

"I figured you for a more aggressive player," Prof said to me in the middle of a hand where I had just matched the big blind. "Dunno why. Just thought you'd bully the play a bit."

Prof responded with a double of the big blind and I promptly folded. I was only getting involved enough to seem involved, but not enough to endanger my stack. I wanted to last in the game. But the five grand buy-in? I had mentally prepared to let that go. If the red-haired guy got knocked out before me, he could be gone – in the wind, so to speak. I'd have to be careful with my own stack, keep a close eye on his, make sure I always had less. But there was no danger of that after the first couple of hours when Airforce's stack dwarfed all others.

I kept pretty quiet throughout. I didn't direct anything Airforce's way. At the same time, I didn't want to appear like I was ignoring him in favour of the other four, so I got involved in conversations he started.

It was a little after one when I had my first and only showdown with Airforce. After the flop – three of hearts, six of spades, six of diamonds – only myself and Airforce remained, fighting it out for the high and the low pots. For the low pot I already had a potential run from three to seven. For the high pot I had two-pair, queens and sixes. Not quite the nut hand in either pot, but I felt I was in a strong position. The best case scenario was that I would win both high and low pots, add just over two grand to my stack. Worst case was that I lost both pots and was down to about fifteen-hundred. The chance of a split with one winning high and the other low was a possibility, too, maybe the best outcome to prolong both mine and Airforce's stay at the table.

The turn card was a good one for me. A queen of clubs gave me queens full of sixes for the high pot, didn't dent my chances in the low pot. I bet the minimum hundred. Airforce doubled it up. I responded by calling his bet, wary not to push either one of us into dangerous territory. The river - four of diamonds - made my low straight from three to seven. I checked. Airforce bet and I called.

I can't say that I was surprised when we showed down. Can't say I was exactly impressed either. I was first to show and I could see from the reaction of the other players that they fancied my chances. Airforce laughed.

"Is that the best you can do, Brucie baby?" he said, sticking the boot in like he literally had in Churchfield.

He turned two of his cards - a five and a two - to reveal a run from two to six. That won the low pot for Airforce. But could he best my full house? He turned over his other two cards to reveal two sixes to add to the two that had come up on the flop for quads. He raked in about two and a half grand and looked to be in an unassailable position.

"Talk about turning a sow's ear into a silk purse," he said, and I couldn't disagree.

I could see the other four cursing under their breaths. I wondered how many times this had happened to them. Wondered if they were too stupid or just too addicted to keep turning up for these games.

The first to be knocked out around two was Quick. He got too deep into a hand with Airforce and lost out to the nut low and a flush. Next to go about ten minutes later was the guy I'd thought would be the first casualty; Fingers got caught in one too many pies and went out with no low hand and nothing better than two-pair for his high hand. This time the Prof hoovered up his chips.

I was now by far the low stack. I was also beginning to lose patience. About who exactly Doc Martins was, other than Airforce One, I knew little. But I knew from the eyes he was involved in the Churchfield robbery. I knew he was a serious guy, clever, deliberate. He was no lackey, of that I could be confident. And maybe that much was worth the five grand I'd lose. If I did crack him, I was sure he'd lead me to something solid.

Jack was the second biggest stack now with nearly eight grand. Airforce had about eighteen. Prof was languishing on about three and a half. I was nearly dead in the water on eight-hundred.

"You'll need to be selective," Prof said to me.

Despite my lack of conversation, he seemed to enjoy the challenge of prising me open like a mussel, to get me to betray a tell.

But he was right. I had to be selective. Would I follow Red Hair or Doc Martins? I gave it some thought. There had been a few things Red Hair, or Jack, had said that made me believe he was full of crap, that he didn't know the first thing about Moolah or his murder. I decided I'd make a last, perhaps desperate, move.

"What happened to that guy in Nohoval was shocking," I said.

Assuming Prof and Jack were crooks, I thought maybe they would sympathize with his plight.

Jack took the bait.

"Getting your throat cut like that? Awful way to go. Just imagine feeling that blade entering the neck by one ear and being dragged to the other side. I'd prefer a bullet to the head myself."

The MO had never been released to the public. Jack was probably playing on that, inventing his own narrative to that dark night in October. He'd probably tell another version around some camp fire somewhere, scare a few kids. But the version he gave at the table was incorrect. Moolah had been strangled, not cut. I knew, then, that Jack was a bullshit artist. My selection became obvious – my target was now Doc Martins.

I'd had enough of the game, wasn't enjoying it one bit. Maybe given an unfettered strategy I might have. I decided then to get reckless, put my chips in on each hand until I lost them all. Then I'd wait outside for Doc Martins.

Inconceivably, I had more luck in the next couple of hands than Manchester United – and they were the jammiest team going. But I didn't want it then.

I threw my chips in on the next hand and fluked a straight

flush on the river, ace to five, to win both high and low pots. Now I had tripled my stack to two and a half. The next hand I hit runner, runner to win the high pot with a king-high flush. No low pot meant I had now doubled up to five grand. Now I was back in the game when it was the last thing I wanted.

The fear of winning made my heart race. Though possible to luck my way to a win no matter what I did, it was highly improbable. But reality did finally kick in and five hands later I had managed to dump my entire stack.

"Good luck, guys," I said as I rose from my seat.

"Good game, Brucie," Airforce said. "Maybe I'll see you around again."

But he'd already seen me again. And he would be seeing me again sooner than he thought.

Jimmy came out of the office. He shook my hand.

"Decent effort first time out, boy," he said. "Better luck next week?"

"Luck doesn't come into it," I said.

"Some people are born lucky," he said. "I'm still sucking air. That's proof enough."

He had a point. He was a bit like Jordan in that respect. You either had good luck or you didn't. The jury was still out on mine.

I smiled and gave the remaining players a wave. At a little after three, I left the card room and let myself out of the pub, latching the door behind me.

Before going into the Steamship, I had done some reconnaissance on where best to keep an eye on the door. Albert Quay joined with Kennedy Quay to the east, but the main road bent around to the south at the join point of the quays and continued on to Victoria Road going south-east.

I had parked by the bend and had a change of clothes ready. I changed quickly into a more casual outfit – jeans, T-shirt, trainers and a warm puffer jacket. All black or navy to blend in with the shadows. I also donned a baseball cap so that I could bow my head to hide my face should Doc Martins look back at an awkward moment.

More importantly, though, I donned my gun – slipped it into a jacket pocket. I took my camera too. I'd brought it in the hope of capturing the red-haired card sharp, but now I wanted a picture of Doc Martins.

There were a handful of cars and trucks parked at the end of Kennedy Quay. I hid behind a truck and kept an eye on the door. Unless Doc Martins left by the back door and climbed over a wall, I would see him leave.

The first to leave was Prof just before three-thirty. He'd lasted another twenty minutes. He headed back west towards the city.

Five minutes later, Red left. On another night he might have won, like he often did, but Doc Martins had been too strong, seemed to have x-ray eyes. I had no doubt he was collecting his winnings inside. However, he shattered my certainty by coming out very quickly after Red and was going in the same direction – towards me.

I was confident of being out of sight, but still I was tingling. Not just in my groin, but all over. Red turned onto Victoria Road with Doc Martins following.

I zoomed in with the camera, had the flash disabled, night vision setting enabled. I wasn't confident the photos I took would show their faces properly, though a couple were taken when they walked under a lamp post, so I had some hope of a well-lit shot or two.

Red slowed and fumbled in a trouser pocket. He stopped at a car and pulled out a set of keys. Doc Martins was closing in. Red never saw the bag coming.

In a fluid motion, Doc Martins took a bag from his pocket, unfurled it and put it over Red's head. He pulled a drawstring to tighten the mouth of the bag around his neck. He heel-kicked the back of Red's knees, forcing him into a kneeling position. He took out a pistol and pushed it against Red's head, told him not to move if he wanted to keep it.

I was blindsided by this, of course, but not as much as when the black van arrived and came to a halt next to them. A side door slid back and another man got out. They manhandled Red into the back of the van. Doc Martins went around to the passenger side of the van and got in. The other man jumped in the back with Red. The van drove off without speeding. The whole thing took less than fifteen seconds from bagging to vanning.

The van drove towards Mahon on the lengthy Victoria cum Blackrock Road. If they kept in that direction I had a chance of catching them.

I ran to the car. It only took a few seconds. The van was well out of sight, though. I turned the key – a misfire, over-revving and then it settled. I drove off in the direction of the van. I was doing about seventy in a fifty zone and hoped the shades weren't around. I was OK on the drinks front – I did a rough calculation that said I was below the limit.

By the time I reached the bridge over the old railway line walk, I had caught up to the van, a brand new Ford Transit to replace the one burned after the Churchfield robbery. They were keeping to the fifty limit, drawing no attention to themselves. The two little windows on the back doors were blacked-out. I wondered if the number plate was a clone – most likely given the sophistication of these guys.

I'd suspected they were specialists after the Churchfield robbery, but now I knew for sure. These guys were a unit, had trained together, gone on many missions together. It screamed army to me.

A half-mile after the bridge they arrived at the Marina turn. At nearly 4 a.m., traffic was non-existent. I kept a distance behind. A car following along a straight road isn't particularly suspicious, but one taking the same left turn is. The Marina turn headed more or less back the way they came, so I assumed they'd stop there or thereabouts.

I didn't want to spook the specialists – three or four guys with pistols were not to be trifled with – so I continued on and hoped for the best. Worst case scenario I had a photo of Doc Martins to fall back on. If the camera was any good at its job, which I doubted somewhat.

I parked a little bit up Castle Road. I'd seen brake lights on the van before it went out of view. They were stopping at the pier. I walked back towards a low wall that was teeming with ivy. The wall was in a gap between a building known as Pier Head House and the trees that grew further along Castle Road. I had a good view of the pier from there.

The van had indeed stopped there. It had been parked in such a way as to block the view of passersby from whatever was going on. But I had a partial view from Castle Road. Red was on his knees again on the edge of the pier. Someone, and I assumed it was Doc Martins, took the bag from his head. I could only see an arm extending from behind the van. Red's head was bowed. He was crying, his chest heaving. The arm retracted and extended again with a pistol to Red's head.

I waited for the shot. I waited for Doc Martins to kick the body into the drink. I waited for a bullet that never came. The arm and the gun disappeared from view leaving Red still on his knees, his palms on the concrete. He was shaking. He didn't look back.

The van turned. I ran back to the car. The Transit headed up Convent Road. I did a U-turn and followed. The road snaked left to right to left to right again before a junction with Ringmahon Road.

The van stopped at the junction. The way was clear. But the van just stayed there. This was a disaster. I came to a stop a couple of car lengths behind. Should I reverse, overtake? The Transit driver made the decision for me. They took a left and accelerated. They no longer kept to the speed limit. At that point I knew the game was up. I'd been rumbled. The van sped off into the distance. It could have been on its way to the Jack Lynch Tunnel to cross under the Lee and connect with the main Dublin or Waterford roads.

A long night was at an end. I was sore and exhausted. It was time to go home and process the night's events.

I drove back via the pier. Red was gone. He could have been walking back to his car, a forty-minute walk at most.

I finally had time to think as I drove. They'd stuck a gun to his cranium, more than likely given him a warning of some kind. Was it something personal, something Red had said at the table to offend Doc Martins? No. You don't have a precision operation involving a crew of soldiers for that. They may have interrogated him in the back of the van, determined he was no threat, and given him a stern talking to. With the bag and a gun to the head as an exclamation point.

At home, I booted up the laptop and connected the camera. I had two usable photos – one of Red and one of Doc Martins. Could I trouble Cotter again, see if these guys were known to him? I suspected Red would be. But Doc Martins? I doubted it.

It was after half-four. I went to bed. I had a dream I didn't enjoy about being bagged, shot and dumped. Like a piece of rubbish. Though I had been shot in the head, I was aware of being kicked into a hole. The hole became the boot of a rusted car. My father wasn't in the boot. Robbie was.

11

Good Old-fashioned Legwork

THE PREVIOUS NIGHT'S EVENTS came to me in flashes. It was overwhelming. I brewed up some Classic Blend and sat at the table. It worked on my brain like a set of jump leads. I began to put the flashes in order, to put some manners on them.

Did I need to trouble Cotter with the photo of Red? From what I'd seen at the table, Red was a mug. The warning at the pier more or less confirmed it. He was small fry, of no consequence. I decided to shelve the photo for now, use it later if I'd exhausted other avenues.

I was on thin ice with Barry, so I decided to use some old-fashioned legwork first to find an identity for Doc Martins. I knew a good place to start.

Ned Fagan was long since retired from service in the engineering group at Collins Barrack's 1st Cork Brigade, but he had seen the comings and goings in or around the barracks for nearing half a century.

How I came across Ned is a long story. The short version involves a girl named Deborah. His granddaughter. That's the link.

The long version is too painful to recall. It inevitably invites the memory of that Valentine's night fifteen years ago.

If there was one man who might identify a soldier, it was Ned. There was every chance he would tell me to take a running jump, but I knew, at least, that he was discreet.

I drove to his house and took my laptop. The house is on the aptly-named Military Hill, which is within pissing distance of the barracks. It's a fine Georgian-style house that was built in the fifties. Pale yellow paint on the walls, the mouldings around the sash windows an antique white.

Originally from Athlone, Ned relocated to Collins Barracks to take up a senior rank. When he retired, he used the skills he learned to start a wrought iron business – gates, railings and such. An impressively bright, black set of iron railings on a low wall seesawed from one end of the site to the other. Each railing was topped with an ornate gold-painted *fleur-de-lis* design. Ned might have been trained to stick someone with a bayonet, but he sure had an eye for detail and a high level of craftsmanship.

He welcomed me warmly. He always did, had a soft spot for me. Despite what happened with Deb. He invited me into his living room.

The living room had wall-to-wall shelving on two of its walls. The shelves were full of books. Biographies were prevalent – De Valera, Collins, Pearse and others associated with the rising and the civil war. Pearse – another guy who died in his prime. Like Gerald Griffin and Dad. There were also biographies of figures from the great wars – Haig, Churchill, Rommel, Roosevelt and a dozen or so others.

The room was exceptionally clean and the furniture in very good order. Deb was mostly to thank for that. She would call most days to help out and I worried she might be there when I arrived. I think I was glad she wasn't. On a side table next to an armchair by the gas fire was what looked like a new book about the Congo by van Reybrouck. Ned saw me studying it.

"Fascinating book. Some of it new to me," he said. Of course, the Congo was writ large in his mind, like so many Irish soldiers of his generation.

"You know," he said, "every now and again I hear someone use the word Baluba to mean a fool or they say *are you Baluba?* instead of *are you mad?*" His mouth twitched. "We lost nine men to those savages at Niemba, so we did. They butchered them like something from the stone age."

I envied his use of the word *we*. I wasn't able to use that word about the Guards.

Ned sat in the armchair and turned down the flame in the gas fire.

"I hope it's not too hot for you, Michael. Old folks like myself get cold so easily."

I said I was fine. I sat in another armchair on the other side of the hearth.

"The year after, I was deployed to the Congo as part of the 35th Batallion. This was before I transferred to Cork. There was only a hundred and fifty or so of us at Jadotville when the Katangans came with thousands."

He had a glass of Lucozade on the table and paused to take a sip. I refused when he offered some to me.

"Forgive me, Michael. I'm getting into one of my war stories again, so I am."

I'd heard several of his stories, but he had never opened up about Jadotville. There were obvious reasons for this.

"Well, we were dug in real good. Quinlan's orders. We had some old Vickers machine guns. We liked those, even though they dated back to the first world war and were heavy as hell to carry around the jungle. We got our own back on the Balubas then, I can tell you. Cut them down, so we did."

He paused again to regain his breath. He was eighty and in failing health. I thought he might have had emphysema. Unfortunately with my hypochondria, I've become a bit of a diagnostician – like yer man House on the TV.

"Six days we held them off. Our reinforcements couldn't break through the Katangan lines. We had no choice in the end but to surrender."

He paused and his mouth quivered again.

"Jadotville Jacks they called us. They mocked us with it. We put up the white flag, you see. There's no honour in that, so there isn't."

"It was a scandal as far as I'm concerned," I said. "Each and every one of you should have gotten medals."

"I could handle it. I largely got on with business when I got back. Transferred to Cork not long after. But what they did to Quinlan was unforgivable. He was a fall guy, so he was. The real blame went much higher up the chain. All the way, in fact."

"And in typical Irish fashion," I said, "his good name was only restored after his death."

Ned nodded. "He saved countless lives. We'd all have been cut down within a day but for his orders. I'd never have met my Mary, for instance." He looked up to the mantelpiece where a picture of his dead wife was. She was smiling. "We knew he was a hero and I think for him that was enough."

I don't know whether I also had Quinlan to thank for Deb. We'd had a good run of it until that day in February all those years ago. But I couldn't look at another woman for years after.

Ned got up from the chair and went to a window. He pushed down one of the sash panels to shut it.

"It's a fine balancing act, so it is," he said, "between the heat of the gas fire and getting in some fresh air."

Before he could get back into stories about the Congo or any-where else, I took my laptop out of its case.

"There's something I would like you to look at, Ned."

I lifted the lid on the laptop and it came out of its hibernation. I thought hibernation was something bears did, but apparently computers can go into a similar deep sleep and wake up as if nothing had happened.

"I'm a welder, Michael," he said. "Computers aren't my thing."

"You're more than just a welder. But I just want to show you a picture of someone. I'm hoping you might know who it is."

I had one worry. Soldiers, the men in green, like the men in blue, closed ranks. If he thought I was after one of his brethren,

I might get nowhere with him.

"Go on," he said.

The laptop booted back into Windows and I opened up the Pictures folder. The photos were sorted by year, month and day, so it wasn't difficult to find the ones from the night before. I loaded the best I had of Doc Martins and expanded it to fill the screen.

"Pass me those, will you?"

He was pointing at a pair of over-sized reading glasses. I obliged.

He squinted his eyes. He examined the photograph intently. He took his time about it.

"There's two types of people I hate most in this world, so there are," he finally said. "Belgians and mercenaries."

I understood why. Chief among the culprits at Jadotville had been the colonial Belgians and the white mercenaries hired by the Katangans. In fact, it is a bitter irony that the commander of the Katangan forces at Jadotville, Mike Hoare, aka Mad Mike and himself a mercenary, spent his early years in Ireland.

"And he's not Belgian," I said. I had taken what he said as an acknowledgement of recognition.

"No, he's most certainly not."

He stayed quiet for a few seconds and I wondered if he would decide to close ranks after all. Then he spoke.

"Hognatt is his name, so it is. Matthew Hognatt. He's an East Kerry man. Retired from the army when his twenty-one years were up."

After twenty-one years of service you were entitled to a full army pension.

"Any idea where he is now?"

"The last I heard of Hognatt, he was working for an oil company in Angola."

I assumed Hognatt wasn't the drilling kind. "You mean working as a mercenary?"

He nodded.

What Ned said only confirmed what I suspected. I needed to

find where he was or what he was up to in Cork. And why his path had crossed mine at least one time too many for it to be just coincidence.

"How do you know Hognatt?"

"He drank up in Sheehan's. I knew all the soldiers up to about the turn of the century. When I was mobile enough to go for a pint up the hill. I only go as far as the Ambassador now, so I do."

"Do you know where he lived?"

Ned shrugged his shoulders and wheezed from the effort. He coughed a smoker-like cough, though he hadn't smoked in more than twenty years.

If I couldn't get to Hognatt directly, maybe I could do so indirectly.

"Up in Sheehan's ... did he hang around with anyone?"

He thought for a few seconds, took off his reading glasses and rubbed his eyes.

"There were two or three lads, alright. One was a guy called Davis. Another was Crowley."

He stopped then. His eyes rose a little in their sockets.

"You know, that Crowley fellow ... I think his mother lives up on Old Youghal Road, so she does. Down towards Dillon's Cross a bit. Anita her name is. I'm trying to remember his name." His face strained. "Ah damn this memory of mine."

"That's OK," I said. "I can go and—"

"Barney," he said. "It's Barney Crowley. He retired about the same time as Hognatt. Never made it past private."

One thought came into my mind from the card game. The nickname – Airforce One.

"This Hognatt guy ... was he into aeroplanes or anything like that?"

Ned laughed and he began to wheeze again, but more deeply this time. I told him to take his time and I picked up his glass of Lucozade for him. He took a sip and composed himself.

"Not exactly," he said. "It was choppers, so it was. He wanted to join the air corps. Ten years in the army and he suddenly decided he wanted to fly. The brass laughed him out of it, told him to cop himself on. It was a running joke for a while."

There was no one better to capitalize on a joke than the Eel. He would have taken some glee from giving Hognatt the Airforce One moniker.

Ned was out of breath. The more he spoke, the worse he got. With a solid lead in the bag and some names to go with it, I decided to give the old guy a break and leave. I asked about Deb before I got up.

"She's doing OK, Michael. She married this guy — gobshite he is — and they have a kid now. I'd given up on being a great grandfather."

The word grandfather had tapered to a whisper. He had no breath left to give. I shook his hand and thanked him for his time.

There was a phone on a table at the front door. In a shelf underneath was a phone book. I took it out and thumbed my way to Crowley. No Barney. No Anita, either, but she wouldn't be difficult to find. I had every right to believe that her son, Barney, was in the van on both occasions. And I believed he would lead me to Hognatt.

It didn't take much detective work to find Anita Crowley's house. Cork folk are very obliging when you ask where so and so is, not being in the least bit suspicious about your intentions. As long as you're not black, Polish or a traveller, that is, in which case it's pot luck.

She lived opposite Harrington Square where a grotto allowed people to pray to the Virgin Mary. The grotto was well-maintained — grass cut, bushes trimmed, and so on. Immaculate, I would say it was, like the good woman herself, apparently. I could well believe there was a Jesus at some point, but him being conceived by magic — that I didn't buy.

I didn't know if Anita was in, or if someone else, including Barney, would answer. I wouldn't pretend to be the most patient of detectives; staking the place out all day wasn't in my script. If Barney had answered, who knows how it would have gone down. I wasn't carrying my gun. That would have been ammunition for

Savage or Halloran to arrest me.

As it happened, nobody answered. As I waited for someone to open the door, a neighbour left her house.

"Looking for Anita?" she enquired.

She had a scarf over her head. A bit young to be wearing one, though. The clear sky had dropped the temperature below ten degrees.

I said I was, said I was there to sort out the paperwork for her life insurance.

"That sounds important," she said.

"Yes, madam," I said, playing the part of the prototypical slimy insurance salesman.

"You'll find her over there in the launderette."

She was pointing to the other side of Harrington Square and Suds Launderette on Ballyhooly Road.

I thanked the neighbour and walked through Harrington Square. It was a minor oasis in an otherwise bustling suburb. An old woman was kneeling on a cushion, praying to the Good Mother. If you prayed long enough, you began to hallucinate, see an arm move, or a tear fall. From the blood pooling and the brain deoxygenated, if you ask me.

On Ballyhooly Road, a number seven bus passed going north. I noticed a kid on the bus – and for some reason I was noticing kids more often – who was blowing a bubble with some gum. On the back of the bus was an advertisement for the re-election of Niall O'Donnell, TD. Corruption, it seemed, had a way of getting around.

I crossed the road. Suds had a lattice grille covering the window and the door was covered with solid steel plate. It looked tankproof.

Inside, there were about ten large industrial washing machines. To the rear a counter accepted laundry – individual items to be cleaned with care and bags to be washed without.

A couple of student types – one with hair in braids, the other with a nose ring and black fingernail polish – were sitting on interlocked chairs. One had one of those tablet things, the other

her nose – and the ring on it – buried in a smart phone. I had to pity them. The best screen of all was the window to the outside world, security grille or not.

There was only the one woman behind the counter. She was around seventy and I assumed it was Anita. The job was for a few extra bob on top of her pension, I assumed. Either that or she was the owner. She was painted more than the statue of Mary I'd seen moments earlier – deep pink lipstick, red blusher, purple eyeshadow. Gold hoop earrings, bottle blonde, the look of a hard woman.

I'd worked on my cover story when walking through Harrington Square.

"Hi there," I said. "Anita, is it?"

She looked me up and down. "It is. What do you want?"

Abrupt, impolite.

"I'm Jerry O'Leary," I said, lacking in imagination. "I was in the 1st Brigade with Barney."

Her demeanour changed completely. She softened.

"Oh, you know Barney?"

"Yeah. I'm trying to get in touch with him. One of our comrades died, I'm afraid. We're trying to get the lads together to honour our fallen brother."

Invoking that kind of brash sentimentality isn't my normal style. Honouring a colleague in the Guards largely consisted of a lorryload of booze.

"That's terrible. Don't you have Barney's address?"

"I lost touch with Barney when he went to Angola," I said. "I was hoping you might help me on that front."

I didn't know for sure whether Barney had gone to Angola with Hognatt, but it would have made sense if they were still operating as a crew. Dropping the name of the country would, I hoped, convince her that I'd kept in touch with Barney up to that point.

"We all lost touch with him. The rotten animal."

Surprisingly candid, even with the harshness of her demeanour.

"Do you have an address for him?"

"I have a number. Why don't you call him?"

I didn't want to talk to Crowley. I wanted to shadow him, get him to lead me to Hognatt.

"I'd like to surprise him. Besides, I need to go over the design of some wreaths with him."

I'd honoured my own father recently with a cheap wreath, put no thought into it. I regretted it at that moment.

"OK. I see. Hang on."

She took a handbag from below the counter. She rummaged in it and pulled out a little black notebook. Like a detective's notebook. She wet an index finger and flicked through the pages.

"Here it is," she said. She read out an address on Blackrock Avenue, a fairly new build of duplex townhouse apartments in Mahon. Or Blackrock, depending on your position on the snobbery scale. It was a Celtic Tiger build. *Townhouse* was a favourite word of that tiger. *Terraced*, it seemed, was too dirty, evoking images of coalminers and the common folk of Coronation Street.

"That's grand, so," I said. "It'll be good to catch up with Barney again."

There was little doubt about that. The closer I got to Hognatt, the more emboldened I got. Crowley was a stepping stone I would happily stamp on.

I went to leave, but turned back.

"It'll be good to surprise him," I said. "I can't wait to see the look on his face."

It was getting on for 3.30 p.m. when I arrived at Blackrock Avenue in the ridiculously named Eden development. Celtic Tiger developments tended to have grandiose names – names that looked good on brochures, names that gave you the impression that you were buying above your station.

I brought my gun with me. I was done messing around. I wanted answers and I wanted them quick; and there's no answer accelerator like the nozzle of a pistol in someone's face.

Crowley's apartment was on the ground floor of one of the

duplexes at the end of a terrace. The orange bricks of the frontage were only a supporting act to the exposed wooden frame
around a floor-to-ceiling living room window. I didn't see anyone
in the living room. I parked four spaces down. I put on my puffer
jacket and slid the gun into my right pocket.

I had waited for a moment like this for days. I had fantasized
about it, played out the many ways things might go down. I put
my right hand in my jacket pocket and clasped the cold steel of
the pistol. My father had warned me off guns, said they were
more likely to get you killed than offer protection. But now I was
the perpetrator; I was the one taking the initiative.

I walked to the door. I paused for a moment to compose myself. I stood to the side of the little head-height window on the
door. *Breath in and out, like the CD said.*

I knocked on the door with my left hand, kept my right on the
gun. Safety off, bullet in the chamber, nine more in the clip.

Just breath in and out. In and out.

The door opened. A woman. Early thirties, dark hair with
blonde highlights – expensive looking hairdo. No make-up, spots
of flour on an old T-shirt and flour paste stuck to her hands.

I must have worn a dozen different faces all at once. She looked
at me with the look of a girl who got Thomas the Tank Engine
for Christmas instead of My Little Pony.

A woman. That wasn't in any of my mental rehearsals. I could
come back later. But I thought again. I had to do this now. I was
done waiting.

"I'm a friend of Barney's," I said.

She looked sceptical.

"From the brigade, back in the day. Jerry's my name."

"OK?"

In other words, *get to the point before I slam the door in your face!*

"I wanted to talk to Barney about a mutual friend who passed
away. A comrade from Collins Barracks."

"OK?"

"I want to talk to him about honouring our fallen brother."

"Look, Jerry. Barney will be back after six. You can call back then."

I felt desperate then. She'd describe me to him. Give him the name Jerry – quite possible there was no Jerry in his regiment or group. He'd put two and two together and get Bosco. I'd arrive with a pistol and he'd trump it with a submachine gun.

"If I could just wait inside—"

"Please call back later. After six."

She closed the door. On my foot. I pushed the door open and forced my way in.

"What are you doing?" she shouted. "I'm going to call the Guards."

I took the gun out of my pocket and pointed it at her. I was thrilled and appalled in equal measure. I gestured towards the living room with the gun.

"Draw the curtains," I said. "Then turn on the light."

She complied. The look of terror on her face made me feel like my head was going to cave in on itself. She was probably a nobody, clueless about Crowley's shenanigans. I had to remind myself that this was necessary. I'd not scare her any more than I needed to.

"I've got some money," she said. She pointed to a PlayStation under the TV. "You can take that. There's jewellery too." She started sobbing. "Just take what you need and go."

"Sit down," I said, using the gun like a laser pointer to indicate the couch. I had to remind her when she didn't move. She sat.

"I'm not here to rob you," I said. "Like I said … I just want to talk to Barney."

I sat opposite on an armchair. The decor was modern. Clean lines – furniture that was angular, boxy. A chrome TV stand. Seven or eight speakers around the room that looked like they would create an exquisite soundscape.

"What's your name?" I said.

"Ju – Justine."

"Good. You see how easy this can be?"

She didn't relax in the slightest.

"Girlfriend?"

She nodded.

"Good."

There was a glass coffee table between us. I nodded towards it.

"Pick up the remote. Turn on the TV."

Her hands shook. She grabbed the remote control and it clinked on the glass a couple of times. She hit the red power button.

The TV was at least a fifty-incher. Along with the rest of the furniture and fittings, it suggested no shortage of income. A regular army guy could hope to earn about five-hundred a week. Now it looked like he was earning at least five-hundred a day.

"Put something on that you like," I said.

She raised her hands up a bit like someone balancing two saucers. It told me she couldn't decide. Probably her brain had seized from the fear.

I wasn't liking this one bit. I used to be a guardian of peace, for fuck's sake. But if there was one thing that was going to make Crowley talk, it was the sight of a desperate man with a gun to his woman's head.

"Sky News, then," I said. "We'll see what's going on in the world."

The channel changed and a flood in Indonesia was the main story. Countless displaced people for whom we had a surface sympathy, but not any deep feeling. I didn't speak to her again until Crowley arrived home at what the Sky News graphic said was six-thirteen.

I stood in the hall when the key turned. I had the gun pointed at Justine in the living room. The door opened and Crowley walked in holding shopping bags in both hands. I turned the gun to him.

"Hello, Crowley," I said. "Justine and I have been waiting patiently. Do join us in the sitting room."

I waved the gun sideways to usher Crowley into the living room and I asked him to sit next to Justine, which he did. He held Justine's hand.

"No touching," I said. "Move to the opposite ends of the

couch, please."

Please? Was I going to be graded by anyone on my manners? No, but I was a civilized man. A civilized man who was terrorizing an innocent – most likely – girl.

"What do you want?" Crowley said. There were nerves in his voice, but he remained steady. I doubted very much that this was the first time he'd had a live gun pointed at him. While his physique wasn't as imposing as Hognatt's, being no more than five-nine in height, he was stocky. He looked boyish, much younger than the mid-forties he must have been, and had tightly-cut strawberry blond hair.

"I just want to talk. You know who I am, right?"

Justine turned her head to look at Crowley. Her eyes had narrowed somewhat, suggesting that if he affirmed, there would be trouble in paradise.

Crowley's expression didn't change.

"I have no idea—"

"Churchfield," I intervened. "Druid."

"I still don't—"

I became very angry then. I remembered the knock to the head. I remembered how it had kickstarted a chain of events – beatings, a shooting, the humiliation in the Bridewell.

"I know about Hognatt. I know about Angola. I know about the red-haired man last night."

Crowley said nothing. He looked like he was strategizing. I didn't like it. I didn't want to give him time to work on any angles. I stood up and approached him. I pointed the gun at his head.

"Speak now or forever rest in peace. I won't hesitate, Crowley. You better believe it."

"Look, yes, I'll admit I've seen you before. But I don't know shit, man. Hognatt gives the order, we carry out the mission. I don't know who Hognatt is taking his orders from. All I know is that whoever it is pays handsomely."

Something inside me changed at that very moment. I'd been two, maybe three steps behind from day one. Now I felt like I was at least even, maybe a step ahead for once.

"Churchfield?"

It seemed like Crowley couldn't get the words out of his mouth fast enough.

"Hognatt said he'd checked out Druid, that there'd just be you there on patrol. He said it would be easy, man. A standard in and out job. We'd suppress you, load the TVs into the van. Simple."

"What did you do with the TVs?"

"We took them to some barn in the ass end of nowhere. We just left them and went. Burnt out the van a few miles later, changed to a new van."

"The black Ford Transit?"

He nodded.

"Those TVs are worth about fifteen K. How much did you get paid?"

He opened his mouth, but nothing came out.

I inched half a step forward.

"How much?"

"Ten thousand."

"You got ten K for yourself? That was your cut?"

Again, he just nodded. I knew there was more to the job than just TVs. That was confirmed now.

"Last night. The red-haired poker player."

"Hognatt said it was a bag and grab. He'd give us the go and we'd grab the guy and stuff him in the van."

"Did you interrogate him in the van?"

"No. The orders were to keep him quiet. When we got to the pier, Hognatt took him to the edge. He told us to get back into the van. I thought the guy was toast. A dump job in the river. But Hognatt just let him go."

"Did you hear what he said to this guy?"

"No, man. I didn't hear jack shit with the engine running."

I put my finger over the trigger. "Jack shit?"

"Jesus, man. I swear on my mother's grave. I'm just in this for the money … to … to pay for the mortgage on this place. To have a good life for myself and Justine."

"Your mother's alive," I said.

"Hey, man, it's just an expression. I'm telling you. I just take orders, get my payoff at the end of the op."

"You better be telling me the truth or you very well might be swearing on your mother's grave."

"The truth, man. I swear it's all the truth."

Justine looked at him with her mouth open.

"Still want to call the Guards, Justine?"

She looked right at me, her eyes wide open like she'd seen a … no, much worse than a ghost. Ghosts don't carry guns. She shook her head. Smart girl.

"Tell me more about Hognatt."

"We joined at the same time. Went through training together. We had each other's backs. You know what I mean, man?"

I did. It had been like that with Cotter.

"Go on," I said.

"The army pays shit, man. We said when we retired that we'd travel a bit, earn some money. I mean, there's always some big company in the third world that needs to keep the natives under control."

"So you joined a private military company?"

He nodded.

"And Angola was the last assignment?"

Again, he nodded.

"How did you end up back home?"

"Hognatt said he knew a guy. Said he paid well. Not as much as Angola, but it was a chance to go home for a while. He said he had to deal direct, that the guy didn't like too many people knowing his business. So like I said, Hognatt gets the orders, passes them on to us."

"Us?"

He looked at Justine, then at me.

"Look, man, you knew about Hognatt. I'm not giving anyone else up."

Again with the closing of ranks, even with my pistol pointed at him. I understood it. He seemed only to tolerate Hognatt, but when it came to his other comrades, I suspected he might take a beating for them. Not a bullet, though.

I considered ramping up the threat, maybe push the gun against his skull. But I decided I didn't need anyone else. Crowley could get me to Hognatt. Hognatt would get me to whoever the guy on top was.

"That's OK," I said. "I don't need anyone else. How many are we talking, though."

"Two others."

Two plus two equals four. Four, for fuck's sake. I was just one. How deep was I prepared to go?

"What kind of heat are you packing?"

"MP7s, night vision goggles, flashbangs."

"ERU issue," I said, referring to the Emergency Response Unit of the Gardaí. Most people weren't familiar with their existence, being more familiar with the term SWAT – Special Weapons And Tactics.

"Like I said," Crowley said, "I don't ask questions. Hognatt gets the orders, the gear, the transportation."

"Where's your weapon now?"

"Hognatt moves them around. When we have a job we gather together and Hognatt brings the guns in a holdall."

"But you've got a gun in the house, right?"

Crowley shook his head.

"I don't believe you."

I looked at Justine, her hands still messy from baking. I pointed the gun at her. Her neck lengthened and her head went back slightly.

"Is he telling the truth?" I said to her.

She looked at Crowley. She seemed to be looking for permission.

"I didn't think so," I said. "Stop messing with me, Crowley. A guy like you doesn't not have a gun."

"OK, OK. I have a gun in a safe in the bedroom."

"I'm not kidding around here. I've been pushed around enough by the likes of you. I won't hesitate to respond disproportionately. No more games?"

Crowley held his hands up in front of his chest, palms towards me like he was surrendering.

"No more games," he confirmed.

"You're going to give me Hognatt," I said. "Where is he?"

His expression changed to one that reminded me of an illiterate pupil being asked to spell the word *acknowledgement*.

"I don't know where he is. *We* don't know. He moves around."

I believed him for once.

"In that case, I want you to arrange a meeting."

Some of Crowley's resolve dissipated. I could see worry in his face.

"It doesn't work like that, man," he said. "Hognatt contacts us. We don't even know how to contact him."

Hognatt was a ghost, it appeared. He blew around on the wind. He was a shadow man.

"We're in for a long wait, then," I said. "Do you have any rope?"

Both Crowley and Justine looked at each other, more alarmed than ever. Crowley twitched and I almost pulled the trigger.

"Don't even fucking think about it," I said.

Crowley eased back into the couch and put his hands into that surrender position again.

"Cool, man. Cool. Look, there's no need for rope. We have a meet to discuss the next op tomorrow morning. We're meeting at five sharp. Hognatt will ring at four with the exact location."

I thought about this for a minute. It was nearly seven. 4 a.m. was nine hours away.

"No, I'm afraid we still need the rope. Guy like you is bound to have some."

I hadn't come prepared for hostage taking. Once Justine appeared at the door I had to begin improvising.

Crowley told me he had rope under a kitchen counter. I got Crowley and Justine to get up from the couch and walk to the kitchen. I asked Justine to get the rope – Crowley might have tried something stupid.

"Wash your hands," I said to Justine. No sense in leaving the paste on her hands. She complied.

I looked at a large mixing bowl with flour in it. There was another large bowl on the counter top with a frothy light brown mixture in it.

"Sourdough?"

Justine looked at me, drying her hands with a towel. I might as well have asked if she was making a bomb judging by her expression. She nodded, though.

"I get the Arbutus sourdough myself. I wouldn't have the patience to make my own. My mother was always a soda bread woman. She'd knock together a loaf in no time."

The couple stared blankly at me. I don't think the idle chat of a man with a gun was something they thought about entertaining.

I made Crowley tie Justine to one of the kitchen chairs. I fixed Crowley to another.

"I'm not a great one for sleep," I said. "But by all means catch some Zs if you like."

I pulled a chair into a corner of the kitchen and sat. I rested the gun on a knee. I had time to look around.

"This is a nice place you have," I said. "Big screen TV, marble counter tops, island unit."

No thanks from the couple. None to be expected. I was jealous, I have to admit. I still had black and white TV. And that had just become useless since the digital TV service, Saorview, launched. I had an outside toilet when they had an ensuite. Porcelain tiles to my cheap linoleum.

"I can see it needs paying for."

I got up and searched the cupboards for glasses. I found them and poured water into two of them from the tap.

"Still, though," I said. "You get the same water as everyone else."

By this point the couple had a dejected look about them.

"Straws?" I enquired.

Justine nodded towards a drawer. I put the glasses in front of them and put straws in them.

"Can't say you were mistreated now, can you?" I said.

There was a thought that had been tugging away at me, like the kid tugging at his father's trouser leg that I often pictured.

"What's the deal with the machete?"

Crowley tilted his head.

"Up in Churchfield. Hognatt approached me with a machete. Seems … out of step with the clinical nature of your business, don't you think?"

Crowley straightened his head. He was about to respond when I interrupted.

"It's Africa, isn't it? Angola or maybe somewhere before that. Maybe Somalia. They like their machetes there."

Crowley nodded. "Hognatt said that a gun would frighten someone, but the sight of a machete would make them wish for the gun. A clean death versus being hacked to death, I suppose."

"Mad Matt," I said, thinking of the parallel with *Mad* Mike Hoare from the Jadotville siege.

Crowley raised his eyebrows. I suspected it wasn't the first time he'd heard the phrase used to describe Hognatt.

I'd had my fill of Hognatt at that point. I decided that silence would be a good idea for a while. I needed to nurse my brain. The thing had been working overtime of late.

A couple of hours passed. Justine began to nod off, then couldn't hold off any more and fell asleep, her head lolling to one side. I could see Crowley was going to hang on till the bitter end to avoid sleep.

Another hour passed. It was already feeling like a long night and there were still nearly six hours to go until Hognatt's phone call. Crowley's head began to drop, then he jerked it back up again. This happened a couple more times until he did finally go to sleep.

Where's the harm? I'll need to be sharp tomorrow. Maybe a bit of shuteye would do me good.

I slumped in the chair to find comfort and closed my eyes.

I woke to find Crowley struggling with his rope. His left arm was almost free.

The gun. My gun! My arteries nearly popped. I relaxed. It was on the ground. How it never woke me when it fell, I will never know. I picked it up. There was a chip in a porcelain tile. The only chip in the kitchen. I felt like apologizing, but didn't. I pointed the gun at Crowley.

"Nice try. Now relax, Crowley."

I checked my watch. Just after three.

"Where's your phone?" I said.

"It's in my pocket."

"Burner?"

"What do you think?"

Of course it was.

I took the phone out of Crowley's pocket. I tightened his ropes, double-checked Justine's. She woke when I disturbed her. She had a strange, distant look at first, then realized she was tied to a chair in her kitchen in the presence of a gunman and flailed for a few seconds before calming.

"My apologies," I said. "I don't like being woken out of a deep sleep either."

I put the phone on the table.

"When Hognatt rings, I'll answer and put it to your ear. You'll say whatever you would have had I not been here. I'll listen in at close quarters. I won't put the phone on speaker. He might notice and think there's something funny about it. I'll have the gun to your head in case you try anything. Just so you know in advance. So you don't sound nervous."

As if that was going to make him less nervous. There was time to eat. I'd gotten used to eating at all hours when working for Solid Security. When I made Weetabix for the couple, they refused it. I ate mine, though.

The time passed quickly. I assumed Hognatt would call bang on the top of the hour, so when it reached five minutes to, I started watching the second hand on my analogue display.

At ten seconds to four by my watch, the phone rang. I went to the table and picked it up. I hit the green phone icon and put it to Crowley's ear.

"It's me," Crowley said.

"I've just sent the coordinates to your phone," I could clearly hear Hognatt say.

The phone beeped to indicate a message had been received.

"Got it," Crowley said.

"Five o'clock."

"Got it. Five o'clock sharp."

"OK. Five o'clock sharp. Should take you thirty minutes. See you then."

Hognatt hung up.

Crowley looked up at me. I took the gun away from his temple.

"Happy?"

I didn't think it was the right word. But I didn't detect anything from Hognatt's end. I believed we would have the element of surprise.

I fiddled with the phone. I managed to find the message. There were GPS coordinates in decimal format. I showed them to Crowley.

"Do I look like a sat nav to you?" he said. I felt like slapping him across the head.

"Approximately," I said.

"East of here somewhere. Maybe twenty miles. I'll have to enter the coordinates into the Garmin in the car to see exactly."

I was satisfied for now. We had about twenty minutes to spare. I looked in a ceramic jar that said TEA.

"What are these?" I asked. I was holding up a plain paper-wrapped stringed teabag.

Crowley looked at Justine as if to say he wouldn't be caught dead drinking the stuff. Justine answered.

"Chasteberry."

I'd never heard of it. She must have spotted the look of ignorance.

"It's a herbal tea. You probably wouldn't like it."

Crowley chipped in with his two cents: "Unless you are trying to get pregnant."

I quickly dropped it back in the jar. Like I was holding a bag of pubic hair.

"Doesn't anyone just drink tea anymore," I said to no reply. *But to each their own. In her world of tea drinking, I'm probably the equivalent of the Heineken drinker, her the equivalent of the Howling Gale drinker.*

I made do with water. We saw out the last quarter hour with all manner of fidgetiness. I was tapping the sole of my right foot on the ground. Crowley looked like he was grinding teeth. Justine was twitching her nose.

At four-twenty I untied Crowley. I instructed him to use his rope to further tie up Justine.

"Don't worry," I said to her. "We'll be back before you know it. And don't think about shouting."

I pressed the gun to Crowley's back to emphasize my instruction.

In the hall, I asked Crowley for his car keys, then asked him to brush his hair. *Nothing out of the ordinary. Invite no suspicion from a distance.*

We went out to the car, a black Saab 9-3 with expensive-looking alloys. I kept the gun on Crowley through my jacket pocket. He got into the driver seat and I got into the passenger seat. Crowley entered the coordinates in the Garmin sat nav. The map centred on a location in Aghada, East Cork. I passed the keys to him.

"Drive," I said. "And no—"

"Funny business. I know. Look, man, we want to start a family."

Don't we all. He was trying to personalize himself, make it difficult for me to put him in harm's way. If he actually had a kid, it might have worked. But my resolve was unbreakable. I wanted to get to Hognatt.

"I'm just a foot soldier," he said. "I'm of no consequence to you."

"Just shut up and drive," I said. "Hognatt's waiting."

Crowley turned the key. The engine started. He reversed out of the parking space and began the journey to Aghada.

12

The Puppet Master

I ASKED CROWLEY TO tune the radio to Lyric FM. I wasn't impressed that it wasn't one of his presets. Jazz was playing. I'm OK with Jazz. I'd take classical over it, though. Beethoven, Haydn, maybe.

After twenty minutes we reached the Lake View roundabout, which I always thought of as the Midleton roundabout. Crowley took the last exit for Whitegate and Ballycotton.

We passed a relatively new estate called Maple Wood. Maples were Canadian. What was wrong with good old Irish Sycamore? Another hangover from the Celtic Tiger – stupid names for housing estates. Names that just made you want to club the property developer who dreamed up the name over the head.

A few minutes later and we were driving through Rostellan, a beautiful village that looks like a picture-perfect entry for the tidy towns competition. To the right was a lake, which was really a piece of the inner harbour that had been dammed by a road to the woods on the other side. Swans spent the comparatively mild winters there and I could see a couple nuzzling on the water.

When we were a couple of minutes' drive away from the meeting point on the far side of Aghada, I asked Crowley to turn onto a lane. At the entrance to a farm, I told him to pull in. It was six minutes to the hour.

"We'll walk from here across the fields," I said.

It hadn't rained, but the ground underfoot was still soft. I supposed the water table was low here with it being so close to the inner harbour. Crowley walked in front and I held the gun down by my side.

"We'll wait until your pals are all there. Then I'll walk you in with the gun to your head. Let's hope for your sake that Hognatt values your life."

"For your sake too," Crowley replied.

He had a point. Just like the poker game, this was all in or all out. Who knows how much Africa had warped Hognatt's mind. He brandished a machete like it was just a toothpick, so God knows what he'd be like with an MP7 in his hands.

We came to a ditch and climbed over. There was another field between us and the farm where Hognatt wanted to meet. I had a close look at the hedge beyond. We were hidden from view.

"This is crazy," Crowley said. "It's not too late to turn back."

"Just keep your beak shut," I said. "Before I shoot it off."

There was a gate in the hedge – not one a tractor could fit through, just a man and his dog, maybe. We sidled along the hedge until we reached it. I peeked around the hedge corner. The main yard had two cars. One was an old Ford Cortina that was in good repair. The other was a Honda Civic hatchback. I asked Crowley to take a look.

"Any of those Hognatt's?" I asked.

"No. I wouldn't know what he might turn up in, but those belong to the other team members."

Team members made them sound like office workers.

"Then we wait," I said.

I had another look. To the far side of the courtyard there was a stable where I could see one man smoking, the other chewing gum. They looked relaxed.

Another couple of minutes passed and I became more nervous.

"Does he turn up late? He doesn't seem the type that would."

"Ah, he might. Now and again."

Crowley seemed evasive. For the umpteenth time I held the gun up, pointing it at his upper chest.

"Look, man, he'll arrive in his own time."

"He better, because—"

The world went dark. I felt something knock the back of my legs and I fell to my knees.

"Drop it," a voice said and I could feel something hard against my skull.

I did consider shooting Crowley. Somehow, and I didn't know how exactly, he had betrayed me. Hognatt was waiting. I'd been bagged. The chord had been tightened around my neck, nearly choking me to unconsciousness. I dropped the gun.

"I warned you," Crowley said and I felt a punch to my left kidney.

I could feel two men drag me by my armpits. The tops of my toes trailed behind me.

I was hogtied.

I was lifted off my feet.

Not a word was spoken.

I landed on something hard, metal probably. I heard an echo. A door closed behind me.

"I'll call tonight," I heard Hognatt say from outside whatever I was in.

Another door closed. There was shaking, then considerable bumping. I was in the back of a jeep or a van. And I was being driven away to only God knew where.

I was alive. I could have been shot and dumped on that farm. I might have been found in some rusting tank, much like my father in that car boot. Could be that I'd never have been found.

We drove for what felt like twenty minutes. We only took a couple of turns. Then a final turn and the ground underneath was bumpy. Not gravel or rocks. Rough like driving through tractor tyre tracks.

The vehicle – car, van, truck, I couldn't say – finally came to a stop.

A door behind me opened. I could hear the hinges squeak.

Someone, something caught my feet and dragged me. I fell sideways onto the ground. My head hit the dirt with a thud. I was dazed and the bag over my head disoriented me entirely.

"Get up," Hognatt said. My arms and legs straightened out when Hognatt cut the hogtie. My hands were still tied together, but my legs were free.

I had difficulty getting up. The backs of my knees ached from Hognatt's heel-kick.

I had naively gone to get Hognatt, done considerable legwork, taken serious risks. All for nought.

Hognatt twisted my body like a top to face in a particular direction.

"Walk," he said and I felt something hard in my back. The distance he spoke from suggested that he was holding a shotgun, rifle, something with a lengthy barrel to my back.

I stumbled over a rut in the ground. Then I fell over a piece of wood or something.

"Get up you fat cunt!"

I struggled to my feet again and Hognatt gave me a shove forward.

"Mind your feet here," Hognatt said.

I took baby steps and found myself against a step. I carefully raised a foot to step up. Then another step and another.

Hognatt came to my side and I heard a door open.

"Go on," he said.

I walked a few more steps.

"Sit."

I had to take it on faith that a chair would break my fall. It did. The funny bones in my arms stung when they hit the wooden arms of the chair.

Hognatt loosened the drawstring and pulled the hood from my head. The light blinded me for a moment and my eyes watered.

A man was sitting opposite. A tall man, his arms high on a similar chair.

"Michael, Michael. It seems I have underestimated you."

I knew at once who it was.

It was Jordan.

We were in the house past Killeagh where we'd met before when Goulding was present.

Hognatt handed something to him. It was my gun. Jordan turned it over in his hands, examined it from all angles. He ejected the clip, counted the bullets and inserted the clip again.

"Such a crude weapon, Michael."

He handed it back to Hognatt.

"Nine-mil Walther," Jordan said. "A little pop-pop gun. Look at what my friend here is carrying."

Hognatt stood next to him with what I knew was an MP7. It was resting in his arms like a baby, the nozzle pointed diagonally to the ceiling, a scope on the top for mid-distance aiming.

"I'd see you as a P90 man, myself," Jordan said. "More up close and personal, but all the lethality of the MP7."

I don't know if Jordan was trying to impress me with his firearms knowledge, but it was wearing thin on me. The pain rose from my knees until it surged into my chest and became an outburst.

"I might have known you weren't retired," I said. "Fucking puppet master pulling all the strings. Robberies, the threat of murder, actual murder if I can assume Moolah was your handy work."

"Wait—" Jordan began.

"And to think I bought into your crap hook, line and sinker. Teaching MMA to disadvantaged kids. I mean, for fuck's sake what a brass neck."

"Wait, Michael. It's not how it seems. You're such a surface man. You don't look beneath. I'm much more nuanced than you give me credit for."

I stood out of the chair. Hognatt aimed the MP7 at me. I sat down again.

"I had nothing to do with Fitzmaurice's murder," Jordan said. "The rest … well, there is truth in it, I'll grant you. But for very different reasons than you might expect. Very different reasons."

He waved Hognatt away. Hognatt looked at him with a double-checking expression. Jordan confirmed his wave.

"Hognatt here is going to take a stroll around the garden. And I'm going to ask for your trust. If I was up to all you say I am up to, do you think you would still be alive?"

I blanked him. He was right, though.

Hognatt closed the door behind him. I had an opportunity to get up and take Jordan out. But Jordan got up first. He walked over to me.

"Hognatt can be a bit heavy handed."

He untied the rope around my hands. I grabbed his wrist tightly. Jordan looked at me with not an ounce of concern.

"Trust me, Michael. Trust me."

I let go of his wrist. Jordan returned to his seat.

"Let me begin," he said.

"No," I said. "I'll begin." I sat upright to show I meant business. "What the fuck happened in Churchfield? Did you sanction that and the knock to my head?"

Jordan put a hand to his chin and rubbed it.

"Yes and yes. Not to do you any harm, though I'm sure some was. The television sets were just vessels for drugs. Meth, to be precise. About half a million street value, I would estimate. I knew O'Brien was up to no good. So I took his televisions. I took his drugs. I wanted to stir things up to see what his movements would be after that."

"Hang on," I said, then stopped. I considered his admission that I was to be banged on the head. I thought about Cotter's suspicions about the link between Jordan, Solid Security and Druid. A triangle that I seemed to be the centre of.

"You own Solid Security?" I continued.

Jordan chuckled a little. "In a roundabout way."

"And Druid."

"Yes."

"Did you request me for the Druid assignment?"

"Yes."

There it was. Not even an attempt to evade the question.

"Did you even have something to do with me being hired by Solid?"

"Yes."

"So this headhunting, the HR guy that asked would I be interested what with me being an ex-Guard and all that – that was your doing?"

"Yes. Of course. Of course."

He said it like I was supposed to applaud. But he'd dragged me into this whole mess much like Hognatt and Crowley had dragged me on my heels like a slaughtered pig.

"You're not just the puppet master," I said. "You're the fucking guy who pulls the strings on the puppet master."

Jordan laughed a loud, long laugh.

"Ah, Michael. I see you are back on form. Good man. Good man."

I didn't join his laughter. I thought it was obscene.

Hognatt prised opened the door, peered in and closed it again.

"I get a bang on the head. I get all riled up ready for vengeance. You send O'Keeffe to kidnap me. You set it up so I couldn't say no to your offer."

"You've got it all figured out, Michael. You got me."

He held his hands above his head in symbolic surrender.

"But … but why?"

"Why?"

"Why me? Why go to all that trouble for a washed-up Guard like myself. You said it yourself. I was damaged goods."

Jordan leaned forward.

"You see there, Michael … *was*. You *were* damaged goods. But you're back in the groove now. I think my pep talk at the gym was the catalyst. Would you admit that much, Michael?"

I was going to admit shit to him. He was right, though. His words had stung and I'd resolved to sort myself out. And to stop taking things lying down. But something still didn't sit right with me.

"You dodged my question, Jim. Why me?"

Jordan stayed still and silent for a few moments. He eased into the chair and placed his hands back in that Abe Lincoln pose on the chair.

"I owed it to your mother," he said and I wasn't sure at first if I'd heard him correctly.

"I'm sorry. Did you say you owed my mother something?"

"I'll explain, Michael, but I'm going to ask you to give me a full hearing. Don't jump to conclusions until you have it all."

I nodded. I felt sick to my stomach. I just knew Dad would be in there somewhere.

"Your father was an inquisitive fellow. And that's putting it lightly. Always out for the big scoop. And he was good. I mean, really good."

He paused as if considering the exact word he needed. One that wouldn't send a spark onto the puddle of petrol I had become.

"Just to cut things off at the pass, to use one of my favourite expressions, I had nothing to do with your father's … rather unfortunate end. I'll swear on my daughter's life on that score. And you know how much I love my daughter."

I was stuck to the seat. My chest tightened and my breathing shallowed. I felt light-headed.

"Would you like a glass of water?"

I refused, told him to continue.

"The first time I met your father, he wasn't investigating me. He was investigating the underground bare-knuckle scene. He was barely in his job at the Standard a wet week. He'd started with tinkers to burst the myth of the king of the travellers. People thought travellers fought in some kind of challenge match to dethrone the current king. But it was all about cash. Thousands of pounds, even in those days."

One thing for sure about Jordan was that he could tell a story. To the point of making you want to spoon your eyes out. But I was riveted to my seat.

"You look a bit cold there, Michael. Can I get you a blanket?"

"No. Actually, yes."

Jordan got up and opened a large wooden chest next to the fire. He took out a tartan blanket. Something like the Queen might have put across her lap when trooping the colours in her carriage.

"Sensible man. Putting up a front only gets you so far."

He passed me the blanket and I draped it over my knees. They still ached, but the warmth of the blanket helped at least psychologically to ease the pain.

"One of the travellers told your father about the bare-knuckle matches I was involved with. I suppose it was an alternative to cock or dog fighting for the more civilized among us. That's a dichotomy if ever there was one. It was an all-comers invitational type event. You could buy in to a bout with your own money or have someone sponsor you."

Jordan's throat seemed to dry up as his words became hoarse, so he took a sip of water before continuing.

"I was only nineteen when I started fighting for cash. I'd fight in the Irish amateur championships one day, go bare-knuckle the next for cash. There was this guy, Paddy. I did odd jobs for him. A beating here and a delivery there. You know how it goes."

I nodded. It was his apprenticeship in the organized crime trade. Jordan was in full flow now.

"Paddy sponsored me. He'd pay the entry fee, give me a twenty-percent cut of the winnings after fees were deducted – referees and such. I never lost. I thought about asking for a bigger cut, but …"

"You didn't go asking Paddy for things he might not like you to ask for," I said.

Jordan nodded with soft, shallow nods. I can't say for certain, but I think there was regret in the way he looked and nodded. Like maybe he recognized he'd been the same way with many of his own men. Some of them had disappeared.

"I did OK out of the arrangement, though. I put some money aside and before long I had enough to start up my own small-scale enterprise. Just a bit of Mary Jane at first. Oh, those were the days."

I disliked his nostalgia for the good old days of drugs. I don't believe in *soft* drugs. My experience on the streets of Cork showed me they were gateways to harder stuff. Heroine, coke, meth. Glue if the money ran out.

When Jordan seemed to be on a transcendental plane, I interrupted him: "And my father?"

He snapped back into reality. "Patience, Michael. I'm almost there."

I reminded myself for the umpteenth time to breathe.

"It might have been my sixteenth or seventeenth fight. One of the last in fact. Your father showed up with a sponsor. Don't ask me how he got this sponsor to back him, but whoever it was put up the three-thousand to enter your father into the bout."

He paused again. He raised up a hand and slowly wagged a finger at me.

"I didn't know who your father was from Adam. And the rules of the fight are the rules of the fight. It was of no consequence to me then what happened to your father. Now, your father was in decent shape, but he was no fighter. No fighter. You have to understand, and I say this as someone who can call himself a true fighter, there's fighters who aren't fighters. Do you know what I mean?"

Despite his minced words, I did. Some fighters only fought the easy fights when they could. But when they had to go into the deep waters with a better opponent, they either drowned or came up too fast for air.

"Maybe I take that back to some extent," he said. "When I say your father was no fighter, I mean he lacked the skills. But he had heart and I respected him for that. He could take a beating, come back for more."

He looked at me. It was as if he was seeing beyond me.

"Like you, Michael. Like you."

He continued to look through me. It was almost trance-like. He only broke his glassy gaze when I spoke some half-minute later.

"And my father's death?"

"I had nothing to do with it. Absolutely nothing. Your father was like that annoying fly that gets trapped inside the windscreen of your car while you're driving. The one that, when you swipe at it, you keep missing and take your eye off the road."

"I don't follow."

"I mean, I would warn him off in the strongest non-violent terms. But it did not deter him. I had a soft spot for him after the whipping he took from me, so I tolerated him. Ultimately, it's probably what got him killed. That he didn't heed warnings."

I'd heard my Dad called reckless. Dirty too.

"Those that have blackened my father's name. Was he into anything? You know … illegal?"

He looked at me with coolness.

"If there is one thing on this good Earth – and it is good, Michael, believe me – one thing that you can believe without hesitation, it's that your father was clean. He got into murky waters more than once, but he always came out smelling of lavender, if you'll forgive my poor attempt at metaphor."

Except for that one time he didn't come out. He was left in the boot of that car not smelling of lavender but decay.

I thought about the note. The one that fell from *Billy Budd*.

"Does the name Starman mean anything to you?"

Jordan's chin lifted suddenly.

"Starman?"

"Yeah, Starman. And don't mention David Bowie or Jeff Bridges to me."

Jordan didn't seem to understand the name drops.

"In the context of your father, I know what Starman would mean."

He paused and I felt like getting out of the chair to rush over and shake it out of him.

"We used to call this guy Starman. He dealt in acid in those days. Tabs, microdots, postage stamps. Whatever you're into."

"Who was it, Jim?"

"He lived up in Farranree—"

"A fucking name!"

Jordan stopped, saw I meant business. I think if he had held out any longer I might have strangled him. What with it being my most basest of reactions and all that.

"Jimmy Dorgan."

The Eel. Starman and the Eel were one and the same. I put a hand to the back of my head, rubbed the nape of my neck.

"Need I ask?" Jordan said.

I shook my head. "It's for another time, I think. Something for me to deal with on my own."

"If you need help, you know where to call. But a warning on Jimmy – you don't mess with the Eel."

I could tell he meant it on both counts. Then I remembered what he had said a few minutes earlier.

"You said you owed my Mam … what did you mean by that?"

Jordan smiled. "Before your father knew your mother, I did. We grew up on the same lane together off Barrack Street. Not too far from The Lough. She was a gas girl. A real tease. She was a couple of years older and I had a big crush on her. But then my parents moved to Ballinlough and we lost touch."

It doesn't rain, but it pours.

I considered asking to go home. I thought I would just grab my stuff and leave the country. After I dealt with Jimmy the fixer. Assuming Jordan ordered Hognatt to give me back my gun.

However, I'd come so far that week. There was another outstanding issue.

"What about Moolah?" I asked.

"Poor old Johnny Fitzmaurice. He was an unfortunate casualty." He held up his palms to me. "But not at my hands – not even indirectly."

"Who then?"

"I've gone from puppet master to all-seeing, all-knowing deity have I? I don't know is the honest truth. But I have my suspicions."

"O'Brien?"

"That's possible. But I always got the sense that O'Brien didn't have the stomach for that kind of thing. Not like I did. Not like I did. He's not a fighter. You know what I mean, don't you?"

I nodded. He continued.

"It'll cost him in the end. You see, when you're on that mountain and the guy below you is hanging from a rope around your waist, you don't hesitate in cutting the rope."

I thought about Savage as a possibility for the murder, but didn't say anything.

"And the man with the red hair?" I asked.

"Doolin. A fatuous man, a fatuous man. All bluster. Thinks he amounts to something when he's not fit to grace the sole of my boot."

"You gave him a warning."

"Precisely. Precisely."

"Not a punishment beating."

Jordan smiled. "No. Just a warning to stop taking my name in vain."

Like the Lord. Maybe he did think of himself as a deity.

"And Hognatt?"

"Hognatt is a results-oriented man like myself. Very black and white, unlike myself now. Unlike you too, Michael, I would like to think."

I didn't know about that. I had become more black and white over the past week. I was done reasoning with people. I'd been discovering that a gun in the face is more effective than any of my old cute-hoorism. But I was sitting opposite Jordan, chastened, a mad man outside with an armour-piercing submachine gun.

"Did you know he had a machete in Churchfield?"

"I saw it in the police report."

"Do you condone that?"

"I cannot say I do and I cannot say I don't. Did he cut you with it?"

I shook my head. But you didn't just cut with a machete. You hacked.

"Then there's your answer. No harm done."

My arms tensed and I gripped the arms of the chair.

"Easy, Michael. Easy does it. I understand your perspective. Really I do. But desperate times sometimes call for desperate measures, as I often say. And if you knew what Hognatt had seen in Somalia, I think you'd understand."

I didn't think I would. But I'd graduated from fist to gun, hadn't thought twice about it, so maybe there was an atom of truth in there somewhere.

Jordan looked at his watch. "How time flies. It's getting on for seven-thirty. I'd say that was breakfast time, wouldn't you, Michael?"

I shook my head and tutted. I was only in the mood for going home.

"Come, come, Michael. A bit of grub, as you would probably say. It can only do us good."

He got up despite my protestations and went to the kitchen off the living room.

"There's plenty in the refrigerator, Michael. Plenty."

I walked into the kitchen. Jordan had the fridge door wide open. I could see an assortment of food, healthy and not. I could see black pudding on the bottom shelf. I don't think anyone would have blamed me for partaking.

Hognatt walked into the kitchen some time later when I was chewing a morsel of black pudding. Jordan had remarked how it was farm fresh. The old secret recipe of an old East Cork farmer. I didn't think there was better than the Clonakilty, but what I ate that morning gave it a good run for its money.

"Grab some breakfast, Matt," Jordan said. "Most important meal of the day, as I like to say."

He said it like he'd invented the received wisdom.

Hognatt took a saucepan from the draining board and retrieved three large eggs from the fridge. While Jordan and I continued talking, he made scrambled eggs with toast.

"You did some solid work tailing O'Brien to Limerick. Solid work. The man you photographed is an interesting man by the name of Moose. I think there's no more to the name than its similarity to Morrisroe, his real name."

It made sense to me. And I suppose it made sense that Jordan would have the resources, the connections to identify Moose.

"Interesting how?" I asked.

"Interesting in the sense that I respect his methods. He's canny. He doesn't sully himself with feuds. No tit-for-tat like the other Limerick gangs. To put it another way, he does what's best for business, and I can drink to that."

He lifted a glass of orange juice momentarily in salute, then took a sip of it. It bothered me the way he could celebrate thuggery, however calculated.

I knew much of this from speaking to Cotter, but I pretended like I knew none of it.

"So he's a gang leader?"

"Yes, Michael. And a good one at that. He started out small in Ennis. There's a parallel with myself that I find endearing. For me it was weed, but for Moose it was X."

"And now?"

Jordan nibbled on a slice of toast like a gerbil. While I was tucking into a full Irish, Jordan was satisfied with two small slices of toasted rye bread. He cleared his mouth.

"Now it's meth. At first he imported through his connections in Shannon. The kind of connections I would have envied back in the day. Port authority, shipping companies, customs – a clear path for his imports."

"And then?"

"Then he started to cook his own. Good purity. Ninety-five percent plus. But only in small batches and he's looking to expand."

"And you think O'Brien could help him?"

A look of disdain from Jordan.

"O'Brien piggybacked on my network. I had connections on the continent. Hard-earned connections. That's what Fitzmaurice was up to. Smuggling crystal from Spain via Mexico. He'd fly out to Spain and bring a load in on a chartered yacht. Nohoval

Cove was his last such trip."

"The stuff in the TVs?"

"Correct."

"That was destined for Moose?"

"That's what I believe, though I can't be certain. I *can* be certain that you photographed him giving Moose a sample from a new batch. I don't have any intel on that shipment or where O'Brien is keeping the stash."

Hognatt scraped the scrambled eggs onto a plate just as his toast popped.

There was a question that had been formulating in the back of my mind about me minding Druid on my lonesome.

"If there was half a mill in drugs just lying around the warehouse in Churchfield, then why just the one security guard?"

"I asked myself the same question. At first I wondered if he didn't want to draw suspicion, satisfied with hiding the drugs in plain sight. But that would be to give the idiot too much credit. Then I heard some chatter."

Jordan took another bite. Even in retirement – if I could believe that – Jordan had his contacts. Jordan cleared his mouth with a sup of orange juice. He continued.

"It seems O'Brien has some Guards on his payroll. Our belief," he said nodding his head in Hognatt's direction, "is that they were patrolling the area to keep an eye on the goods. Matt here had done his reconnaissance."

Hognatt sat at the table to eat his scrambled eggs. He had eaten only a single mouthful when Jordan brought him into the conversation.

"Tell him about that night, Matt. About how we nearly called it all off. The whole thing was done at such short notice. I had only learned of the drugs that morning."

Hognatt looked at me like I didn't belong at the table, then looked at Jordan. He didn't waste any more time.

"Two hours before the operation I checked the perimeter of the distribution centre, assessing the fencing, the lighting, the view from other buildings."

I realized then that Hognatt had been out there that evening. He'd watched me pace around, smoking my cigarettes, urinating, scratching myself no doubt. I felt violated.

"It didn't take long," Hognatt continued, "to realize that there were two separate patrol cars keeping an eye on the place – one marked, the other unmarked. I timed the distance between them – always at least six minutes and never more than eight. But it wasn't like clockwork, so I couldn't be certain of any gap."

The first marked Garda car had arrived only a few minutes after I made the call. It had seemed suspicious then, but now I knew why. Savage and Dominic arrived two minutes later in their unmarked car. Again I made the decision to keep Savage for myself. Could have been that Jordan knew about him anyway.

"There's great credit due to Hognatt for the precision of the operation," Jordan said. "He assured me that they could get it done in less than four minutes."

After the crack on the skull, my command of time awareness had been unreliable, but I could well believe it had been done in that time.

"We didn't mess around," Hognatt said. "As soon as the unmarked car was out of sight, I cut through the fencing on the eastern side to distract you, Bosco. So that Crowley could stop you raising the alarm. The others came through the gate in the van."

Jordan chipped in with an impish wink. "A little inside knowledge helped with the keypad on the gate."

Hognatt finally had a chance to properly tuck into his eggs, which he did with gusto. The smell of his ultra-strong coffee nearly knocked me out. African beans, no doubt.

Jordan had admitted to taking the drugs. What I needed to know was if he had done so for profit. At the expense of the tweakers on the street for whom meth was a scourge.

"What happened to the TVs and their contents?" I said, directing the question to Jordan.

"I've got them in a safe place. But don't worry, Michael, I have no plan to gain from them financially. Let's just say for now that they are part of a larger plan. And before you enquire any further, I plan on involving you in my plan, so you'll have all the details in due course. But things are strictly need to know for now, as I'm sure you'll understand."

I did. But I could feel my veins hardening again with the frustration.

"You're asking me to take a lot on faith here, Jim. Up to now I've been a pawn in your megalomaniacal fantasy. Now I'm going to be what?"

"Once again, Michael, patience, patience. I said you'll have all the details in time. I didn't say I wouldn't give you any details now. I can tell you that Morrisroe, despite appearances, will be an asset. He just doesn't know it yet."

"And the drugs you kept are your leverage?"

"Need to know, Michael. Need to know."

Jordan's mobile phone rang. His ring tone was the *Rocky* theme tune. I wasn't surprised.

"Terence," Jordan said. He listened intently to what was obviously Goulding on the other end. "Uhuh. Uhuh."

Hognatt sat calmly by eating his eggs. He took a slice of toast and cut it into strips. Into soldiers. I thought things couldn't get any more surreal, but then I reminded myself that they most certainly could.

"Oh," Jordan said. "Uhuh. They found what?"

I looked at Jordan. There was concern on his face. It worried me.

Jordan held up a hand to me or Hognatt or both of us, I couldn't quite tell. Be with you in a minute, I assumed it meant.

I got some more fragments from Jordan's end: "By the marina"; "When do they think it happened?"; and then the one that made my back straighten up, "And cause of death?"

Jordan finally thanked Goulding for the call and hung up. Hognatt had sat there for a few seconds with a forkful of egg halfway between his plate and his gob. I felt like a statue again, my legs somehow growing into the chair.

"There's been a development," Jordan said. He looked at me.

"Michael, would you mind waiting outside for a minute while I talk to Matt?"

I stared at him for a moment. Then I thought, what with Hognatt and his gang of mercenaries, that I'd sod this for a game of soldiers.

"You've got to be fucking kidding me," I said. "There's no way I'm going out that door, so you better tell me what the fuck Goulding was telling you about. Who's been killed?"

Hognatt looked down to his plate to avoid eye contact with anyone. Jordan gave me a look that suggested I had crossed a line, but only by a small enough amount that I could move the line with me.

"OK, Michael. Let's go with the unedited version. But you've a habit of jumping to conclusions, so please keep your counsel like a good man. Like a good man."

I nodded.

"Terence has just told me that a body has been found by the boat club on the Marina. A dog walker came across it yesterday evening. The ID has been confirmed as Brendan Doolin."

Hognatt looked up from his plate suddenly. Doolin. The red-haired card sharp. He'd been threatened by Hognatt less than half a day earlier.

"And the MO," I asked.

Jordan just shook his head.

"The MO, Jim," I said.

Jordan took his time about speaking. "According to Terence, the cause of death was strangulation."

I'd have been lying if I said I was surprised. First Moolah, then Brick, and now Doolin. I knew there was a connection from Jordan to Moolah and Doolin, one way or another. But Brick? I didn't think there was. Strangely enough, Jordan attempted to answer the question for me.

"You came across a gentleman by the name of Alan Brick before, didn't you, Michael?"

This is it. The moment Jordan reveals Brick as a piece on his crooked little chessboard.

"I wouldn't call him a gentleman. He's small beans. Prescription pills, ecstasy."

Jordan nodded. "Yes. Of no concern. But odd that he was strangled also, don't you think?"

Now things were beginning to click into place for me. Somehow Jordan was going to hang me – in the sense that I was to be his fall guy to take heat off him.

"Look, Jim, there's obviously some attempt to try and fit me up. I know how it looks, but—"

"I know"

"What?"

"I know you are being made a patsy."

Was he admitting to being the one behind the fit up? The puppet master pulling his strings?

"How do you know?"

"Call it intuition. I've gotten to know you, Michael. And I'm a good judge of character. Besides …" He took a sip of orange juice. "The evidence collected from the latest murder is too convenient."

"Evidence?"

"Hair between the man's fingers. Dried blood under his fingernails."

I didn't follow.

"Stand up, Michael."

I didn't. I just stared at him.

"Please, indulge me. Trust me."

He stood. I decided I would trust him and stood up. My knees ached again.

Jordan went behind me and I had a clear vision then of my demise at the hands of The Gentleman. He would throttle me, cut the blood supply to my brain. Maybe put me in a bed next to Chambers.

Instead he examined my head, parted the hair.

"Savage had a good go at you, didn't he? Drew blood from you."

I nodded as he came back to face me. I remembered the pain

in my jaw and spitting cheek blood on the ground.

"And Dominic, his eager sidekick, held you?"

Again I nodded.

"He pulled your hair?"

I was too stunned to nod. He'd grabbed a good hold of it. Probably took a chunk of it with him.

Jordan said: "And now hair and blood at the Doolin crime scene. Evidence when there had been none before."

"Jesus Christ."

"When exactly were you going to tell me about Sergeant David Savage?"

"I don't see—"

"Come on, Michael. You've been holding things back from me since the beginning. Savage, Moose, Doolin. What was your plan?"

I looked at him. I didn't have the wherewithal to form an expression.

"I don't believe you had one, did you, Michael? You've been making it up as you go along. I mean, you can't arrest them. Were you going to shoot them?"

He had my gun. How could he have concluded any different. And maybe he was right. Maybe I was so thirsty for vengeance that I would have fired the damn thing, gunned someone down that I felt deserved it. Maybe Halloran was right: I wasn't just the Bruce Lee of Cork, I was the Batman of Cork, a vigilante bent on mayhem.

"Well I can't shoot them now," I said.

Jordan sighed.

"I thought you were a man of subtlety. Isn't that what I said when we first met? That I didn't have such men in my employ. I'm disappointed, Michael, really disappointed."

Hognatt left the table and rinsed his plate under the tap. Like O'Keeffe, Hognatt was a speak when spoken to type of guy.

"I'm sorry to disappoint, Jim, but I wasn't exactly a willing employee, was I? You inveigled your way into my brain, planted the seed of revenge. I wanted to mind my own business, had done for a couple of years, planned to for the rest of my days. It was pitiful, but I was only of harm to myself, no one else. But you fucked all of that up for me. You're responsible for all of this."

Jordan seemed taken aback by what I said. "I gave you a second chance, Michael. A second chance. I had such plans for us. You have no idea."

He got up and took his plate and glass to the sink, then returned for mine. He plugged the sink, turned on the hot tap and reached for the Fairy liquid.

"I have some thinking to do, Michael. If they can link you to the murders, then they can link me by extension. They can play the conspiracy card." He turned his back to me and began to wash the dishes. "Hognatt will take you home. Wait for my call. I'm not done with you yet."

I thought better of speaking. I followed Hognatt to his jeep. I noticed O'Keeffe sitting in a car. When he saw us getting into Hognatt's jeep, O'Keeffe got out of his car and walked towards the house to take up his position as Jordan's bodyguard.

Hognatt drove me back to Blackpool with not a word exchanged between us.

13

Apples and Bananas

THERE WERE NO GUARDS waiting for me at home. But Savage and Halloran would be biding their time gleefully. It took time to process evidence for DNA, then to match it and get a warrant. However, I knew time was running out.

I had felt for just a brief while, just a couple of days really, that things were in my own hands. That I'd wrangled them like wild horses until they had been tamed. But I'd only held a gun to the horses' heads, forced their compliance. Now the gun was gone and the horses were stampeding.

My DNA would probably be available from evidence in the Chambers inquiry to match to the new evidence. If my hair and blood had been planted at the Doolin crime scene, it would be hard to deny that it was at my hands. There was no one to alibi me. I had been following Hognatt and his crew in my car. There would likely be CCTV footage from the area showing me driving around. The Transit van would have been of no consequence in that footage. There were also witnesses that could put me with Doolin at the card game not long before he was killed.

I felt very alone then. Felt that I had no one to turn to. Cotter would no longer be able to shield me from the other Guards if there was evidence linking me to Doolin. Mogs was still in hospital. I wasn't going to put my mother in harm's way. And I didn't even have my gun for company.

I knew there was one person I had been able to open up to like I had never done before. Someone in whose company I felt very comfortable. That was Grace. It didn't seem so important then that Jordan might end me for getting involved with his daughter. For dragging her down into my murk. He had other reasons to do that now.

I took out my phone. I looked in the call history for her number and moved my index finger to the call button. I paused. This was madness. It was selfish. But I hit the button anyway.

"Michael?"

Hearing her voice was like ten doses of Valium.

"Hi Grace. I'm sorry for calling."

"Why are you sorry?"

"I'm trouble, Grace. I'm bad news. You can do well without the likes of me calling you up."

"What are you talking about, Michael? Are you OK?"

I thought for a moment. Open up or shut down?

"Actually, I'm … I'm not OK. But I'm better now that I can hear your voice. Have you spoken to your father?"

"Not for a couple of days. He's been pretty busy with the new academy. What's wrong? Why are you not OK?"

"I don't want to involve you, Grace. I just wanted to hear your voice."

"You're starting to scare me, Michael."

"Don't be scared. I'm going to be just fine."

"Does this have something to do with my father? Because if—"

"No, Grace. Your father is actually a pretty decent man under it all. He's seen right by you, you know."

"Then what is it?"

"This isn't a great idea, Grace. They might trace the call back to you. And I don't want you to get caught up in all of this."

"All of what? Why won't you tell me what's going on?"

"Because ..." *I love you.* "... you're a good person. Too good for the likes of me."

"Michael—"

"Goodbye, Grace."

I hung up before the pain in my throat took my voice away, before the tears came. I turned off the phone and gave myself a minute to finish crying before wiping my eyes and steeling myself. Talking to Grace was just the fillip I needed. It was high time I copped on to myself and started acting rationally. Having a gun had made me feel invincible. But Grace had highlighted my vulnerability and it made me think straight again.

I was being framed for something I did not commit. I would have to do my damnedest to ensure that the culprit was revealed. Somehow Savage's actions had to come to light. But how? I had no evidence. All I had was hearsay, the conversation in Carrignavar, which from the mouth of the accused would seem like desperation.

I didn't feel like waiting around to be arrested. I decided a trip to the local was a good idea. I'd drown my mental hurt with drink, I decided. If I was to go down, it was down into oblivion I would go.

I sat at the bar in An Capall Bán. I ordered a Howling Gale. I was given a fresh pint, the head nice and white and frothy. I sipped it and closed my eyes. Heaven. It would be the first of many, I resolved.

I turned the phone back on. There were three missed calls and one voice message from Grace. I decided the time wasn't right to listen to it. I decided that if an arrest happened and I was thrown in jail, that I never would. I'd refuse her visits. I'd tear up her mail. It would be too painful. A reminder of what I could not have. Besides, I didn't deserve a happy life. I was no less a piece of dross than Savage.

Jordan had asked me to wait for his call, so I left it on. I mulled over this point. Jordan still wanted to talk. But about what? Surely at this point I was dead to him.

"Are you well, Mickey?" the barman said absently as he dried pint glasses.

I thought about his question. I considered telling him about the hurricane of hurt I had endured. Poor me, I would say. I'm to be pitied. The world and his granny have it out for me. Instead I did the opposite.

"Fantastic, Willy. Just fantastic. I've chased villains, been a high roller, and met the girl of my dreams. A girl as beautiful inside as she is out. A girl who would make me happy even if the entire world was desolated by a zombie apocalypse as long as she was still in it. A girl I … I have fallen in love with."

Willy raised his eyebrows and eased back from the bar. He wanted no part of my mania.

A voice from behind: "In love with?"

Holy Christ in Heaven. It was Grace. I turned around. She stood there with a look of anger.

"Grace … my God, what are you doing here?"

But I knew. I had turned off the phone. She was worried. She knew where I was because I had joked about An Capall Bán over dinner. About how despite it being full of the Northside's detritus, I was still proud to call it my local.

"You said in love with. You barely know me, Michael."

There was truth to that at a surface level. But I'm a believer in soul mates. It took Grace for me to believe it, but I was certain of it then. There was a harmony between us that couldn't just be pure chance. I was like a planet orbiting around a star. I felt like I *knew* her.

"I'm sorry, Grace. I didn't mean for you to hear that. It was just … it was just the ramblings of a washed-up loser."

She grabbed a stool and sat next to me. She nodded to the barman. "G and T, please."

"Look, Grace, you'd be better off just going before—"

"Before what? And you better start talking, Michael. I don't want any of this closed-book shit."

She cursed. I'd never heard her do it before. It shocked me more than when Hognatt put the bag over my head.

"You don't—"

"I do. Start talking or so help me God I'll walk out that door and you'll never see me again. Tell me what's wrong."

I looked at Willy. He may have caught some of the conversation. There was to be no shaking Grace, so I would give her the full story. Damn and be damned. Lay it all on the line and see if she was still sitting there by the end. And if she was, maybe then we had a chance.

Willy served Grace's G and T and we took our drinks to a quiet corner. A fire was lighting and smoke billowed out now and again as gusts came down the chimney.

"I'll tell you all, Grace, but I don't think you'll like it. I don't think you'll like me after the story either."

So I told her everything. The robbery in Churchfield. Her father's mercenaries and how they had ripped off O'Brien and terrorized Doolin. The tailing of O'Brien and how it had revealed Sergeant Savage as corrupt. My encounter with the Eel and how the gun changed me. How Moolah, Brick and Doolin had all been murdered by strangulation, the same method I'd used on Chambers to put him in a coma. About the likely fit up for the murders – about the fight, the tearing of my hair, the drawing of blood and the planting of evidence. I told her about taking Crowley and his girlfriend hostage, about tracking down Hognatt, how he had blindsided me, bagged me and taken me to her father. I told her about her father's admission that he had beaten up my Dad and as a result had a soft spot for me. Lastly, I told her I had been warned off her. That I was a lame horse fit for termination.

"Is that all?" she said. I thought I might have detected the merest smile.

"You want to hear how I shot JFK too?"

Then she did smile. Properly. "That's a lot to have bottled up. I can see why you came here for a pint."

"You seem to be taking this in your stride. I mean, what I told you about your father …"

She laughed. "My father. Yes, my father."

I don't think she needed to elaborate. She had been making allowances for him for years. I wished I knew what that was like – having a father to make allowances for. I think I'd have tolerated a lot just to have mine around for one more day.

"Like I said … you shouldn't be around me. I'm like a freshly painted fence – you lean on me, you're going to get paint on your dress."

She sighed. "Enough with the metaphors, Michael. My father got you into this mess, he damn sure better get you out of it."

"What do you mean?"

"I mean we are going to drive out to Killeagh right now and sort things out. Everything. I know what he says to people, about everyone being on their own when it comes to the Guards. Well, I've had enough of his bunker mentality. We're going to Killeagh and we're going to sort it."

She got up from her seat. I didn't.

"Michael … up you get."

She held a hand out to me. I hesitated before taking it.

"Your father isn't a man to be trifled—"

"Ah, trifle, schmifle. I'll put him straight. In case you didn't know it, he listens to me. I mean, he doesn't have anyone else. He's so paranoid that he's shut everyone else out. That's why I think he reached out to you. I think he craved a kindred spirit of sorts. Someone he could respect enough to be himself with."

"He did seem rather disappointed I let him down."

"You see? He doesn't get disappointed by people. They simply live up to his expectations, or lack thereof. He talks about you differently. Maybe … maybe that's the real reason he doesn't want to see us together. Because if it didn't work out, he could lose the both of us."

"You better be right, Grace. Because if you're not, he has a private army that can make me disappear."

"Just trust me."

Jordan said that a lot too. The other Jordan. I had to remind myself that she was a Jordan. She was his heir, his only child. But what if it really did come down to a choice between Jim Jordan and me? A gun to the head kind of a choice. I didn't know the answer.

She held my hand all the way to her Volvo outside.

"Are you sure about this?" I said.

"Yes," she said with a certainty that put me at ease.

We got into her car and she drove down Blarney Street and on towards Killeagh.

When we arrived at Jordan's bungalow, O'Keeffe got out of his car.

"It's OK, William. Michael and I are just going in to have a civilized chat with my father."

He looked at her with his eyebrows raised. I don't think he bought the *civilized* part of what she said. All the same, he didn't get in our way.

Jordan was still inside. He was sitting at the kitchen table reading The Irish Times. When he looked up from his paper, for the first time ever I saw surprise in his eyes.

"Daddy," Grace said. "We need to talk."

"Then you'd better sit."

Grace sat opposite her father. I sat next to her.

"Michael has told me everything."

A look from Jordan that said I was dead meat.

"Stop it," Grace said. "I'm tired of all these secrets. Stop being so fucking paranoid."

Even the second time she cursed I was shocked. I mean, the F word coming from her usually cultured mouth!

"I have every reason to be paranoid," he said. "Have you any idea how many have lined up over the years to take a pot shot at me? Do you know how much of a struggle it is to maintain a sunny disposition with all of that heaped on top of me?"

"I know, Daddy, but you've got to let me in at some point. You never let Mum in. And look what—"

Jordan quickly put up a hand to stop her. I held Grace's hand under the table out of his view.

Jordan said, "I know what happened to your mother. It's been eating away inside of me. I've never been able to trust anyone since. But look at me, Grace … I'm still here. I have the Guards running around in circles."

I chipped in. "What about O'Brien?"

He looked displeased with my interruption. "O'Brien is small beans, as you like to say. Leave him to me."

At this point, I decided Grace and her father needed some sorting out time. Besides, my bladder was fit to burst after the pint of Howling Gale and the drive to Killeagh.

"Excuse me," I said. "I need to visit the little boys' room."

Along the hall to the bathroom, I could see pictures on the wall. Jordan, Grace and another woman, obviously her mother, were in them. Some were taken against the backdrop of famous monuments: the leaning tower in Pisa, the Colliseum in Rome, the Acropolis in Athens. It made me wonder why Grace's skin was so alabaster white, while Jordan's glowed like Sunny Delight. In the bathroom I could hear the conversation continue in the kitchen. It seemed to get heated, then quietened down again.

When I went back to the kitchen, both were smiling.

"Michael, Michael," Jordan said. "You have been too quick to judge me. Grace tells me you think I'm going to feed you to the wolves. Nothing could be further from the truth."

I looked at Grace. She nodded.

Jordan continued. "I have a plan, you see. A plan. Not just for O'Brien, but one to solve your own little problem with the Guards."

"What is it?" I asked.

"Patience, Michael. Let's go outside for some fresh air. I always find it brings new perspective on things."

He got up from the table and ushered us out into the garden.

It was bitterly cold and our breaths were so foggy that we would disappear from each other's view momentarily. Jordan walked towards a tree in the middle of the back garden.

"My wife planted that tree," he said. "I think it's supposed to be an apple tree, but I've never seen it bear fruit."

"It did one year, Daddy," Grace said. "I remember Mum cut down an apple and gave it to me. All I can remember is how bitter it was."

"Must have been a cooking apple so," Jordan said. "Happy times. But only inside that bubble we created."

"You mentioned the stash," I said, attempting to get the conversation back on the plan.

"Always the pragmatist, Michael," Jordan said. "Always with the eyes on the prize. Much like the bare-knuckle fighter." He stopped under the tree where the leaves had browned and some littered the grass. He looked down. "These need raking."

"The plan, Daddy," Grace said.

"Yes, the plan. The stash is hidden in the Cardoso banana wholesaler down by Tivoli docks. Let's just say that it wasn't only bananas we imported back in the day, so we have our little hidey-holes."

Jordan kicked at some of the leaves.

"Where do I come into the plan, Jim?" I asked.

He looked at Grace, then back at me.

"You will stay with us. Hognatt will get in touch when the operation is complete."

Grace seemed calm. I wondered if she had spoken to Jordan about keeping me out of harm's way. She would have had the opportunity when I needed to go for a piss earlier.

"Hang on," I said. "Savage might be there. He's trying to frame me. Do you really think I can stay here and just hope for the best?"

He looked at his daughter. I sensed some resignation in his eyes. But Grace was having none of it.

"Michael. Are you mad?" she said. "Hognatt and his men are trained for this kind of thing. You could—"

"You're forgetting I was a Guard, Grace. I can handle myself."

It didn't seem to reassure her. She turned to her father.

"Talk some sense into him, Daddy. He could … he could get himself killed."

Jordan sized me up. He obviously made the judgement that I wasn't going to budge. I think maybe he respected me for it.

"I'm sorry, Grace," he said. "A man's gotta do what a man's gotta do, as I often say."

Grace gave me a cold look that warmed up as she spoke to me. "You better not take any chances, Michael Bosco. Or you'll have me to deal with when you get back."

I smiled. "I'll just stay behind Hognatt and his MP7."

The van could be heard arriving out front.

"That'll be Hognatt. Let's go over the finer details with him, Michael." He turned to his daughter. "You don't need to be involved in this. Why don't you go inside and prepare lunch?"

Grace pondered what he said for a moment. "No. I'm done with you shielding me from the business end of things. I need to know more than just the numbers."

Jordan took a little time to consider what she said. I guessed he'd kept her at a distance from the compromises that needed to be made when running such a large business empire.

"OK," he said.

We walked around to the front of the house. Hognatt was standing next to a white van. Another new one. He was dressed in dark clothing – black leather jacket and dark grey camouflage cargo pants. He wore black Doc Martins, of course. He wasn't carrying a weapon, but I assumed there was an arsenal in the back of the van.

"Hello, Matt," Jordan said. "Let's go over the plan again for Michael and my daughter's benefit. And, by the way, Michael will be going with you. But for God's sake make sure he stays well behind you."

Hognatt gave Jordan another of his questioning looks, then looked at me.

"He's dead weight, Mr Jordan. What if things go south?"

Jordan chuckled. "Just make sure they don't then. Besides, he can – how did you put it, Michael? – *handle* himself."

Jordan gestured for Hognatt to open the side door of the van. Hognatt slid it back. Inside was a holdall and a small rucksack.

Hognatt nodded towards the bags. "MP7s, goggles, walkie-talkies and flashbangs. Crystal in the rucksack."

"Good, good," Jordan said. "Then let's go through the finer details."

"Moose has arranged to meet O'Brien at nine to collect two kilos of ice. What O'Brien doesn't know is that we've offered Moose five kilos just to draw O'Brien out into the open with his stash. Moose said he wanted to meet with O'Brien personally at the handover, so it gives us the perfect opportunity to set him up."

It sounded like a decent plan, but I wondered if Moose could be trusted.

"How do we know Moose won't double-cross? Maybe he fancies seven kilos and the continued supply of meth from O'Brien."

Jordan nodded. "Like I said, Michael, you are a canny man. I can't give you a one-hundred percent guarantee. But I trust Morrisroe. I've explained to him that, one way or another, O'Brien is going down."

"The other way being a hole in the ground?" I probed.

Jordan shook his head. "That's not how I operate anymore, Michael. Let's just say that O'Brien would have gone to sleep in his bed one night and woken up somewhere in Eastern Europe the next morning. With a bundle of cash and a note telling him that it was in his family's interest that he enjoy an extended holiday."

It seemed Jordan would go out of his way now to avoid murder. But the threat of thuggery was still thuggery in my estimation.

"What happens when we have O'Brien and the drugs together? And what about Savage?"

I'd used the word *we*. I was part of this now. And the last time I had felt part of anything bigger than myself was in the Guards.

"Go on, Matt," Jordan said.

Hognatt continued with the plan. "Let's deal with O'Brien first. And this is where you come in, Bosco. I believe you are friendly with a Guard named Barry Cotter? He's an organized crime cop, right?"

I nodded.

Hognatt went on. "You'll tip him off about a time and location. But we'll already have suppressed the site. They'll be presented with O'Brien on a plate."

I wondered whether it would work. Cotter knew I was up to something. The photo of Moose was proof enough of that. I guessed – no, I knew – that Cotter would come good if I gave him what I said was solid intel.

"The MP7s, the flash grenades … are they strictly necessary?"

Jordan added his two cents at that point. "Fail to plan, plan to fail, as I like to say. There's no way O'Brien is walking away tonight. If O'Brien smells a rat, takes an early bath, then we'll take him and carry out plan B."

I assumed plan B meant shipping him out in a container or something. Using his *contacts* in the Tivoli docks, no doubt.

"And Savage?"

"There's a chance he might turn up at the meet, but I doubt it. We'll get to him beforehand."

"How?"

Hognatt spoke. "Jimmy Dorgan – I believe you know him as the Eel – has been on his payroll for years. He tipped off Savage about Doolin."

I nodded. That more or less confirmed to me that Savage had gone so far to the dark side that he was willing to kill with his bare hands to fit me up. And likely his intention was to implicate Jordan to give the NBCI and the CAB every opportunity to take him down.

Hognatt continued. "Dorgan will plant some information for us. Something that will get Savage to a location of our choosing."

"What information?" I asked.

"That you are meeting with his pal Sham to pick up an assault rifle."

It made sense. I'd graduated from fist to gun and gotten nowhere. Graduating from handgun to assault rifle was a natural next step. For the Batman of Cork, anyway.

"Again … how can we trust Jimmy?"

Hognatt smiled. "A bag over the head can be very persuasive."

The bag. The pistol. The threat of a swim with Davy Jones.

"So we get Savage to a location … then what?"

"We grab him. We take him to the meet in Charleville with us. We literally tie him to the drug deal."

It would tie him to the drugs, get him arrested, but the planted evidence was still out there.

"What about Doolin? What about the DNA?"

Jordan spoke. "Goulding is a master of the dark arts. I've no doubt he'll have you out on bail at the very least, if it comes to it. Remember what I said about everyone for themselves with the Guards?"

I nodded.

"I'm suspending that indefinitely. That was the old me talking. Remember what you said the first time we met about not having that trust gene in your DNA? Well, I'm trying to discover mine. Grace will help me find it."

We went over some more details. About nabbing Savage. About the meet near Charleville, the roads in and out, the specific instructions for the crew members such as positions to take up when the van door opened. It was a thorough plan that I believed had a good chance of success.

All that was needed on my part was to play the role of bait for Savage and then call Cotter to tell him where to pick up the pieces at the end of the night operation.

14

Two Syllables is One Too Many

THE HOURS BEFORE THE Savage op started were excruciating. There was very little conversation among myself, Jordan, Grace, Hognatt and O'Keeffe.

At about twenty minutes past one, Hognatt made the call to the Eel. He gave the time and location where I was supposedly collecting an assault rifle from Sham – five o'clock in the blocked lane to a demolished factory in Little Island.

Finally at four, Hognatt gave the go ahead. We went to the van outside and I got in the passenger seat. The location was only about a fifteen-minute drive. It would only be myself and Hognatt for the first operation.

"What if there's more than just Savage?" I asked.

"There won't be."

"How can you be so sure?"

"Jimmy told him that he'd get no more intel if Sham was nicked by the Guards. What Savage thinks is going to happen is that Sham will turn the weapon on you and wait for him to arrive. He arrests you for possession of a deadly weapon and sends Sham on his merry way with some cash for his trouble."

"And you get to play the part of Sham?"

He nodded. "It's simple really. I turn the MP7 on him and unless he's lost his marbles, he should surrender."

"There's a lot of ifs and maybes about tonight, though?"

"You always allow a margin of error on any operation. You always need an exit strategy."

"And you have those?"

Hognatt just grunted as if my question was an insult to his years of training and combat experience. But I wondered if any of the exit strategies involved shooting his way out of trouble. Killing a Guard, dirty or not, was liable to get you put inside a prison for the rest of your days.

We arrived at the old lane with twenty-five minutes to spare. We drove by to ensure Savage wasn't already there. It looked clear. We turned around and drove up the lane. It was lined with thick hedging and would make a good funnel.

Hognatt said, "There's a nice hoodie in the back. By Mantaray, I think. Just in case he knows what Sham looks like."

"And if he suspects something's up?"

"It'll be too late anyway. I'll have the gun pointed at him with the scope to my eye. And I don't miss."

We got out. Hognatt went to the back, donned the hoodie, and took an MP7 from the holdall bag. He pointed it at me.

"Don't worry," he said. "The safety's on. I'll only take it off once Savage arrives."

We stood like that for twenty minutes.

"Your arms must be tired," I said.

He shook his head. "I can hold this up for hours."

A minute or so later a car passed by the lane.

"Someone had a good look up here," Hognatt said. "Get ready."

The car came back and drove part-way up the lane before stopping. A man got out of the car and approached.

"Sham?" he said from about fifty yards away.

I was caught off guard. It wasn't Savage. But I knew the voice. I'd heard it that night in Churchfield. It was Dominic.

Hognatt nodded. Dominic approached a bit more.

"Good man," Dominic said. "I'll take it from here."

"You will in your fuck," Hognatt said and turned the gun on him.

Dominic froze. He seemed coiled, ready to run.

"Down on your fucking knees," Hognatt shouted. "Now!"

Dominic didn't move. Hognatt walked forward slowly. About twenty yards between them. Dominic looked to one side and then the other. The kid had some balls on him – he made a run for a gap in the hedge between him and me.

At the Bridewell he'd surprised me, taken me from behind. Now I was ready for him. I charged towards him. Dominic tried to climb over the ditch to go through the gap in the hedge, but I grabbed a leg. Then I grabbed the other so that I had a hold of him around his knees. He struggled and I pulled myself along his body until I mounted him.

"Bosco!" Hognatt said.

I struggled with Dominic. I took his back, rode him. I wrapped my arms around his right arm and his head. It was like the choke hold O'Keeffe had on Jordan in the cage. I squeezed.

"Bosco! Let him go. I have him."

I squeezed harder. Dominic tried to buck me off. I applied more pressure. He went limp. With Chambers I'd lost control, choked him for too long, denied his brain oxygen to the point of brain damage. But I let go of the rag doll that Dominic had become.

I got up and looked at a disbelieving Hognatt. "He's all yours, Matt."

Hognatt took a bag from his back pocket, placed it on Dominic's head. He tightened the drawstring.

"Jesus, how many of those things do you have?" I said.

Hognatt shrugged me off. He put plastic ties around Dominic's ankles and wrists and tightened hard. We carried him to the van and dumped him in. Like a piece of rubbish. Hognatt chained his arms and legs to the wall of the van.

Where Savage had gone was a mystery. Dominic had some

questions to answer when he came to.

Hognatt spoke. "Mr Jordan's right. It seems you are easily underestimated." He searched Dominic's pockets and threw a set of keys to me. "Follow me in his car. We'll dump it out of sight."

We drove off and I followed Hognatt deeper into Little Island.

Hognatt drove the van to the end of a road through one of Little Island's oldest industrial estates. We arrived at what looked like a storage area for tools and machine parts. Several shipping containers, some full-length, others half-length, were stacked at odd angles. Most were open, but some were locked with padlock and chain.

Hognatt got out of his van and came to my window.

"You can drive right in there," he said pointing to one of the half-length twenty-foot containers. "There's room enough to get out if you park it tight to the left side."

I drove Savage's Mondeo into the container and used the passenger wing mirror as a guide, scraping it on the corrugated interior of the container. I had about a foot and a half on the driver side to open the door and squeeze out, though it was a tight fit with my gut.

Hognatt came over to the container doors.

"I assume you'd like a chat with our friend in the back of the van. Do you know him?"

"His name's Dominic. I don't know his second name. Savage has been showing him the ropes. I wasn't sure if he was dirty or not, but I guess he answered that question himself."

Hognatt nodded. "That was some stroke he pulled, trying to escape. That move you put on him … where did you learn that?"

I didn't want to get into the story about the display in the cage, so I blew him off.

"I just hugged him and squeezed the bejaysus out of him. I'm not sure how much I had left in my arms when he passed out."

"Well, he woke up a couple of minutes ago. He's just lying there, not a word out of him."

"You going to lock the doors?"

Hognatt nodded. He went to the back door of the van, opened it and took out a chain and a padlock. He came back to the container and closed the doors. He locked the handles in place and wrapped the chain around the steel poles attached to both doors. As he applied the padlock I thought I heard something – an echoey metallic sound.

"Did you hear that," I said.

"Hear what?"

I held up a hand to get Hognatt to stay still. "Listen."

A few seconds passed. Traffic from the N25 Cork-Waterford road could be heard in the background, some heavy machinery operating nearby also. But then the noise again.

"It's inside the container."

Hognatt nodded in agreement. He removed the chain, unlocked the handles and pulled back the doors.

"It must be the car," he said. "Did you switch it off properly?"

The noise again, only louder. Then a muffled voice.

"Eh ee ow!"

We looked at each other in bewilderment. Hognatt took a pistol from a holster on the back of his pants.

"Eh ee ow!"

"It's from the fucking boot," I said. "It's *let me out, let me out.*"

"Jesus Christ," Hognatt said. He raised his gun, pointed it at the boot. "Open it."

I released the catch on the boot and it sprung up. It was quite dark in the container, but the shape of a man could be seen.

"Ah Jesus! Help me! Get me out!"

It was Savage. What was he doing in the boot of Dominic's car?

"Get me the fuck out!"

"Get out yourself," Hognatt said. He gestured upwards with his pistol.

"Ah God! Ah Jesus!" Savage grabbed onto the lip of the boot, raised his head up like a demented jack-in-the-box. He looked dazed.

I put a hand under his armpit and lifted him up. I pulled him and tossed him head first onto the floor of the container. Savage whelped.

"Get up," Hognatt said and stuck a Doc Martin into his side. "Get up."

Savage struggled to his feet. He was in full Garda uniform, dusty and dishevelled. A couple of shirt buttons were missing. He'd pissed himself.

Hognatt waved the gun towards the container door. "Get out."

Savage walked wearily. Hognatt pushed his back to hurry him up. "Get a move on."

"Where is he?" Savage said. There was terror in his voice. Then it became anger. "Where is the cunt? That fucking runt. I'll kill him!"

"Hold on, Dave," I said. "Slow down. What happened?"

He looked at me, his eyes wide like he was on the very drugs O'Brien was trying to sell.

"Dominic. The lousy bastard. He tried to kill me." He was pointing to his neck. "Tried to fucking throttle me. I thought I was done for."

"He tried to strangle you?" I said. I looked at his neck. Bruising could be seen.

Savage nodded briskly, then winced and put a hand to his neck. "Ah fuck! The pain!" He looked around manically. "Where is he? You have him, don't you? Let me at the bastard."

He ran to the van, slid the door back. Dominic was still lying there, the bag over his head. Savage leaped into the van and began to kick Dominic in the ribs.

"You lousy bastard. You lousy bastard."

Hognatt ran after Savage, wrapped his arms around him, dragged him from the van and onto the ground. He took a plastic tie from his pocket and secured Savage's wrists.

"Make a move like that again," Hognatt said, "and I'll put a bullet in you. Understood?"

Savage sat on the ground, his back to the rear tyre of the van. He was out of breath and sobbing. He nodded.

"Good. Now my friend here, Mr Bosco, would like a word and

I expect your full co-operation."

Hognatt closed the van door. I got onto my haunches next to Savage. His head was bowed, tears dripping from his chin.

"I know you're dirty, Dave. I heard you myself in O'Brien's. What I want to know is why. Why did you fit me up?"

Savage coughed. "I don't know what you're talking about, Bosco. You're fucking delusional. Who the fuck is O'Brien?"

I nodded to Hognatt. He gave Savage a kick to his right kidney.

"Again," I said. "Why did you try to fit me up?"

"You've finally lost it, Bosco. You're a fucking joke!"

I nodded again and this time Hognatt put the gun to Savage's head.

"Ah fuck. I swear to you, Bosco, I wasn't trying to fit you up. I was just helping O'Brien with security. But then he suspected Fitzmaurice of snitching on him."

"And was he?"

"I don't know. But O'Brien wanted it taken care of. I told Dom to go and rough him up, beat a confession out of him. When I heard he was killed, I thought maybe things had gotten out of hand and Dom had defended himself."

"But then Brick."

"Brick wasn't even on my radar. That was all Dom. I think he got a taste for it after Fitzmaurice."

"For what? Strangling people?"

Savage nodded.

"Jesus Christ. And he picked Brick from one of my old arrest reports?"

Savage shrugged his shoulders. "Makes sense. Brick had nothing to do with O'Brien, so I didn't put two and two together and connect Dom to it."

"And Doolin?"

"I was interviewing O'Keeffe about the Fitzmaurice murder when—"

"You were trying to put O'Keeffe in the frame for Moolah."

He nodded. "Then Dom came rushing in, said he'd seen you leaving. I lost it. I couldn't believe you were in the Bridewell behind my back."

"Dominic tore my hair. You punched my face, drew blood."

"And Dom must have strangled Doolin and planted the evidence."

I sighed. "How did Dominic find out about Doolin?"

"I met with Jimmy Dorgan around the corner from the Steamship the day before the poker game. I asked if he'd any new information to justify his retainer. He boasted about you being in the game. He said you were like Bruce Lee. Bruce Lee, for fuck sake! I used to love Bruce Lee movies."

"Dom was in the car with you?"

Savage nodded.

I supposed that it wasn't such a leap from there to Dominic nabbing Doolin, choking him, dumping his body and planting my DNA. He was probably watching Doolin's car that night, saw the kidnapping, happened across him when he followed after us.

"So what did you do to piss off Dominic?"

Savage shook his head. "I don't know why he turned on me like he did. I had a slight suspicion after Doolin, but I said nothing. Maybe he sensed my suspicion. I turned my back on him for a second and the next thing I remember is waking up in that boot."

I had my own suspicions about why Dominic decided to strangle Savage and keep him in the boot.

"He was with you when Jimmy called about the assault rifle?"

He nodded.

I looked at Hognatt. "Get Dominic out here."

He opened the van and got in the back. He unchained Dominic from the van wall. He dragged him by the ankles and sent him flying to the ground, landing on his back. He loosened the hood and pulled it off.

"What was the plan, Dominic?" I said.

Dominic gave me a cold stare. There wasn't a flicker of emotion. He said nothing. I looked in his eyes. It was like looking into Chambers's eyes.

"You enjoyed it, didn't you? Was Moolah your first?"

Nothing from Dominic but that icy stare. I decided to change tack.

"It was an amateur job. I'd know. I'm the Bruce Lee of Cork. I'm a legend – did you know that?"

I thought I might have detected a flinch in his eyes.

"What I did to Chambers … that was something special. I mean, a child killer. For fuck sake, boy, I choked a child rapist, a paedophile. And what did you go after? Twopenny corner boys. Not worth the time of day. It's all so … forgettable. That's the word – forgettable."

"Stop," he finally said.

"What?"

"I said stop." Genuine anger.

"And then I got to strangle *you*. I thought Chambers was a special feeling, but then I got my arms around your neck. It was like … it was like making love. Do you know what I mean? Isn't that how you felt?"

"I said stop!" I'd rarely seen such rage. Dominic thrashed, kicked his legs and flailed his arms. Blood was streaming from where his wrists were tied. He stopped and looked in my eyes – his were wide open, maniacal. "You're the one going to prison, Mickey. I set it up good and tight. There's a fucking new Bruce Lee now, man. You're going down." He started laughing.

"You had a great plan. Jesus, I mean, setting me up as a cop killer? I'd never have seen the light of day again."

Dominic kept laughing. "You don't know the half of it. What are you going to do about it? Are you going to kill me? Dave too? It's your word against a Guard."

Savage spoke. "No, it's your word against mine, Dom."

Dominic stopped laughing suddenly. He looked at Savage and his eyes narrowed. He didn't have an answer.

"You're done," Savage said. "I'm done. The game's up."

"W–wait, Dave. We can work our way through this if we just—"

"Save it, Dom. I've had enough. You're one sick freak. You need to be cleaned off the streets before you murder some other poor fucker."

"But they're scum, Dave. They're all scum. How many have walked free from court? How many get out of prison early because they can't fund enough prison spaces? I thought you'd be impressed."

"Enough, Dom."

Dominic looked up at me. "You understand, don't you?"

In a way I did. But I hadn't calculated Chambers's end – I had become lost in the frenzy much like Chambers had with Robbie O'Meara. Dominic, on the other hand, had planned his killings meticulously. I knew there would never be an end to his killing spree until he was locked up for life.

I looked at Savage. "You'll testify against him?"

Savage nodded.

"And you'll confess your own deeds?"

Savage paused, but then nodded.

I believed him. I saw it in his eyes. And I'm good with eyes, me.

I looked at Savage. "My friend here is a demon with a machete. You should see him bone a chicken. Don't even try and double-cross us."

I turned to Hognatt. "Change of plan. After the next op I'm going to take these guys in. I've got to clear my name."

He nodded. "We can tie them up in the container, padlock it closed, return later."

I helped Savage to his feet. Hognatt took him into the container and secured him. He returned to help me with Dominic. He put the hood back on Dominic's head and we dragged him into the container.

"Hang on," I said. "Let's give him a taste of his own medicine."

I opened the boot of the car. Dominic kicked and screamed, but Hognatt was a beast and slung him into the boot head first, slamming the boot door down on top of him. Hognatt closed the container doors and chained them.

We decided to change location, just in case. We got into the van and headed towards the Jack Lynch Tunnel.

We took the exit to Mahon and drove up past Mahon Point shopping centre, then turned right and continued on until we reached Loughmahon. Hognatt parked between two groups of houses in a *cul de sac*.

We had about an hour to kill. Hognatt turned on the radio, hit a preset for 4FM Classic Hits.

"This must be just another day at the office for you," I said.

Hognatt responded with a grunt. "Every op is different."

"Business must be booming," I said. "There's always some little war going on somewhere that needs hired guns."

Hognatt curled his lips. "As long as there's oil, there'll be no shortage of work. But it's good to be home for a bit."

"Have you considered another line of work? One that takes you out of harm's way?"

Hognatt shrugged his shoulders. "I'll always be a soldier. I don't know any different."

I understood him completely.

Something had been rattling around in my brain. I was wondering how he had grabbed me.

"How did you know I was going to be in Aghada?"

"We have a code word. If you're under duress on the phone, you use the word *sharp*. Crowley said five o'clock sharp."

I nodded. "A bit like a safe word during kinky sex. You know … when the dominatrix has your balls in a vice."

Hognatt laughed.

To pass the time, we listened to a number of songs that included Eddy Grant's 'I don't wanna dance', Abba's 'The winner takes it all' and Tracy Chapman's 'Fast car'.

At seven we left to pick up Crowley. When we pulled up outside the apartment in Blackrock Avenue, Crowley came out immediately. He opened the passenger door with a look of shock on his face.

"It's all good," Hognatt said. "Get in the back."

"You can't be serious, he's—"

"In the back, Crowley."

Crowley relented. He gave me one final look of disdain and got in the back via the side door. He sat glumly on the floor.

"Don't worry about him," Hognatt said to me quietly. "He's motivated by money. He won't do anything stupid to jeopardize it."

I nodded.

We drove off and picked up two more men, one in Douglas, the other in Rochestown. We took the N27 back to the city centre and then the N20 Blackpool bypass to get onto the Limerick road.

I got glimpses of Blackpool village from the bypass. People smoking outside pubs. Cars filling up at O'Callaghan's garage. Then the shopping centre where people were emptying bags from trolleys into the boots of their cars. *Good people*, I thought. *Good people.*

The three in the back said little as we drove. I supposed I'd seen their quiet nervousness only in war movies. Like paratroopers waiting for the call over Normandy. They were probably mentally rehearsing their planned actions, much like a professional slalom skier would sway his hips while queueing before the start gate.

The destination was the old Jennings animal feed plant on the Limerick side of Charleville. There seemed to be an agricultural feel to Jordan's recent land acquisitions. Maybe it was a reaction to his failings during the Celtic Tiger.

As we passed through Buttevant, I was reminded of my tail of O'Brien. I wondered if O'Brien would stop to fill up at the same petrol station again. I wondered if he would buy cigarettes and put one in his mouth before getting into the car. I could imagine his nervous energy. How he fidgeted his hands, paced around in circles. He would be doing that now, I thought.

I suppose it was my own nerves that made me talk to Crowley between Buttevant and Charleville.

"How's Justine getting on?"

Crowley looked at Hognatt. "Is he trying to wind me up?"

Hognatt put a hand on my lap. "I'd just keep my trap shut till we reach our target."

Charleville was closer to Limerick than Cork. That made sense with Moose supposedly taking the initiative on the meet. We passed through the town and took a right about two minutes later. Shortly after the turn was a facility surrounded by chain-linked fencing. A sign that had all manner of dirt on it, from diesel fumes and whatnot, read JENNINGS FEED COMPANY — SPECIALISTS IN BOVINE AND EQUINE NUTRITION. A picture of a horse adorned the sign also. Then it made sense, I suppose. The love of horses. Maybe Jordan had made an acquaintance in need of a quick sale.

Hognatt stopped and got out. He took keys from his pocket and opened a padlock. He pushed back two chain-link doors to make plenty of room for the van. He got back in and we drove up to the main building.

He looked back. "O'Brien will know about this place within the hour. We'll make sure no one's here now and hide the van."

The crew in the back nodded.

He looked to me. "You stick with me. Don't leave my side."

I had no other plans.

The men in the back took their MP7s and walkie-talkies from the holdall. Also in the holdall were balaclavas and helmets fitted with night-vision goggles. They were every bit as well equipped as the Garda ERU would have been. It gave me some reassurance. Hognatt went around back and took his own equipment, then came back to me at the front of the van. He was holding a handgun in his hand. He held it out to me. It was my P99.

"Try not to shoot this if you can."

"And if I have to?"

"Well, in that case just shoot the fucking thing. Just make sure I'm out of your way."

I thought maybe he was underestimating me. But he'd probably seen the actions of greenhorns in the army. You didn't know how they would react until they were under live fire.

Hognatt and his men checked the feed plant. They pronounced it clear and we all went back to the van.

"Pass me the nocks," Hognatt said to Crowley.

I had no idea what he meant until Crowley handed him a set of binoculars. Army guys and their one syllable names for things. Maybe they thought two or more syllables took so long to say that they got you killed.

Hognatt pointed to positions for Crowley and the other two. A grain silo and outbuildings that surrounded the inner courtyard.

Hognatt asked them to double-check their LAMs. I enquired and he explained that a LAM was a laser aiming module. The red dots I saw when the men targeted their MP7s made it clear – not only did they enhance aiming, they scared the shite out of anyone who saw a dot on their chest.

Hognatt drove the van around the back of the main building and came back to the group in the courtyard. He directed the others to take their positions and then I followed Hognatt to the main building. He took out his mobile and called Moose.

"We're ready. If the operation succeeds, I'll text you the location of your reward."

O'Brien had been instructed by Moose to wait in Buttevant for a call with the meet location. The instructions also included a warning to bring no more than two people with him.

Hognatt put the binoculars to his eyes. He pointed them to the turn off from the main Limerick road.

Fifteen minutes passed. I was getting nervous.

"What if he doesn't show?"

Hognatt kept looking through the binoculars, said nothing.

A minute later a car turned off the Limerick road. Hognatt raised his walkie-talkie to his mouth. "Possible target sighted."

A hundred yards from the gate.

"Target confirmed. Wait for my command."

The car was a dark-coloured SUV. It stopped at the gate facing in. A man got out of the back and walked a few steps inside the gate. He took a good look around. He got back into the SUV. The SUV didn't move.

"They smell a rat," I said. "The operation's blown."

"Steady," Hognatt said to me.

The SUV moved forward. It drove into the courtyard and

stopped about forty yards from the double doors of the main building.

Hognatt pulled his balaclava down over his face.

"Look the other way," he said to me.

He took a flashbang from his pocket and threw it towards the car. He raised the walkie-talkie. "Go. Go. Go." He gave the command calmly. Like he'd given it countless times before. Just then there was a flash of light and a bang milliseconds later.

"Stay here," he said and at first I complied.

Hognatt walked briskly forward with the scope to his eye. I could see two dots on the windscreen of the SUV.

Hognatt shouted, "Police! Don't move! Hands up!"

Crowley and the others closed in with their MP7s aimed at the occupants of the SUV. They were most likely blinded by the flashbangs, maybe hearing ringing in their ears.

Hognatt's men shouted over each other: "Don't fucking move!", "Get out of the car!", "Drop your weapons!".

They reached the SUV without a shot being fired. Almost in unison, Hognatt's men opened doors and pulled out three men. They forced them to kneel at gunpoint. They searched the men and took handguns from their pockets. Hognatt stayed in position to cover them.

This was my moment to move in. I took the P99 from my pocket and released the safety. I came up behind Hognatt.

"May I?" I said.

"What the fuck, Bosco? I said stay behind."

"The bag."

"What?"

"I'll do the bag, if you'll indulge me."

"But I like doing the bag thing."

"Just this once."

He sighed. "In my back pocket."

I took it out and walked to where Crowley had his MP7 pointed at O'Brien's head.

"Up here, O'Brien," I said.

O'Brien either didn't hear or he ignored me. I reached down

and grabbed his hair and forced him to look at me. There was terror in his eyes.

"Who the fuck are *you*?" he said.

"The Gentleman says hi," I said.

I was fiddling with the drawstring on the bag, loosening it. I didn't notice O'Brien moving his hand to his ankle. I didn't see the flick knife. The weapon of a hoodlum.

O'Brien lunged the knife towards my gut. I parried it, but it pierced my shirt, sliced into my love handle a bit.

I lifted a leg and kicked the knife from his hand. I swiped him across the jaw with the P99 and he fell face first into the dirt. A tooth fell from his mouth and lumps of congealed blood dribbled from the side of his mouth.

I slipped the bag over his head. I tightened the drawstring.

It's difficult to describe what I felt then. Scoobs might have called it closure. But closure is just modern psychobabble. It was more cathartic than that. If you could imagine the sensations of biting into an Arbutus bread, Gubbeen cheese and Italian cured ham sandwich, drinking ice cold Howling Gale Ale on a hot summer's day, and Clonakilty black pudding melting in your mouth, then wrap them all up together, you might come close to understanding.

Hognatt and his men got to work on tying up O'Brien and his men in the main building. Crowley searched the SUV and found five bricks of meth in a hidden compartment. He took the bricks into the main building and put them on the ground near O'Brien.

Hognatt retrieved the van and we got in.

"Good work, men," Hognatt said. "Bonuses all round."

The men cheered, then laughed. The bagging of O'Brien was a release of sorts for me. Cheering and laughing was theirs.

A mile after Charleville, Hognatt stopped the van.

"Pass me the rucksack," he said to one of the men.

He got out next to a road sign that said there were sixty kilometres to Cork. Sixty klicks in military speak, what with their preference for single syllables. He tossed the rucksack over a wall into a field. He took out his mobile and keyed in a message for

Moose.

He tossed the phone to me. "Call Cotter."

I got out of the van to make the call. Cotter answered almost immediately. Before I could tell him about picking up O'Brien and his drugs, he spoke with urgency.

"Jesus Christ, Mick. We're missing two men. Savage and Mangan."

"*Dominic* Mangan?"

"Yeah." There was silence for a moment. "Do you have something to do with this?"

"Yer man Halloran? Can you get a hold of him?"

"Since Savage and Mangan went missing, pretty much everyone's been called in."

"Tell him to expect me. Tell him there's about to be a break in his case."

"What is it, Mick? You're not ..."

"What? Confessing? Fuck no. Just tell him to stay where he is and wait for me. And there's something else you need to know too."

I explained about O'Brien, his two heavies and the drugs. I gave him the location. I was vague about the means of capturing them.

"Jesus Christ. It's Jordan, isn't it?" he said.

I remembered the Jordans' love of horses. Somehow it filtered into my response.

"Don't look a gift horse in the mouth, Barry."

And with that I hung up.

Hognatt dropped off his men and drove me back to the container where Savage and Mangan were. He stayed until I had Savage secured in the back of the car.

"You need any more help?" he asked.

"I'll be fine from here."

"Well ... maybe our paths will cross again someday."

I didn't think so at first, but then I realized that trouble had a habit of inviting itself around. Maybe I would see him again. I hoped it wouldn't be after he took a bag from my head.

"Maybe. And maybe you should stick around a bit longer."

Hognatt looked around. It was like an emigrant from a century earlier taking a last look before boarding a ship in Queenstown for a one-way trip to America. I knew then he planned on going back to Africa.

"Take care, Bosco."

I nodded. He got into the van and drove off leaving a dust plume behind him.

I got into the Mondeo. There was a smell of urine. Despite everything, I felt some pity for Savage.

"Are you ready for this?" I asked.

How could he have been? He said nothing in reply. He just stared out the window as we drove towards the Bridewell.

When we arrived at the Bridewell, I pushed Savage in front of me, his hands still bound by the plastic ties. There were stunned looks from Guards as we walked in the front entrance. Though I had no right to manhandle a Guard into the Bridewell like I did, no one confronted me. At the desk I asked for Halloran.

Halloran came out, looked at me with the look of man that's found out his lottery win was a hoax.

"What is this, Bosco? Release him this instant."

He gestured to a uniformed Guard to take action.

I whispered in Savage's ear, "Remember what I said about my friend's machete?"

"Wait," Savage said, directing his words to Halloran. "I'd like to … I need to … I'm handing myself in."

Halloran's mouth dropped open.

I took the car keys out of my pocket. I threw them to Halloran and he caught them instinctively.

I said, "If you think the shit's hit the fan now, wait until you open the boot."

Halloran spoke to the uniformed Guard. "Untie Savage's hands and take him to interview room two."

He walked to me and said, "I have an arrest warrant pending for you, Bosco. You're not going anywhere."

"Then you'd better call my solicitor," I said. "Goulding's his name. Terence Goulding."

Halloran spoke to another uniform. "Take Mr Bosco to inter-view room four."

I was happy to oblige.

Halloran went outside. A moment later, as I was being led to the interview room, I heard him.

"Bosco!"

EPILOGUE

BARRY COTTER WAS LOOKING out at the estuary when I arrived at the Rochestown walk by Hop Island. Some birds were searching for worms in the mud. An onshore breeze brought the rank smell of decaying seaweed. I greeted him and we started to walk towards Passage West.

"It's a crisp morning," I said. I hunched my shoulders to emphasize how cold it was.

Barry looked at his watch. "It's afternoon, you dozy twonk."

I grunted. "How many is it now – four?"

"Five, including Bracken this morning. I think they are anxious to cap it there if they can get away with it. The last thing we need is another witch hunt. Not after the whistle blowing thing."

They. The brass. The recent whistle blowing cases that had highlighted corruption in the Guards had shown just how much they all closed ranks, brass included. A dead rat had been hung from the door of one of the whistle blowers. It wasn't proven, but everyone suspected it was a Guard. It was just one way to underline that omerta in the Guards was alive and well.

"And Halloran?"

"Taking as much credit as he can. To be fair, he's pursued the others with Savage's assistance."

"If it hadn't been for Goulding's sorcery, I might have been shackled to Savage and Mangan. Halloran would have loved it."

"There's history there, I believe?"

I remembered my mother's face. About how Halloran had re-floated memories like a sunken cruise liner full of skeletons being salvaged.

"I'm not done yet with Halloran."

A young woman, her arse tight in an Under Armour baselayer pants, zipped by on roller blades. Barry ogled her.

"That's a sin if ever there was one," he said. "Putting it out there on show like that." He was practically drooling. "But you've your eyes elsewhere, I hear."

I didn't enquire as to how he knew about Grace. I didn't want to know about sources anymore. I didn't want to be paranoid like The Gentleman.

"We'll see. There's hope for me yet."

As we walked, the wastewater treatment plant across Lough Mahon at Carrigrennan, on the south tip of Little Island, came into view. I thought about how, much like the plant did, I had at least helped clean up some of the effluent that had been poisoning the city – Savage, Mangan, O'Brien. But there was plenty more where it had come from. Moose would be busy dealing his new poison in Limerick thanks to Jordan's ruthless pragmatism. The Eel would continue to pursue his loan book by any means necessary. And the Gentleman? Well, as far as I was concerned, the jury was still out on him.

I said, "How did you explain O'Brien and the meth?"

"I told O'Brien that if he pleaded to the drugs charges that we wouldn't pursue conspiracy to murder. His two associates were offered lesser charges. The brass wanted to have a win, so they turned a blind eye to exactly how it went down. We agreed on a simplified version of the truth, if you know what I mean."

I did.

"You know, Barry, one of these days we should go for that pint. Events seem to have gotten in the way in recent times."

Barry laughed. "And you don't think they will again?"

He was right. What with trouble being a close relation of mine, practically immediate family.

We walked to Passage West and back sharing some blue jokes along the way.

Somewhere fancy we had agreed. I didn't know anything about restaurants, so I chose a five-star hotel, Hayfield Manor, near the university.

Grace arrived wearing a long purple dress that only had a strap on one shoulder. She'd had her hair done. She wore a broad smile on her face. She looked angelic. The right kind of angelic.

I looked over the menu and tried to hide my shock when I saw the prices.

"We can split the bill," she said.

I'm a man of tradition. I told her I'd take care of it. Jordan had paid well and I needed a way to start spending the cash I was accumulating under my mattress.

"That's not how I operate," she said. "I pay my way."

I wasn't going to argue. I guessed if I was to have a chance with her, I'd need to compromise.

"What catches your eye?" I asked.

"The terrine for starters and tart tatin for the main."

She sounded like a food critic the way she said it. I felt embarrassed about replying with my own choices and appearing agricultural.

"Mickey? What are you going to order?"

I picked the most pronounceable items. "Soup of the day and Salmon."

"Ah take a risk, will you?"

I waved her off. "I've always wanted to try a nine Euro soup."

The waiter took our food order and Grace chose a fifty Euro bottle of wine. Like father like daughter.

We made light work of the starters and continued our conversation.

"I've talked to Daddy," she said.

"Go on."

"He's in good form. He talks a lot about you. Says that he has plans."

I'd had enough of Jordan over the past three weeks. Every punch, cut, rise of my blood pressure had been down to him. By him looking out for me in a twisted way, because of his soft spot for Dad.

"Tell him I'm grateful for his consideration, but that I'd like a little vacation time. I think I've earned it."

She smiled. "He's decided to step back from much of the business to concentrate on his pet project."

"The MMA academy."

She nodded. She leaned in closer and whispered, "I think it's his Mother Theresa complex. He wants to save the children. You know?"

I did. But I believed it was sincere. Maybe ill-gotten gains could be cleansed if they brought hope to an area decimated by governmental apathy.

"He said I should train there with O'Keeffe. Work on my cardio and combat skills."

She frowned. "Not so you can start fighting. Have you seen Daddy's nose?"

I was touched by her concern. "It's just for fitness." *So the likes of Savage can't beat me up.*

"What's going to happen the rest of the business?"

"I'm going to take on more responsibility. I'll hire a couple of good managers, though."

I nodded. "Your father tried to pull too many strings. Best to delegate."

The main course arrived. My salmon was on top of some chive mash for some bizarre reason. I used a knife to put it back on the plate where it belonged. I tucked in.

"This is good," I said. "Beats a battered cod any day."

An embarrassed smile from Grace. "Certainly it's healthier. What with your new fitness regime."

I nodded. I'd keep to the healthy eating plan. But on Saturday mornings I'd allow myself a portion of Clonakilty. Something to keep me straight for the rest of the week.

"Can we do this more often?" I said. "The dinner, maybe the occasional drink?"

Her face lit up. "I think that would be nice."

I put my hand across the table. She flinched slightly, but then allowed me to hold her hand.

"You're too good for the likes of me," I said. "But I'm good people."

"A good person," she said, trying to correct me.

I laughed. "Sorry. It's an expression. That a single person can be good people."

Her brow furrowed. I didn't think she watched much gritty American TV.

I said, "Like a horse could be good horses."

She laughed and there was a snort. "Oh God, Michael. Are you always going to tell bad jokes?"

"If you'll tolerate them." I squeezed her hand. "I might slip a good one in now and then, though."

We finished our main courses and most of the wine. The waiter returned and asked if we wanted dessert. We refused, but asked for another bottle of the wine.

While we waited, I took the note my Dad had written from my wallet. The crisp one that had *Starman* written on it. I rubbed my thumb over it.

"What's that?" she asked.

"Ah, it's nothing. An old note I found."

"What does it say?"

"It's a reminder that I have a job to do. But it's for another day."

"Another week, another month, I hope."

I nodded. "There's no rush with history."

She took a final sip from her wine glass. "You know … they have vacancies."

"I don't know that I'm qualified to work—"

"Room vacancies. Not job vacancies!"

I felt like a tool. "Oh." Then it hit me like one of Hognatt's Doc Martins. "Oh!"

"Shall we?"

She stood up and offered her hand. It had been years. Many years. I took her hand and stood. I felt a tingling in my groin. A nice tingling.

We left to get a room.